Countries of Origin

Countries of Origin

JAVIER FUENTES

PANTHEON BOOKS
New York

All rights reserved. Published in the United States by Pantheon Books, a division of Penguin Random House LLC, New York, and distributed in Canada by Penguin Random House Canada Limited, Toronto.

Pantheon Books and colophon are registered trademarks of Penguin Random House LLC.

Library of Congress Cataloging-in-Publication Data
Name: Fuentes, Javier, author.
Title: Countries of origin : a novel / Javier Fuentes.
Description: First edition. New York : Pantheon Books, 2023
Identifiers: LCCN 2022042643 (print) | LCCN 2022042644 (ebook) | ISBN 9780593317587 (hardcover) | ISBN 9780593317594 (ebook)
Classification: LCC PS3606.U375 C68 2023 (print) | LCC PS3606.U375 (ebook) | DDC 813/.6—dc23
LC record available at https://lccn.loc.gov/2022042643
LC ebook record available at https://lccn.loc.gov/2022042644

www.pantheonbooks.com

Jacket photograph: *Boy on a Raft* by Peter Hujar.
© 2022 The Peter Hujar Archive /
Artists Rights Society (ARS), New York

Printed in the United States of America
First Edition
2 4 6 8 9 7 5 3 1

Mayka

Countries of Origin

1

I grew up loving a country that didn't love me back. The United States had been my home since I was eight years old, and for more than a decade, I believed that a strong will would make things right. But a country can't love you back, and a strong will only gets you so far.

I had changed into my street clothes and was throwing my chef's whites in the hamper to be dry-cleaned when Chef called asking me to meet at his apartment. It was on the top of the town house whose other floors were home to Le Bourrelet, Manhattan's first Michelin three-star restaurant. None of the employees had ever been to his home, not even the occasional hostess he brought into his office. I kept the invitation secret to avoid giving more ammunition to my coworkers, already jealous of our relationship. Looking at my spotless station, I feared that Chef had finally learned about my fake Social Security number. It was an illogical thought after so many years working at the restaurant and paying taxes, but I was undocumented, and logic only applies when you have papeles.

Instead of taking the interior stairs that connected the restaurant to his apartment, I said goodbye like every other night and left through the service entrance, making sure not to slip on the frozen loading dock. As I turned the corner of Eighty-third Street and Fifth, the bitter March wind stung my face with slivers of ice.

I made my way up the narrow staircase, my winter boots barely fitting on the steps. I had expected the upper floor of the town house to be well maintained, but the white walls had yellowed and the paint on the door was peeling, as if the wood was shedding its skin.

"Entrez!" Chef said after I knocked. He was so proud of being Parisian that he not only kept his strong accent but spoke French to every customer whether they understood him or not. He read *Le Monde* every afternoon, mostly drank wines from Provence, and wheezed from smoking two packs of Gauloises a day. Living abroad seemingly had only made him more French.

I pushed open the door and took off my boots before entering the apartment. Holding an empty glass in one hand and a cigarette in the other, Chef paced the room cradling the phone with his shoulder, the creaking of the wood floor muffled by several Persian rugs. Faded issues of *Paris Match* were piled up against a balcony door, the light of the lamppost across the street faintly filtering in. He pointed at a sofa, and I sat next to a stuffed red fox as Chef, speaking softly, crossed into the other room.

"Au revoir, princesse," I caught before he hung up. Dressed in his signature three-piece black suit and burgundy loafers, Chef looked exhausted. His forehead was lined with deep wrinkles, his eyes no longer sparkled. Maybe he had looked that way for a while, and it was only now, away from the kitchen, that I was able to see it.

"Eight-thirty in Paris," he said, glancing at a grandfather

clock that marked half past two in the morning. "I'm the first voice they hear when they wake up, haven't missed one matin."

"That's nice," I said, unsure how to continue.

Chef unfastened his collar and loosened his tie but kept his jacket on. He grabbed a bottle of cognac from a bar cart and poured two glasses. "So, how are you?"

"I'm good, Chef. It was a busy night."

"So I heard. I can't believe I've had this cold for so long."

"Yeah, it's pretty crazy. Are you any better?" I asked because I wanted to know but also to keep the conversation going.

"Comme ci, comme ça. Tell me, how long have you been working for me?" Chef, speaking more slowly than usual, seemed to be struggling to find the right words.

"It'll be eight years in May, Chef."

"C'est pas possible!"

"Yeah, right?" I said, not wanting the awkwardness to sink in. I took a long sip of cognac and felt the muscles in my right leg cramp.

"Well, Demetrio. I've been thinking a lot about you lately. You've pretty much learned everything I have to offer. I think it's time for you to move on." He dragged on his cigarette for a while.

Moving on could mean many things but at that moment, it only meant one thing: I was being let go. The cognac, which had traveled smoothly down my throat, suddenly burned its way through my stomach. I could feel beads of sweat forming on my face. I turned my head and looked at the stuffed fox with its defiant teeth, its mount covered in dust.

"Santé, santé, santé," Chef said, refilling his glass.

I grabbed a folded paper towel from my back pocket to control my sneezing.

"What do you mean, Chef?" I smiled as if I did not understand what he was trying to say.

"Oh, you're not getting fired, if that's what you're thinking. That's not at all what I meant."

I released a nervous laugh that didn't sound like me.

"At this point, you're in charge of our dessert menu and I can't even remember the last time I suggested something you hadn't already explored. You're one of the most talented pastry chefs in the city, and it's not just me saying it. It's fucking Frank Bruni. If you were in Paris, that'd be a different story. The competition there is brutal. You know, it's part of our ADN. DNA? Whatever."

He sucked one last drag from the cigarette before stubbing it out in the ashtray. Not knowing what to do with so much silence, I took another long sip from my glass, lighting my throat on fire and wondering whether his words were truly what he thought or he was just now trying to make up for the misunderstanding.

"In any case, my friend Marcel Boisdenier, one of the heads of the Culinary Institute, said you should apply for a scholarship. There are very few of them, but that shouldn't be a problem," he said triumphantly. "You would only need to fill out some forms to get Federal Student Aid."

It was so quiet, I could hear Chef's breathing and the distant murmur of voices coming from the bar downstairs. Looking into his eyes, I felt ashamed, small, and expendable. It had been so many years of living with the secret, and there had been periods when I didn't think about it for a whole day, though the fear was always there, lurking in shadows, waiting for the right moment to come back with renewed force. Even though the decision to become undocumented had not been mine, but made by others, I was the one forced to live with it.

At first, Chef seemed confused by my lack of excitement, but he might have thought I was overwhelmed by the news.

"To the future," he said, pouring more fire into our glasses and raising his.

I fixed my gaze on a marble bust resting on a side table and heard the words trapped in my head slowly being released into the air. "I don't have papers."

He kept his glass up, taking time to interpret what I had just said.

"The right papers," I added, as if it needed an explanation.

Now it was Chef who did not understand.

"How so?" he said after a long pause. "You've been here for so long." He put the glass on the table and stood still for a while. His face looked as if he were going through a long list, then he said: "We'll get you the right papers."

We polished off the bottle of cognac while I told him about a part of my past I had shared with very few others: growing up in the Loisaida, going to Public School 64 on East Tenth, and losing my accent watching *M*A*S*H*. He was surprised that I had been able to attend school and that many of my classmates were also undocumented. I talked about Mr. Banks, the head of the school, a local hero who helped all students who were recent immigrants navigate the bureaucracy of their new country and find aid that wasn't dependent on the color of their passport. And how, in trying to fit in and become American, we avoided speaking Spanish except when we cursed, when we fought—which was more often than I would have liked—and when we cried.

Since Chef seemed genuinely interested in my past, I went on about my first job cleaning pots and pans at Rio Mar, a long-gone Spanish restaurant on Little West Twelfth whose kitchen was forever under siege from an army of gigantic roaches. How every Saturday at two in the morning, after the dining room had emptied and the tables were set for brunch, I would buy a phone card at a nearby deli and talk to my mother from a pay phone, always in alleys and dead-end streets, so when the tears began to flow down my cheeks no one could see me.

IT WAS FOUR in the morning when I left Chef's apartment after agreeing to meet an immigration lawyer, a friend who had helped him with his own naturalization process. I was surprised to learn that Chef had become American, seeing how often he looked for opportunities to unfavorably compare the United States with France.

Thinking about my past, and reliving moments that I rarely revisited, had me feeling wired. I opened the door of the building, and stepping into a soundless city covered in snow, I decided to walk home. The streets were so desolate that for the first time in a while I was able to hear my thoughts. With snow up to my knees and a harsh, stinging wind, I crossed Park Avenue, looking at the yellow light of a taxi that had risked one last ride and was now stuck in the middle of the road. Extreme winter storms only came every few years, but that night, in the midst of this apocalyptic sight, I realized that I enjoyed the city most when it was paralyzed.

It took me three hours to make it back to the Meatpacking District, where I had been living for years. I remembered bicycling as a kid through the meandering cobblestone streets, when it was a neighborhood of people living on the margins, their existence doomed to long nights in dark, inhospitable alleys, on decaying piers, or in reeking bars. When artists squatted in abandoned buildings, turning walls into art that years later would be shown at the Whitney, runaways sold their youth, and junkies sold what they could.

By the time I got home, the early morning light revealed a Carrara-marbled sky. The façade of my building was covered in graffiti again. As I pushed open the heavy metal door, a cold chill traveling down my back made me run up the five flights of stairs. My apartment, with its high ceilings and massive windows, gave the illusion of being outside, and on nights like these, it was almost magical. I took great pride in having a rent-stabilized place because it was an earned right, proof that one had stuck around during the tough times, when nobody had wanted to live in this neighborhood.

After peeling off my wet socks, I poured myself a glass of water. A blinking red light across the room signaled a message from Chus, the only person I knew who insisted on using landlines and answering machines. Chus was my uncle, my mother, and my father. Mamá, unable to provide for me, had sent me to live with him when I turned eight years old. He had been in New York since 1967, after fleeing fascist Spain when his name appeared on a list of students organizing against Franco. Chus walked through the Pyrenees into France, spent time in a Paris commune with other Spanish exiles, and then made his way to New York. He took an active role in the civil rights movement and belonged to the Socialist Party of America. Chus believed in free love, so almost every morning growing up I shared my Frosted Flakes with a different man. He had lived in the same run-down tenement on Avenue C for more than two decades. Most of our neighbors, Puerto Ricans, Dominicans, and Colombians, had begun retreating to Spanish Harlem, Sunset Park, and Corona in the mid-eighties. He was one of the few who remained.

I glanced at the blinking light, his gentle voice boxed in, waiting to be released. I did not want to hear any words other than *We'll get you the right papers*. Having already met with an immigration lawyer once, I knew there was little to nothing that could be done to regularize my immigration status. But that morning, lying down in bed, the snow gently landing on the windows blurring the lights across the street, I pretended otherwise.

THE CITY SLEPT IN. A silence that belonged to early dawn extended through the Meatpacking District into midday. Even though it was my day off, I called the restaurant to make sure no help was needed. During blizzards some cooks had the nerve to not show up for work, whereas the washers and cleaners, who were the lowest-paid staff in the kitchen and lived deep in Brooklyn and Queens, made it to the restaurant even if it required hours of walking on side roads and bridges.

I stopped by Florent, my favorite spot for breakfast, a French diner about to close its doors after twenty-two years of consistent food and outrageous nightlife. The owner, a Frenchman and resilient queer activist, was a big fan of my desserts. Every Bastille Day I made him a massive, elaborate cake with the face of Marie Antoinette, which guaranteed me free food for the year. The diner had lost its unbridled downtown energy a while ago, and now the regulars spent most of their time gossiping about rent increases, offers and counteroffers. The closing of such a landmark restaurant, rumored to be happening at the end of the year, was one more sign that we would all be kicked out of the neighborhood sooner or later.

I pierced the yolk of my breakfast sandwich and waited for the plate to turn yellow, wondering if Chef, who had clearly been successful dealing with the USCIS and owned a world-renowned restaurant, would be able to help me. I flipped through the pages of a *Village Voice* someone had left behind, going over our conversation in my head. The check being slipped next to my plate brought me back. I looked at it knowing that it would total zero, left a tip that doubled the cost of my breakfast, kissed the hostess goodbye, and walked into the cold.

Stepping on a powdery, unplowed patch of sidewalk and kicking the snow, repeating the words *We'll get you the right papers,* I experienced a strange happiness, a distant memory from my teenage days. I walked around the Village until the bottoms of my pants were soaked and heavy. Despite his aversion to talking about our lack of papeles, I decided to tell Chus about my conversation with Chef. Near Washington Square the traffic was almost back to normal. I flagged down a cab and gave the driver my old address.

I rang the buzzer three times, a code I had used for years to let Chus know I was coming up. Even though I had keys to the apartment, he usually got up to crack the door open so he could return to his reading. After climbing the stairs and seeing it was closed, I knew something was not right. Chus rarely left in the mornings, only when he ran out of Café Bustelo or if one of the rich kids who had moved into the building had stolen his *New York Times* from the lobby. The two weekly classes he taught were always in the evening. Shutting the door behind me, I stealthily entered the living room. Nothing looked unusual, the floor covered with leaning towers of books and issues of the *New Republic,* the open kitchen neatly scrubbed. I called his name several times and stomped on the hallway floor to alert him I was walking toward his bedroom. The door was wide open. Chus was lying in bed deeply asleep, the nightstand full of cold medicines. I grabbed an open book resting on his chest like a bird in flight, turned off the light, and went back to the living room.

Two hours later, Chus entered the kitchen in his pajamas. I was reading an article on Serena Williams. And simmering on the stove was a lentil soup with chorizo, his favorite winter dish.

"Nothing like waking up to this smell," he said, and then coughed several times as if wanting to convey that he was sick.

"I didn't know you had a cold," I said. "I'd have come earlier."

Chus walked up to me, and as he was about to kiss my forehead, I pulled my head back.

"Wait, I don't want to catch a cold."

"Sorry. You're right, you're right."

We had seen each other a couple of weeks back, but he appeared to have aged all at once, the skin of his face no longer tight, his step unsteady, as if he were hesitant to put his full weight on his feet. For the first time, he looked his age, a man who had already lived his best years.

"How are you feeling?"

"Oh, I'm okay," he said dismissively, as if it were a silly thing to ask.

"Did you see Dr. Boshnick?" I asked, knowing the answer. Chus had been keeping a strict watch over his T-cell count since becoming HIV positive and visited his doctor frequently.

"I did. This cold is not the one taking me to the other side," he said.

I knew that colds terrified him. He feared his immune system would not be strong enough to fight them. For more than twenty years he had been taking antiretroviral drugs, long before the abrasive, debilitating cocktails had been replaced by a small, gentle pill that was advertised by hot Latino guys in their underwear.

"By the way, Alexis contacted me to write him a letter of recommendation. He's decided to apply to Brooklyn College."

"I'll never understand why you always side with my ex-lovers."

"Deme, I'm not siding with anyone. The kid is applying to college, he needs a little help. It's not like he's moving in."

"The kid, as you call him, is a grown-ass man who still lives with his mother. And in case you forgot, he's a cheater. But I guess every gay man in this city is a cheater, so that makes it okay."

"You were together for almost two years, Deme. He *tried* to be monogamous."

"Well, he didn't try *that* hard."

"Not everyone wants a monogamous relationship."

"That's clear to me. You, certainly, don't. That's why you're all alone."

The radiator hissed but not loud enough to cover the sharp edges of my words. I looked at my plate, embarrassed.

"I'm sorry. I didn't mean it."

Chus began serving the lentils.

"I said I'm sorry."

"And I heard you the first time."

"I really didn't mean it. I'm just still very hurt. A whole year without having sex and then I find out Alexis was hooking up with people left and right."

"I know, I know. He should have been up-front about it."

"You forgive me? I really didn't mean what I said."

"Yes. Apologies accepted," he said, though I could tell he was wounded.

His ability to forgive always made me feel a bit of a lesser human. After my overreaction, now was not the right time to bring up my conversation with Chef.

"How's work?" Chus said.

He liked hearing about it. I thought his initial exasperation about my not continuing my studies after high school would be permanent, but it didn't last long. My commitment to baking and the early write-ups that appeared in different publications praising my desserts, which in retrospect were premature and a bit overhyped, convinced him that maybe I was not destined for the academic life he had envisioned for me.

"It's been pretty crazy, which I guess is a good thing. If you own the restaurant, that is," I said with a smile.

With Chus's laugh, a small window of opportunity opened up. I considered that maybe it was not too late to bring up Chef. Taking one big breath, I pulled my shoulders back to ready myself. But as I passed the bread and noted how fragile he looked, his eyes buried in skin, I reached over the table to turn on the radio. The *All Things Considered* theme filled the room. Chus moved his long fingers as if playing an invisible flute. We began to eat.

2

The next couple of days, I lived in a daze. My conversation with Chef was all I could think about. Every time we happened to be alone in the same space, which was not often, I felt my whole body turning into wet cardboard. After plating a dessert, I worried about the plate slipping from my hand as I placed it on the line for the food runners to pick up. The awkwardness reminded me of the only time I had made the mistake of having a one-night stand with a server. For many weeks after, I felt uneasy and distracted, constantly thinking about when I would bump into him next, not able to get over the fact that the kid knew what I looked like without my chef's whites on, the kind of underwear I wore, the face I made when I came. Thankfully, he did not last long and moved back to Wisconsin to marry his high school sweetheart.

Chef was a soccer fan and loved talking about whatever European league was happening at the moment. I was never into the sport even though I had been born in Spain, which apparently comes with an allegiance to either Real Madrid or Barcelona. I learned about the game so that when he started talking about women, I had something else to deflect his attention and keep the conversation going. He knew that I mostly slept with guys, but apparently, the fact that I once mentioned I had sex with girls growing up made me straight enough for him to confide in me.

My best friend, Richard, who had worked at Le Bourrelet almost as long as me, had recently left to become the sous-chef at Clement, the restaurant at the Peninsula Hotel. When he gave notice, Chef demanded that I convince him to stay, which I found odd and didn't even try because I knew it was hopeless. Unable to persuade him with words and a marginal raise, Chef took him to Eleven Madison, and when it was clear that no food would help to change his mind, he stormed out without having dessert. Now, one week after my conversation with Chef, I feared that his silence could have to do with my failure to persuade Richard to stay.

"I don't think he knows how close we are. He's too self-absorbed to notice anything other than himself and the food sitting on the line," Richard said as we waited for dumplings at Nom Wah.

"I don't know. I'm getting a weird feeling about it."

"You and your weird feelings. Drop it. It's all gonna be good."

When our order arrived, I remembered how generic the food had become. Gone were the days when it was still a tea parlor and the best bakery in Chinatown. Chus and I used to come regularly for mooncakes, and during the Mid-Autumn Festival, a Chinese celebration of the moon, the line would wrap around the block. We would then walk to the basketball court and sit under the Williamsburg Bridge while Chus told stories about his time in the commune and how he paid bills by posing nude for an old Spanish painter living in Montmartre whose only talent was opening his wallet.

"I *can't* with these, Deme. I just don't get your fascination with this place," Richard said after taking a bite.

"No, I know. I was just thinking that. It's just a nostalgic thing."

"I said it before. You feel too much."

"Yeah, and you, too little."

"Where did that come from?"

I smiled and took a sip from my beer.

"What's that supposed to mean?" he said, laughing. "You talking about Erica? The fact that she went psycho because I don't want to be exclusive? That's not my fault. Not everyone is interested in domesticity."

"I was just kidding."

"Sure you were. Any word from Alexis? Are you two staying friends?"

"Not for now. We decided—I mean, I decided for both of us—that it's better to not have contact for a couple of months. Time will tell if we can rebuild the trust."

"You mean if *you* can rebuild your trust."

"Yeah, that's what I meant."

Richard shook his head.

"What? Say it."

"You know you're borderline puritanical, right?"

"Because I think that sex is more fulfilling with someone you actually love and respect?"

"Yes! You're so corny."

"If you had grown up with a polyamorous uncle, you'd feel differently."

"Fair point. For the record, I just want to say one more time how much I liked the guy even if he's a horny fuck. I mean I get it. I'm like one of those dogs with their dicks out in Tompkins

Square Park, humping everything that moves," he said, then laughed.

"God. You're such a class act."

"I'm telling you, it's so fucked up. You and I were born with the wrong sexual orientations. You're the most committed, loyal man I know, every girl's dream. And I'd die to get online and be able to get some pussy delivered to my door."

"Jesus, Richard! The amount of offensive stuff you can pack into a couple of sentences. It's nuts."

"That's Yale for you, buddy. Thirty-four thousand a year," he said, waving at the waitress.

We kissed goodbye before bundling up and exiting the restaurant. The temperature had dropped considerably and the walk to the subway in a leather jacket felt like walking naked into the cold room at the restaurant. Before heading to his new apartment in Queens, which I had promised to visit soon, Richard kissed me on the lips a second time, a fascination that had started years ago when he learned it was the way some gay men greeted each other. I remembered the day. The restaurant had closed, and we had polished off a second bottle of a Grüner from Slovakia he was obsessed with at the time. He called me a heterophobe.

"Wait, what?" I said.

"Yeah. You kind of are. Why do you never kiss me on the lips when you see me and give me a lousy homie handshake instead?"

"Just because."

"Just because what?"

"Just because you're not gay, Richard. That's why!"

"Exactly my point. You're blatantly heterophobic."

"You're drunk," I said, urging him to move on.

"Well, I feel insulted. I want you to treat me like any of your gay friends," he said.

"Okay, I'll kiss you from now on. Are you happy now?" I said, and though I pronounced the words with exasperation, the fact was that I was touched.

Richard then leaned his face toward mine.

"Come on, Richard. Don't be annoying!"

He closed his eyes. As I kissed his lips, one of the washers pushed a bucket behind us.

"¡Pinches putos!" he said.

"Putísimos," I said, pulling back, Richard cracking up.

Needless to say, the rumors that we were possibly fucking caught on like a skillet on fire.

THIRTEEN DAYS AFTER I met Chef in his apartment, we went to see the immigration lawyer. The office was on the top floor of an Art Deco building in midtown, with a heavy brass revolving door you had to lean on with your whole body to get it moving. We went up an elevator operated by a guy dressed in a green uniform with polished gold buttons. Tattooed on his neck, peeking over the white shirt collar, was a crown that I had seen on many kids from my old neighborhood, a sign generally marking a life that included time at Sing Sing. When we reached the twelfth floor and the doors opened, we exchanged a glance that made him pull the collar a little higher.

The office was spacious and filled with cold winter sunlight. In the center of the room there was a long table covered with tall piles of manila folders that looked like rooftops seen from above.

"Nice setup," Chef said, taking a seat. "He must be doing well."

We had exchanged few words since meeting at the front of the building. I was about to agree when a thin, nervous-looking man entered the room. He smelled like cigarettes.

We stood up. They greeted each other in French and kissed three times. I shook his smooth hand. His nails were manicured and glossy. He introduced himself to me in English. His name was Frédéric and the way he spoke made me feel I was already wasting his time. I explained my situation but spared him the details I had shared with Chef. He asked for specific dates and the port of entry, his voice indicating a lack of hope. I answered sparingly, mimicking his tone. Then I told him that I had been paying taxes for almost eight years, which to me, despite using a fake Social Security number, had always felt like a redeeming act. While I was midsentence, he raised his hand, signaling me to stop.

Framed by Harvard diplomas and photographs of handshakes with heads of state, Frédéric spoke with a rehearsed iciness. "You have been breaking the law for sixteen years. Whether you are paying taxes or not is absolutely irrelevant. The only way for you to legally settle in this country is to leave the U.S., accept a ten-year ban, and then apply for a working visa." He sounded less like a lawyer and more like a judge delivering a verdict.

"But there's got to be a way," Chef said, uncrossing his legs. "What if I adopt him and claim a permanent residency for him?"

"Unfortunately, that's not an option. You can only do that when the individual is underage."

"What if he gets married?" Chef asked, unwilling to give up.

"Arnaud, mon ami," he said in a patronizing tone. "Things changed drastically after 9/11. The USCIS would find out he's been breaking the law for years. Not to mention he'd be breaking the law again, and I can't possibly advise him to do that."

"Merde!" Chef yelled, as if he were talking to one of the cooks.

"Unfortunately, there's nothing to be done. Ten years is not a long time," he said, glancing at his BlackBerry.

I smiled at him to hide how devastated I was. These words were not new. But hearing them in front of Chef made them irreversible and permanent. I no longer felt capable of keeping them at bay. I knew that from now on, every time Chef looked at me, he would see someone lesser, limited, someone with an inability to go further.

The elevator ride down felt endless. I was filled with anger and despair for having deluded myself these past couple of weeks into thinking that at some point the door would open, when in truth the door had shut the moment I entered the country. Since learning about my undocumented status almost a decade ago, I had been fabricating possible scenarios that would grant me some kind of amnesty and had lost myself in the fantasy.

"Fucking Frédéric. He's so fucking incompetent," Chef said as we walked out of the building.

"Sorry to have wasted your time, Chef."

"Don't be silly. We'll figure it out."

We both knew there was nothing to figure out.

Walking in silence, we found ourselves at Columbus Circle. We sat down on a freezing bench and admired the massive globe sculpture against the blue sky, its continents connected by concentric steel bars. I stared at the winter sun filtering through the shiny plates, forcing myself not to blink until my eyes hurt. At one point, Chef gave me a hug, mumbled something about Bush's being an idiot, and walked briskly away.

THE WINTER WENT BY at a glacial pace, seeming even longer and colder than others, so that at the beginning of March, I began to count the days left until the clock would officially move forward one hour, an idea that I thought brilliant at the time and only made waiting even more torturous. Our kitchen had needed an update for years and Chef decided to close down the last two weeks of the month for the renovation.

Never having been off for more than a couple of days at a time, I debated whether to go down to Miami, where my friend Lucio had recently moved to run the kitchen of Acqua. But when the time came, dreading the long bus ride and afraid to navigate an unfamiliar city with a New York ID card, I decided not to go and spent the days in my pajamas, mostly leaving the apartment to grab wings from my favorite Irish bar and take walks in the middle of the night.

Maybe it was all in my head, but after meeting the lawyer I sensed that something had changed between Chef and me, as if he couldn't overcome the fact that, in the eyes of the country, I was and would always be a second-class citizen. It was known in the industry that Le Bourrelet was the kind of place where people came to build their résumé and then moved on to other jobs with better pay and benefits. After almost a decade working for Chef, the momentum of my career gone and the best years of the restaurant seemingly behind it, I felt as if my friends had left the party at the right time and I, having stayed for too long, was now stuck helping the host clean up with the lights on, the beginning of a hangover already piercing my head.

The last day before returning to work, taking advantage of the unexpectedly warm weather, I forced myself to do something, mostly so I could talk about it at family meal with my colleagues. Biking along the Hudson, looking at the water changing colors as it traveled south toward the Atlantic, had been one of my favorite pastimes for years. Something about being near water soothed my anxiety.

I went downstairs with the bike on my shoulder and headed to the Nicholas Roerich Museum, a town house in Morningside Heights that held most of Roerich's work. I could not stand swarms of tourists, so I always searched for more intimate, less well-known collections. I learned about this and other small museums from Ben, Chus's longest romantic partner. They had a twenty-year relationship but never lived together. For a while it included a third lover, and though Chus and Ben went without seeing each other for long periods of time, they remained partners. Ben had always been a father figure, the person waiting for me outside of school to take me home. He was, with Chus, the most constant presence in my life growing up. When he died of complications from pneumonia in 1997, it felt as though I had lost a parent.

When Ben was alive, I had not been particularly moved by Roerich's work. Now, looking at the heavenly landscapes of the Himalayas in their dreamlike pastel colors, the mystic depictions of Mount Everest with its peak high above the clouds, the darkness that had overcome my life momentarily lifted. I wandered around the town house, whose walls, including the entry foyer and stairs, were covered by paintings. In one of the rooms, a baby started bawling. The mother behind the stroller looked like she could have been from Spain, something about her features that I could not quite pinpoint. And as I was having that thought, in a soothing voice, she began to sing a Spanish lullaby I had heard before. I closed my eyes and focused on the song, slowly drifting back to a street in Seville. My mother was cradling me in her arms as we watched a parade of sinister-looking people wearing dark-purple habits and pointed hoods dragging enormous crucifixes. They were walking barefoot for Easter penance, their feet swollen and bloody. The images were suddenly so vivid and haunting I had to open my eyes. Heading to the exit, I thought how much I would have loved to have known my mother as an adult, what I would have given to be able to go back to the alley behind the restaurant after the last shift and tell her one more lie about how happy I was living in America.

THERE WERE SOME RITUALS that Chus and I continued to observe, as if the survival of our two-member family depended on it. One of them was Ben's birthday. Every year, I made an extravagant cake that we ate while flipping through old photo albums and watching the same tapes that had become grainy and scratched with age. Imagining Ben's reaction as he opened the cake box while I explained its contents filled me with joy. Chus treasured the memories of when we were all together, and I often sensed they were what kept him going.

That year, I made a lemon meringue cake inspired by Alexander McQueen. Chus and I had decided that had Ben lived long enough to see McQueen rise to prominence, he would have adored his work. Staying up late two days in a row after the restaurant had closed, I sculpted a high-heeled shoe made of candied clementines, smaller meringues crumbled on top, edible gold leaf, and candied lemon-peel feathers. This was one of the most elaborate cakes I had ever made. The shoe straps, which I created using spun sugar, kept breaking, and I redid them over and over until they finally achieved the right consistency.

On Ben's birthday, I took the shoe out of the cold room, snapped some photos for my archive, and built a scaffolding of cardboard and Bubble Wrap. On the way to Chus's apartment, sitting in a cab with the box on my lap, I looked at the unrecognizable East Village, the old tenements on Thirteenth Street replaced by horrific condos that seemed dated even before they had been completed. An ambulance passing by, invading the opposite lane, brought back the morning I found Ben writhing in pain on the kitchen floor. He had a high fever and a rash on his neck. After laying him on the sofa, I called Chus, who was on Fire Island. He told me to take him to the emergency room at St. Vincent's while he made his way back to the city. We spent July and August sitting by a hospital bed that by the end of the summer had turned into an open casket. During our time there, a friend whom we had Thanksgiving with died on the same floor. Not eight weeks after Ben checked in, we rolled him out of his room under a white sheet stitched with a blue cross.

The day Ben passed away, Chus never made it home from St. Vincent's. Devastated and at the beginning of a depression that would last for years, he went back to Fire Island and didn't return until classes resumed. I went back to our apartment and discovered outside, at the top of the stairs, lit by flickering candles, an altar made of Tupperware containers piled up against the front door. Some of the food was still warm. I surrendered to the pain that I had concealed for weeks. Crying uncontrollably, I grabbed the sympathy cards that I would not be able to read for months and struggled to put the key into the lock. When at last I managed to open the door, I sat on the floor with my back against it.

I spent the rest of the day listening to old records of María Dolores Pradera, Ben's favorite singer. When the sun started to go down, I realized that I would not be able to sleep in the apartment. Up on the roof, I screamed until my voice was hoarse. Lying under the stars, wrapped in a blanket, I fell asleep to the distant sounds of trucks hitting the potholes on Fourteenth Street.

These memories were always lurking, waiting for me to lower my guard, so I was forced to relive their painful moments. Sometimes they lingered for days or came over me during sleep, waking me up with a strange feeling that was hard to dispel until I was back in the kitchen, occupied with repetitive tasks.

CHUS WAS SITTING on the sofa surrounded by books and stacks of papers, preparing for a class. I put the box on the kitchen table and took off my coat.

"I haven't seen you in ages. Is the beard a new look or just laziness?" he said in a catty tone.

He was dressed in a djellaba, a summer uniform that Ben and he had worn for years on the island. I remembered how embarrassed I was by their outfits when I was a teenager. Now nothing would have made me happier than to see them walking down the beach dressed in their Moroccan robes.

"It's definitely a new look that maybe comes out of laziness?"

"You look much cuter without it, if you're interested in my opinion," Chus said, but changed his tone when he saw the box. "What do we have here?"

Then he noticed I had left my coat on the chair again. "I don't know how many times I've told you about the coat," he said, grabbing it and walking to the entry closet.

"You told me a million times. Like the good old bourgeois lady you've become."

I heard him laugh while I looked for the scissors.

"They're in the sink!" he yelled from the entrance.

I rinsed them off and cut the cords, hoping the feathers were still in one piece.

"Voilà!" I said, pulling down the flaps and dismantling the cardboard structure.

"Oh my god, Deme! This is outstanding," he said, admiring the cake from different angles. "A shoe!"

I let an uncomfortable silence break in between us. "Just any shoe?"

Chus twitched his nose and inspected it with a worried look. I felt bad for putting him on the spot.

"Designed by . . ."

"McQueen!" he yelled, and began to clap. "A McQueen shoe! Oh, Deme. It's gorgeous. We shouldn't eat it." His voice clouded momentarily: "Ben would have loved this."

I cleared my throat. "Okay. So, here's what we have," I said, pointing to its different parts. "Candied clementines, meringue, lemon peel, and raspberries."

Though Chus was staring at the cake, I knew he was no longer present.

"How do we feel about Negronis?" I asked, opening the fridge and seeing he had oranges.

"We feel great. And we'll feel even greater after we drink them," he said. "Wait, I don't have gin."

"Do you have tequila?"

"Yes, I have a bottle somewhere."

"Great, I'll make them with tequila. They're really yummy."

I excused myself to go to the bathroom and went to my room instead. I switched on the light and sat on the bed. Some of my old photos still hung on the walls that I had once painted a canary yellow. It was hard to believe that at some point I had found that color appealing. The images that remained had been happy moments growing up that now made me sad. The view from my window, which back then had been of brownstone roofs where some of my neighbors raised chickens, was now blocked by a tall, ominous building made of dark glass. Even the sunlight that used to illuminate the table where I did my homework could no longer get through. As I looked for familiar marks on the walls, I heard Chus fighting with the ice tray. I turned off the lamp and glanced at the stickers on the ceiling, a group of glow-in-the-dark stars that had once been bright.

"Everything okay?" Chus asked, back in the kitchen.

"Yes, I'm just tired. Work's been insane."

I observed him washing the shaker and considered bringing up my meeting with the lawyer. But what would be the point? Chus was right. Talking about something that cannot be fixed is a waste of time.

"Here, do the honors," I said, handing him the knife.

"No, no. I'm going to destroy it."

"Come on, here," I said, cutting a small portion and breaking off one of the feathers.

We raised our glasses.

"To Ben." Chus gave me a look I recognized. "And to you." He was feeling blando.

"To us."

3

The clock had officially moved one hour forward and the sunlight, beginning to cast shadows as one walked down the street, promised that warmer days were ahead. The hope was crushed when the first day of spring welcomed us with another snowstorm, the fatigue of the longer-than-usual winter showing on people's faces. I blamed my dark mood and lack of energy on the weather, on too many nights sleeping next to a boiling radiator that had turned my skin into sandpaper.

At Le Bourrelet, I had earned currency helping others and being a reference for colleagues who interviewed for other jobs, currency that I would never cash in because I had assumed that I would stay with Chef forever. The washers always knew everything about who was hiring and where. One day, I overheard Los Managuas, two brothers who had been with Chef longer than me, saying that Thomas, a sous-chef who had moved to London for a job at the Dorchester, had returned to the city to become head chef at the Four Seasons restaurant. Knowing Thomas's passion for contemporary French cuisine, I was surprised he would be interested in doing New American. Without the freedom to switch jobs, I was used to ignoring this kind of information, but this time, I started to fantasize about working at the Four Seasons.

Richard and I had been wanting to meet for weeks but our schedules, especially his, had been unpredictable. We always took turns picking places, and maybe because he wanted to get back at me after the disappointing food at Nom Wah, we met at Hogs & Heifers on Washington Street, the whitest and straightest bar in New York City. At a tall table drinking three-dollar cans of beer surrounded by thousands of bras hanging on the wall, I mulled over the best way to get in contact with Thomas.

"Would you keep your U.S. phone number if you lived abroad for two years?" I asked when Richard came back with the next round.

"I don't know. Probably not. Why do you ask?"

"Remember Thomas Shultz? He's the new head chef at the Four Seasons."

"That's so funny. I just saw him doing a bump in the bathroom."

"Wait, what?"

"Look," he said, pointing at the bar. "He's ordering a drink now."

"I'll be right back."

I walked up to him as a new group of girls climbed on the bar.

"What's up, buddy? It's been forever," I said, slapping his back.

"Demetrio, my man! ¿Cómo está usted?"

"All good, all good. Are you back?"

"Fuck yeah. London is a fucking drag. Are you still getting used and abused at Le Bourrelet?"

"It's not that bad. But yeah, still there. Let's swap numbers."

"I have the same one, text me. I'm at the Four Seasons now."

"That's awesome, man. Congrats!"

"Yeah, swing by. I'll hook you up."

LATER THAT WEEK, I did something I would have never thought myself capable of: I texted Thomas and asked whether they were looking for a head of pastries. He responded almost instantly and said that he was about to mention it the other night but didn't believe that I would be open to leaving. His comment, though well intentioned, made me feel like a traitor. He assured me that if I wanted to come on board, given that my name had been brought up a couple of times but discarded because of my known loyalty to Chef, the job was practically mine. We then discussed different dessert options and agreed that I would make two of my newest creations for the executive chef: the Meyer lemon and saffron tarte au citron served with handmade ricotta and sweetened with honey from the Hudson Valley, and the matcha nonnette filled with raspberries and served with black sesame ice cream.

The thought of working at the Four Seasons, the idea that my desserts could be enjoyed in one of the most exclusive dining rooms in the world, was hard to fathom. Ben took me to the restaurant once, not to eat but to admire the spectacular curtain that Picasso had designed for the Ballets Russes and that he wanted to reference for a set commissioned by Merce Cunningham.

The day after my conversation with Thomas I received a call from the human resources director. Bettina treated me as if we had played in the same band growing up and made the chances of getting the position feel so real that, halfway through the conversation, I contemplated hanging up. I knew that pursuing a job in such a corporate place came at a risk and did my best to not let fear cripple my decision.

I was looking forward to baking in the Four Seasons kitchen, but when I got the address for my appointment a week later, it was not the Seagram building but rather a nondescript postwar building near the West Side Highway. It was a freezing April afternoon and the path along the river was almost deserted, with the exception of some red-nosed runners crammed into thermal suits, and disoriented tourists looking for the *Intrepid* aircraft carrier turned museum. Every time I biked by it, I thought of Walter, a childhood friend who joined the army during the War in Afghanistan to pay for college because his dream was to become a philosophy major at Sarah Lawrence. He never made it back. Slowing my pace, I prayed, "Dios te salve, María, llena eres de gracia," and turned right on West Forty-fourth toward Tenth Avenue.

When I entered the building, even before I had a chance to show my ID to the security guard, a woman dressed in a black business suit walked up to me.

"Demetrio?"

"Yes," I said, discreetly trying to wipe my runny nose.

"It's *so* great to meet you. As I mentioned on the phone, it's such an honor. Thomas speaks *so* highly of you," she said, extending her hand.

"Thank you," I said, not quite believing she had used the word *honor.*

"Let's go to my office." She made a gesture that indicated I didn't need to sign in. "You'll *love* the view."

There seemed to be at least one word in every sentence that

she felt it was imperative to stress. Her scripted mannerisms and over-the-top praise, which at another time I might have found off-putting, somehow made me feel appreciated. We took the elevator to her office, where I was given a blue folder with my name printed on it. Bettina handed me the application, asked me to fill out all the forms, and said she would be right back.

The moment she shut the door, I flipped through the pages looking for the word *E-Verify*, the name given to a system put in practice by the Bush administration to prevent undocumented immigrants from obtaining employment. Then I went through the forms again and this time read every line.

I could not find the word anywhere, but I did have to write down my Social Security number several times as well as the names of two professional references. I put down Richard and Lucio and experienced a strange sense of importance after writing down the Peninsula and Acqua next to their phone numbers. I was also asked to sign a form that stated I had no criminal record, my desired compensation and current salary, which, given Le Bourrelet's low wages, following Richard's suggestion, I inflated by 30 percent.

"All done?" Bettina said, opening the door. "Wonderful. As I mentioned, this is all mere formality."

I wondered if that meant they were not going to verify the information.

We then went up to the top floor and crossed a dining area into a kitchen overlooking the Hudson River. I pretended to be lost in thought inspecting ovens and utensils, my mind filled with the signatures I had added on the forms that, given my quivering hands, in no way resembled my actual handwriting. Once I was left alone and started prepping, I began to relax.

Mixing icing sugar with orange flower water to spoon over the nonnettes, I noticed how the distant murmur of the West Side Highway became louder and what had been a subdued sound had turned into a heavy roar of cars battling through rush hour.

Moments after I had plated the tarte au citron, Bettina materialized again. I wondered if I was being watched. I had expected she would come with the director of food and beverages, but she was alone and looked somewhat different. I could not figure out what it was or whether I was imagining things. As I went around the prep counter, I noticed she had changed into sneakers.

"Mr. Benet is caught up in a meeting."

"Oh, okay," I said, thinking there couldn't have been enough time for them to check the forms.

"It's very common. Don't worry about it. He's *always* running late," she said, and then rolled her eyes. I was surprised she would do something so disrespectful in front of someone she had just met.

"Oh, I'm not worried about it," I lied. She reassured me once again that baking the desserts was a mere formality, the decision was entirely Thomas's. Before we said goodbye, I considered mentioning that it had to be more than that, otherwise I wouldn't be there. But I let that thought pass and smiled instead.

THE NEXT DAY I got up early and went for a long bike ride. On my way back from Nyack, crossing the George Washington Bridge, I got a text message from Thomas saying that I had gotten the job. An adrenaline rush took over my body, making me pedal frantically, a biting wind pushing me forward. I looked up at the clouds flying through the sky and screamed, "I got it, I fucking got it!" When I entered Hudson River Park, I got off my bike and wandered to the far end near the water. I lay down on the yellow grass, grabbed my phone, and considered calling Chus. Knowing that he would have advised me against pursuing the job, I had decided not to tell him. But now that it was mine, an irrepressible need to share the news made me dial his number. When I heard his voice, I hung up as a Circle Line boat cruised by. I waved at the tourists standing on the deck. No one waved back.

That evening, stressing about my future conversation with Chef, I thought about splurging on a bottle of 2000 Taittinger Comtes de Champagne but ended up buying cava at a liquor store. A steady rain spread over the streets of the Loisaida, slowing down cars. Every time I returned I could not help being astonished by how the neighborhood was now overpopulated with coffee shops, restaurants that served mediocre food at hiked-up prices just to pay rent, and dingy bars designed to replicate the grittiness of the 1980s. Only the stealthy rats going about their business in overflowing putrid trash cans had survived gentrification. I crossed Tompkins Square Park toward Avenue B, which back in the day had been taken over by junkies in need of temporary shelter and now was full of young rich kids playing poor, their porcelain faces and perfect teeth illuminated by cell phone screens.

I stood at the corner of Avenue C and Eighth, from where I could see the dim light coming from Chus's nightstand. He was probably asleep, an open book resting on his chest. Even though I knew that no matter what I said, Chus was going to disapprove of how recklessly I was pushing my luck, I rehearsed different ways to tell him about the interview until my clothes were completely drenched.

WHEN I ENTERED my apartment, I was so exhilarated that I didn't notice the heat wasn't working until I took off my coat. I called Richard, though he always left his phone in the locker room so as not to get distracted. In the last couple of weeks, I had been consistently avoiding everyone, and now not even the washers asked me to join them for tacos and micheladas at Tacuba.

Sitting on the kitchen counter, I turned on the stove, opened the bottle of cava, and poured myself a glass. I took long gulps and the bubbles, quickly rising to my head, made me feel warm and fuzzy. The window framed a section of the building across the street, with its dilapidated water tank covered with grime, and a dark sky where blinking red lights vanished into the clouds on their way to other countries. I wondered if any of those planes were on their way to Spain. As I kept drinking, my momentary happiness, fueled by steady sips, began to disappear. A strong desire to be surrounded by people overtook me, so when the screen of my phone lit up with a message from Bondi saying that he was bartending at APT, I grabbed my jacket and two fifty-dollar bills from underneath the kitchen sink and rushed out of the apartment.

THE STREETS OF the Meatpacking District were full of stretch limos. A group of drunken girls were fighting on the corner of Little West Twelfth and Hudson. One of them, shoes in her hand, was trying to hit another with her high heels. Just as I crossed to the opposite sidewalk, two undercover cops pulled out their badges and broke up the fight.

The crowd waiting to get into the club was a mix of rich NYU kids and Eurotrash. There was not even a line, because Samantha was working the door. She loved chaos and being the center of attention.

"Hi, gorgeous," she said, opening the rope.

A roar went up.

"Hi, babe."

"What's up?" she said, planting a kiss on my cheek with her brand-new lips.

"You know, same old, same old."

"Did you bring me a cupcake?"

"You look like you've had too many cupcakes lately," I said.

"You bitch," she said, laughing loudly. "Bondi's bartending abajo."

"Yeah, I know. Do you think I walked over just to see your pretty face?"

"Asshole," she said, grabbing my crotch. "You know you love me."

"Of course I do. Everything okay?"

"Fucking tired of these niñatos pendejos," she yelled.

When Samantha spoke in Spanish, her delicate voice turned into a rasp in which some of us recognized Manny, the lanky kid we grew up with playing pelota. Manny lived in our neighborhood until his father found out that he liked to wear his sister's dresses and spend time on the Christopher Street Pier. During her teenage years, Samantha survived on a couple of hundred dollars a month that her abuela sent her from Puerto Rico, and by living with older men.

"Okay, guys. Listen up. If you don't know me like he does, go home," Samantha yelled.

"Samantha, you're insane," I said, pulling the door open. "But I adore you."

"There's a lot to fucking adore here," she said, feeling her ribs with her hands, the muscular biceps I had admired when I was a kid momentarily flaring up. "It's New York City, honey. We're not in Kansas anymore," she yelled to the crowd again. "That's how it's working tonight. Let me help you out. If I don't know you, you're not getting in."

The club was designed like an old Upper East Side apartment with long chesterfield sofas and vintage armchairs against walls covered with landscape paintings in gold frames. Downstairs was a dance floor and a bar made of pale wood, like the inside of Scandinavian restaurants in the pages of *Saveur*, with rows of bottles lit from behind. The small patio where people smoked and did bumps behind the lush bamboo was almost empty.

It was too early for any of my friends to be out. I scanned the dimly lit dance floor looking for familiar faces anyway and walked up to the bar. Bondi greeted me with a tequila soda and two silver shots that we knocked together and swallowed in one gulp. I considered sharing the news right then, but he was busy. Once the dance floor began to fill up and the bar became less hectic, he came over and handed me a bag of molly. I wet my finger and stuck it inside. It had been months since I had done ecstasy. Shortly after Twilo was closed down and Body & Soul evicted from Vinyl, I had stopped clubbing. Having spent most Sunday mornings of my late teens in a K-hole, I was grateful that the nightlife crackdown coincided with my promotion to pastry chef, when I could no longer afford the sluggishness that followed intense partying.

I danced until the early hours of dawn. At about six in the morning, Samantha locked the door of the club and turned it into a private party. She dissolved a bunch of molly in a bottle of water that was passed around. I made sure to take long sips, and soon after the music flooded my body, short-circuiting conduits and nerves, a familiar tingle caressing my spine.

As the morning wore on, old faces from my clubbing days began to materialize, faces I never encountered buying groceries, riding the subway, or biking around the city. Faces that only appeared at night. A group of older club kids I knew from the Tunnel, Palladium, and roller-skating at the Roxy didn't recognize me. Unwilling to accept the passing of time, these now middle-aged men were still wearing the same flashy clothes that had once heightened their youthful beauty but now exposed their used-up bodies. As I kept dancing, I said to myself I would never become the older guy who didn't know when to stop.

A bunch of skinny Russian models with impeccable hairdos and shiny jackets captured the splintered light coming from the disco ball and everyone's attention. I was convinced I had been dancing next to my friend Matt wearing his black, worn-out motorcycle jacket. But at one point, a spotlight illuminated his face, and I realized the guy looked nothing like him.

The bamboo on the patio was slowly turning a brighter shade of green as a shy morning light descended on it. The music had transitioned into diaphanous selections that heralded closing time. We were submerged in a deep, aquatic track that suddenly turned into a shriek blaring out of the sound system. Throughout the feedback, people kept moving, although now, instead of swimming, they seemed to be trapped and fighting to escape. I opened my mouth wide as the blaring noise pushed down my throat, the reverberation fierce and rough. I walked closer to one of the speakers and let the waves of dry sound crash onto my sweaty face. Then the music stopped, and the lights turned on. Seeing so many disfigured faces in disarray, I imagined mine. I grabbed my jacket from the top of the speaker and snuck out of the club without saying goodbye.

It was a crisp Sunday morning. Mixing in my brain like a perfectly arranged song were the sounds of leaves rustling, a car alarm, the beeping of a van backing up. My jaw was sore, my pupils so dilated it was impossible to find the hands on my watch. Time had disappeared.

I took small steps as if, waking up from the longest dream, I had forgotten how to walk. The sidewalk looked welcoming and mushy. I was sure that I was near the river when I found myself in front of Pastis, just a block away from the club. Looking through its windows, I stared at the typical brunch customers who happily paid for overpriced eggs but always refused dessert. Slowly beginning to feel like myself again, I reviewed what had happened after I received the text from Thomas, biking along the river, strolling through my old neighborhood, drinking cava. It felt like a long-ago memory. A desire to leave the city right then was sinking in. I wandered off for a couple of blocks without a destination, and when I couldn't bear the cold slapping my face any longer, I took a cab to the South Street Seaport.

The car slipped down Washington Street while a smooth jazz tune played on the radio. As I looked out the window, the images seemed choreographed to the rhythm of the music: a construction worker waving a reflective orange flag, a delivery boy pedaling against the strong wind, barely moving, and a flock of white birds gliding toward the river. When the song ended, a familiar voice announced the beginning of *Weekend Edition*. I closed my eyes and saw Chus in his pajamas leaning over the kitchen table tussling with the *New York Times* crossword puzzle, drinking café con leche, a cigarette on the ashtray burning on its own.

Only a couple of tourists huddled against the freezing wind were waiting for the ferry. Soon after I got on, the boat began pulling away from the dock and pointed its prow toward Staten Island. Leaning against the frosted glass, I became engrossed in the tumultuous water and the thick white strips of foam gradually dissolving behind us. I looked back at the city in the distance. Thinking about the job, I felt adrenaline flood every crease of my body.

4

Six hours later I woke up with my clothes on, tired and depressed. The sun was setting, and lying on the couch, the last rays slowly sweeping the floor, I was overwhelmed with anxiety. Feeling Bettina's business card in the pocket of my jeans, I turned over and tried to fall asleep again. I considered calling everything off but instead I took a shower, got dressed, and went down to Florent.

My usual corner was taken, the place full of yuppies and unfamiliar faces. I waved at the bartender, who was busy making cocktails as the clock ticked toward the end of happy hour, and signaled I would be back later. As I left the diner, I imagined a life as the head of pastries at the Four Seasons and fantasized about my future: traveling around America, writing a dessert cookbook, and then opening my own pastry shop.

Toying with the idea of calling Chus but afraid that he would raise all the questions I had managed to avoid, I walked north on Eighth Avenue. The streets were pulsating with people rushing home. As I walked east toward Fifth, I chose the exact location for my future shop at the corner of Avenue C and

Ninth, where Barrio, a Puerto Rican bakery that had the best pastelitos de guayaba when I was growing up, used to be.

Midtown was buzzing. I made my way to Clement to see Richard. After several missed calls from him, I figured he would be excited to see me. Many people working in that kitchen had trained with us, something Chef hated. But he paid poorly, and the workers who stuck around were mostly on sponsor visas or had no visas at all.

I fist-bumped the security guard standing at the employee entrance of the hotel and walked down the spotless long corridor that led to the kitchen. Richard was yelling at a nervous young cook who had overbrowned a duck. As soon as he saw me, he pushed two fingers against his tongue and whistled loudly. Everyone began shouting and hitting cast-iron pans against the metal counters. A line cook grabbed two mixing paddles, turned around a pot, and played it like a drum. The sound was deafening. Though this lasted for less than thirty seconds, it seemed much longer. My smile was so big it felt as if my face were a canvas stretched over a frame. When everyone resumed their duties, Richard pulled off his apron, and instead of giving me a kiss, he hugged me so hard that he squeezed all the air out of my lungs.

"Fuck yeah!" he said before walking into the cold room. "Hold on one second."

Waiting for him, the effects of the momentary happiness that seconds ago had pulled me into an incredible high suddenly pushed me into a dark abyss.

Richard came back with a plastic bag and a mischievous look on his face. He yelled that he was going for a smoke with the best pastry chef in America. I followed him to the service elevator, and we skyrocketed to the fifty-second floor, my empty stomach turning upside down. Up on the roof, we climbed a small ladder to the top of a cornice.

"Straight from the Caspian Sea," he said, opening the bag and pulling out a can of beluga caviar. "Only the best for the best."

"Richard, you're nuts. Don't they keep track?"

"They do, but don't worry about it." He pulled two spoons from his back pocket. "Do the honors."

I took a spoonful and pushed the eggs against my palate, the roe bursting like fireworks, the multilayered texture of different buttery flavors flooding my mouth. "This is the real deal."

"We got it this morning."

He pulled a thin, shiny flask out his pocket. His face was gleaming. "To the new head of pastries at the Four Seasons."

After taking a swig of the vodka, I looked down at the yellow cabs rushing along Fifth. Hundreds of feet aboveground, suspended in an ocean of flickering lights, it seemed that anything was possible, and "anything" included becoming head of pastries at the most exclusive dining room in the world.

WITH THE TASTE of the beluga still lingering in my mouth, I walked along Fifty-seventh Street thinking about Alexis. Maybe because I wanted him to know I had gotten the job or because I wanted complete closure, I sent him a message and we agreed to meet outside Tourneau, a store that specialized in vintage watches. Every now and then, I would go in to browse their inventory, and if they happened to have my dream watch, a stainless-steel Rolex Datejust from the eighties, I would try it on and walk around the store, marveling at the simplicity of its design. This time, they didn't have any, and I was secretly glad, because given my new salary, I would have put down a deposit.

Only Alexis knew about this fixation, a secret he had promised to keep, especially from Marxist Chus. When I got out of the store, he was already waiting, his long, skinny body leaning against the marble wall.

"What did you do to your hair?"

Alexis's curls were the most defining part of his look. They dangled around his neck, caressing his shoulders, except on hot, humid summer days, when they shrank so much that people asked him whether he had gotten a haircut.

"Chopped it all off. I was sick of it," he said, and then offered his cheek for a kiss.

His shaved head made it feel as if we had been separated for much longer.

"See anything you like?"

"Nah. They only had one in white gold, but it's too flashy," I said, as if I could afford it.

We headed north on Madison until we were in front of Barneys, where we had spent so much time together. Before Samantha became a nightlife person, she was the hostess at Freds, the restaurant on the ninth floor, until the wife of the manager caught them having sex in a fitting room and we were no longer welcome to drink for free. We would also go right before the sales went up to 70 percent off to try on clothes that we hid on different racks so people could not find them. That was how I scored a Helmut Lang coat, to this day my favorite piece I owned.

"Do you want to go in?" he asked.

"No. Do you?"

"No, if you don't want to."

I thought about sharing the news but suddenly worried he would tell Chus.

"I miss you, Deme. I miss hanging out. Going to Jacob Riis on our bikes, lying down on the pier, reading my poems to you."

"Do you also miss fucking other guys in our bed when I'm not home?"

Alexis tilted his head down as tears began rolling down his cheeks. Without the curls, his eyes and lips had become more prominent, and I felt as if I were seeing them in all their splendor for the first time. I hated being so vengeful, my desire to hurt him also part frustration for falling in love with guys whose idea of loyalty included a weekly visit to the bathhouse.

"I guess you're never going to forgive me."

It was not a question but the sound of a thought. I stopped walking and gave him a hug. He began bawling on my shoulder. We didn't move until he calmed down, then I dried his face with the back of my sleeve and headed to the subway. As I descended the stairs, he waved his hand from across the street. I did not wave back.

WHEN THE PHONE RANG on Monday, I knew it was Chef without looking at the screen. By the quietness of his voice, it was obvious he was trying to act calm. He said to be ready in half an hour and hung up the phone without saying goodbye.

My mind was racing. I went to the bathroom and turned on the hot water, then made the bed. The phone rang again. A number I did not recognize blinked impatiently. I grabbed Bettina's business card from the pocket of my jeans and compared the matching numbers, letting the phone vibrate in my hand until the voicemail icon lit up. I spent twenty minutes under scalding water, and when the steam was so thick it became impossible to see my reflection in the mirror, I turned off the shower and sat in the tub.

By the time I walked out of my building, Chef was standing across the street. I pretended to act normal. My legs were shaking. He stared at me as if he were seeing my face for the first time and was trying to memorize it.

"Hi, Chef." My voice was trembling.

"How are you doing?"

I wasn't completely sure if he knew, so I didn't respond. He looked at me with gloomy eyes, put his arm around my neck, and gently pushed me forward. Neither of us said anything for a while. He drew on his cigarette and each thick mouthful of smoke seemed to contain the words he was unwilling to say. I listed off the ingredients of the lemon meringue cake in my mind and then repeated them backward.

I pretended that I still had a choice, that I could still go back to my old life and forget all about the job. But even if that possibility existed, I knew I could no longer take it. We strolled down Gansevoort in silence. Looking down, I noticed how his loafers were made of thin, soft leather.

"So," I said, accepting that I wouldn't find words to lessen the impact. "I've applied for a job at the Four Seasons."

He grabbed my elbow, climbed the first steps of a stoop, and sat down.

"I know," he said, and slid his hand back and forth as if he were caressing the step.

A couple of seconds went by. People around us rushed down the street, their necks wrapped in scarves.

"I understand you wanting to move on. I even feel that I was the one who started it. But what if you get caught, Demetrio? Have you *thought about that?* Have you already forgotten the meeting we had with the lawyer?" he asked, raising his voice.

"I haven't forgotten the meeting with the lawyer, Chef. In fact, there hasn't been *one single day* since that meeting that I haven't woken up or gone to sleep thinking about it."

"Okay," he said.

"Don't okay me, Chef. Don't *fucking okay* me!" I yelled, pointing a finger at his face.

He began making noises with the coins in his pocket. "I'm sorry, Demetrio."

"No," I said, getting ahold of myself. "I'm the one who's sorry."

"I understand why you did it, I do. And I'm really proud of you."

I appreciated his kind words, his help over the years, but I knew that if I tried to speak, no words would come out. After Ben's death, Chef had been like a father to me, especially while Chus struggled with depression. I had always done everything to impress him and made sure to put the restaurant and his well-being before mine. But that time, as we stood up and began walking north, I accepted that I had only thought of myself.

After fighting the biting wind for a couple of blocks, Chef suggested going to Del Posto. When we walked in the door, I noticed the hostess tensing up at the presence of Chef. She gave a nervous grin and made a quick call. The general manager appeared almost instantly and ushered us to a spacious corner table with a *Reserved* sign sitting on top. We passed the kitchen, and I smelled a lemon and chocolate pudding being made. The phone kept vibrating intermittently in my pocket.

I was grateful for the oversized menu that I was able to hide behind for a couple of minutes.

"Look at this," Chef said. "Noon and it's already packed."

As usual, Chef was drawn to the most elaborate dishes, the white-almond soup, the seared squid stuffed with meringue sauce, the Hudson Valley foie gras, and the rainbow trout with currants and relish. I was interested in the grilled octopus with sweet potato and caramelized onion salad, and wanted to save room for the mille crepe with Grand Marnier, Bavarian cream, and orange-vanilla reduction.

After we placed our orders, I excused myself to go to the bathroom. I locked myself in a stall and listened to the voicemail. Bettina's voice sounded less friendly. *There has been a mistake that is probably nothing. Call me as soon as possible.* I turned off the phone and went back to the table. The moment I sat down, I remembered I had to pee.

I gave Chef a detailed account of everything that had happened thus far, minus the voicemail. While we tried a couple of bites of the dishes that the runner rushed to the table, we acted as if things were going to be fine.

"Did they ask for your Social Security?"

"Yes, and I gave them the one I've always used."

"Okay. Who knows? It might work."

I considered not sharing that Bettina had already reached out.

"I don't think so."

For a moment neither of us said a word.

"They have left me a voicemail saying that something's up with my application."

"When?"

"This morning. I just listened to the voicemail."

Chef stared at me with sullen eyes. "Did you sign anything that allowed them to do that?" he said, the first part of the sentence hardly audible, as if the words were coming from a distant place.

I went silent. Chef let the silence last, then asked again. "Did you?"

The general manager, who had been roaming around our table for a while, decided it was a good moment to make an appearance. Chef waved his hand dismissively.

"Yes," I finally said.

TWO DAYS AFTER Bettina left the voicemail, I biked to Chus's apartment. As I pedaled south along the Hudson River, sandwiched between the roaring West Side Highway and the water, a familiar thought returned: *Maybe it's time to leave.* On this occasion, the words didn't end with a question mark.

I headed north along the East River, unsure if wanting to leave the country immediately was an indication of weakness or just pure fear of being put in a detention center. The notion that this administration would finally pass the DREAM Act, a bill I had renamed the NIGHTMARE Act, now seemed childish and irresponsible.

I slid through the East Village, avoiding potholes and streets with happy memories, and locked my bike on the corner post so I could see it from the kitchen window. I walked up to the building, feeling a calm, steady inner force, pressed the buzzer, and climbed the stairs, as if these actions and the conversation that followed were acts of a play.

"Loosening up my lower back!" Chus yelled from the living room as I closed the door.

Lying on the floor reading the Pasolini biography I had given him for his birthday, Chus had his butt elevated on a pillow. His legs were propped against the wall, making his pajama pants roll up. He was wearing his Pink Panther socks.

"What's wrong?" he asked.

I turned around, walked back to the entrance, and hung my coat in the closet. When I entered the living room again, Chus was sitting on the floor with his back resting on the wall.

"I can't do it anymore," I said, kneeling down next to him. The thought that I had made the decision on a whim crossed my mind but didn't stay long. As I sat down it became clear that it had been in the making for months.

"I've just landed a job as head of pastries at the Four Seasons, but I can't take it. A couple of months ago I was offered a scholarship to attend the Culinary Institute of America that I also couldn't take. What am I going to do? Stay at Le Bourrelet until I retire? And with what money? I won't be getting a dime from Social Security even though I've been funding it since I was sixteen."

Chus stayed still for a while. On his face, I could see the effect of my words. He hugged his legs.

"But the bill might pass in the Senate soon." His voice was so low that it sounded like a thought passing through his head.

"You know nothing will happen with Bush in power. I mean, for Christ's sake, nothing happened when *Clinton* was in power."

The longer we stayed silent, the more difficult it became to say the words: "I have to go back." The most painful sentence I had ever uttered because what it truly meant was: I'm abandoning you. "I know it sounds strange to you. It sounds strange to me too. Because when I say 'go back,' I talk as if I know what 'back' is."

Chus opened his arms.

I crawled on the floor and laid my head in his lap.

5

Three weeks later, walking along the jet bridge, I looked down through a scratched plastic window. I was no longer touching the ground. My last steps on American soil had happened without my noticing, unceremoniously. I suddenly felt like running back into the terminal. Instead, I dried my palms on the sides of my jeans and opened the shiny burgundy passport I had picked up at the Spanish consulate, the expiration date ironically coinciding with the day I would be able to reenter the States. I flipped through its blank pages and remembered my childhood fascination with flying, the dream of collecting stamps from every country. For many years, Chus and I took the subway to the Rockaways on weekends to watch planes take off from JFK until their lights became tiny flashing specks that could have passed for shooting stars. But that fascination was destroyed when I learned that people like us did not take planes. People like us took buses for twelve bucks that left from Chinatown.

I distracted myself by guessing the nationalities of the passengers slowly trickling in. It was an easy game. The Spanish spoke loudly, and many carried enormous Century 21 bags they crammed into overhead compartments. I tried to imagine the kind of lives they were going back to and what their country, my country, would be like. This moment of departure failed to resemble the nightmare I had had for years, where I was driven to a remote "detention facility," a temporary jail with a fancy name. The trip happened at night, and because my hands were tied, I couldn't hold on to anything, my body bouncing freely inside the ICE van. When the doors finally opened, I recognized the faces of the correction officers, people I had argued with, coworkers, neighbors, an angry cabdriver I had given the finger after almost being knocked off my bike.

Now, looking out the window, I hoped this recurring nightmare, always creeping up when I least expected it, would remain here, in the country that had created it. The flight attendant, speaking English with a thick Spanish accent, announced it was a full flight and no more space was available in the overhead compartments. Some passengers carrying suitcases down the aisles became furious. I glanced at my watch. It was ten past seven. The kitchen would be in full swing. I had spent eight years slaving in that inferno, which often reached over one hundred degrees, and where the only semblance of sunlight was the radiance of a twelve-burner range, my only companion a gallon of water to get me through the shift. I closed my eyes and heard the machines buzzing with orders.

A Spanish-looking guy slipped into the seat next to me. I couldn't tell exactly what made him Spanish, but I was certain he was. He appeared to be my age, with carefully disheveled blond hair and a strong jaw accentuated by a five-o'clock shadow. His green eyes were bloodshot.

"Hola," I said after he got settled.

"Hola. Visiting Madrid?"

"Yeah," I said, shoving my passport underneath my right thigh.

He grabbed a pair of headphones and an NYU water bottle from his backpack and stuffed them into the mesh pocket in front of him. He had a gold Rolex Submariner on. If it was real, my yearly salary was on his wrist.

"Are you on vacation?" he asked.

"Not really. I'm actually moving to Spain."

"Oh, that's cool. Isn't it funny? Americans love Madrid and Spaniards love New York."

I smiled and turned my head to the window. A white plane with a golden crown was taxiing next to us.

"That's the royal family," he said.

"What?" I recognized the Spanish coat of arms. "They have their own plane?"

"Yeah, well kind of. It's paid for with taxpayers' money. So technically it's also my plane," he said with a laugh.

"Are you from Madrid?"

"Yeah. I'm heading back for the break. I go to school in New York."

"Oh, great. Where?" I asked, playing dumb.

"NYU," he said, pointing at the water bottle. "How about you?"

"It's a long story. I was born in Seville and came to the U.S. when I was a kid. I've never been back. I'm kind of moving to Madrid for good."

"What do you mean 'kind of'?"

Looking into his eyes, I surprised myself with what I said next: "I'm being deported."

Even though I was not technically being deported, because I

was leaving voluntarily, that was how I felt. The moment I said it, I regretted lying to him. I hated myself for trying to elicit sympathy.

"Wow. That's pretty intense. Sorry about that."

He tried to look unperturbed but glimpsing the full sleeve of tattoos on my left arm and the burns on my hands, his nostrils began to expand.

"These are from the kitchen," I said, pointing at the scars. "I'm a pastry chef."

"Oh, cool."

"Yeah. Don't worry, I'm not a convict on the run," I said, trying to make him laugh.

"Oh, I wasn't thinking that." His smile showed rich-kid teeth. "I love your tattoos. I've been wanting to get one for a while, but my dad would kill me."

"Really?" I frowned.

"No, he literally would," he said, keeping a serious look for a moment, then grinned. He had an easy smile, and his tone betrayed an inadvertent intention to please.

After all the passengers had taken their seats and the comforting voice of the pilot thanked us for our business, the flight attendants walked through the aisles slamming shut the overhead compartments. The plane began to move toward the runway. A few minutes later, we were in the air, with a view of the Manhattan skyline at sunset. No one living in this city, especially those who spent their days working underground, should ever be deprived of such a view. A view that instantly made you feel freer, lighter. Mesmerized, I watched the skyscrapers effortlessly reaching for the clouds until the last buildings of the Financial District were replaced by the dark blue of the Atlantic.

The small TV screen in front of me showed a map of North America and Europe connected by a blue dotted line, and a blinking plane riding on it. I pressed the buttons and zoomed in and out of the image, the widest framing displaying the entire journey, which we would be completing throughout the night. Looking at the vast ocean separating both continents, I thought about crashing into the black, frigid waters and tried to remember the emergency demonstration from the flight attendants I wished I had paid more attention to.

"Excuse me," I said when the seat belt light turned off.

"Sure," he said, standing up.

I was excited to explore the plane. As I unfastened myself from the seat, my passport fell on the floor. I shoved it in my back pocket and walked to the rear of the plane, trying not to think about what the future held for me in seven hours. I couldn't visualize landing in my homeland, a homeland that didn't feel like home.

I lined up for the bathroom and glanced at a big screen in the middle of the cabin. Our plane had moved over the ocean. Staring at the line that connected New York and Madrid, I imagined all the planes that were suspended in the air at that moment.

By the time I returned to my seat, *M*A*S*H* was playing on the screen.

"Isn't this show like twenty years old?" he said while I took my seat.

"At least."

I turned my head to his screen and looked at his beautiful face and long neck, the skin smooth like a child's. Glancing at my reflection in the window, I wondered if spending so much time in a kitchen, deprived of sunlight, had aged me prematurely.

"What are you studying?"

"Well, I'm planning my own major. It's a little abstract."

"Are you at Gallatin?"

"You know about it?" he said, opening his eyes wide. "Not a lot of people do."

"Yeah, of course."

"Are you at NYU too?"

"No, but I know a lot about the educational system," I said, wishing for the first time I was also in college. "I grew up with my uncle, he's a professor of humanities at City College." Chus would have been happy to hear that, since I constantly joked that his job was teaching millennials how to spell.

He nodded and flashed his teeth. "Very cool."

A flight attendant pushed a cart down the aisle, spreading a smell of hot plastic through the cabin. Some of the passengers started to fiddle with their armrests. As I struggled to find my tray, he leaned over me.

"Excuse me," he said, pulling the tray out.

"Gracias."

"Everyone hates airplane food. But I actually love it."

"Beef or pasta?" the flight attendant asked.

"Pasta," I said, wanting to get the Castilian accent right but sounding too over-the-top, the way some of my Latino friends talked to make fun of me. My Spanish had lost its original sound and was now a combination of Caribbean and Mexican Spanish, a strange mix that made me feel self-conscious.

"Can I get some wine?" I said in English.

"Red or white?"

"Rojo," I said with an exaggerated American accent.

He started laughing.

"Don't you love when Americans say that?" I said.

"I thought you were serious."

The flight attendant impatiently raised her eyebrows at him.

"Beef, and I'll have some rojo as well." He turned his head and smiled complicitly. "I'm Jacobo, by the way."

"Demetrio."

We shook hands, his grip intense, as if he wanted to prove his manhood.

"Has anyone told you that you smile a lot?"

"Yeah, I've heard that before. It's my insecurity."

Since we had just met, I found his airing something so personal both strange and charming. I unwrapped every container, picked at everything, but ate little. I mostly rearranged the food on the tray. Looking for pieces of chicken buried under the pasta, I now understood why Chef brought his own food for the plane every time he went to France.

We ate in silence, staring at the soundless main screen showing people having stunning accidents where they miraculously didn't get hurt. Isolated guffaws echoed in the aircraft. I looked at Jacobo out of the corner of my eye and noticed him taking small and deliberate bites, wanting the food to last.

A puffy white line hovered in the sky, the trail of a distant plane flying our same route in the opposite direction. I wondered if there was a kid on board like I had once been: a kid about to become a second-class citizen. The flight attendant stopped the cart at our row. I handed her my trash and observed how Jacobo folded his tray, then imitated him. He excused himself to go to the bathroom but walked to the front of the plane.

I put my hand on his seat and touched the empty space. The final weeks had been particularly intense; all I had done was stress out about my departure and feel guilty for leaving Chus, who kept reminding me that ten years was not long in the context of a lifetime. Now, talking to Jacobo, I experienced a vague sense of hope and a desire to be liked, two things that I had lost since breaking up with Alexis. On the floor, I noticed, next to his olive-green espadrilles, a worn leather wallet. I kicked it gently with my foot and leaned forward. As I was about to grab it, I looked up and saw Jacobo coming down the aisle. I worried that he might think I was stealing it, so I put it back on the floor and retied my laces. When he sat down, I picked the wallet up, feigning surprise.

"Is this yours?" I said casually.

"Yes! Thank you! That would have been the second time I'd have lost it in a week."

Jacobo pulled six small bottles of Johnnie Walker from underneath his sweatshirt.

"Welcome to first class, señor Demetrio. Glad to have you on board," he said, putting two bottles on his lap and stuffing the rest in his bag. He twisted them open and handed one to me.

"Where did you get them?"

"Don't ask, don't tell," he said, flashing a smile again.

I wondered if he was flirting.

Outside the window, there were different shades of misty black. The light from the airplane reflecting on the clouds gave the darkness a life of its own. The night had also extended inside the plane. Except for an old Hasidic Jew, who kept walking up and down the aisle despite the steward's repeated attempts to make him stay in his seat, most passengers were asleep. I closed

my eyes and imagined our blinking plane following the thin
dotted line moving faster than time itself.

AS WE TRAVELED through time zones and the hands on our
watches lost their meaning, our conversation went from speak-
easies and after-hours to world-class restaurants and the political situation in Spain. Halfway over the Atlantic, I found
myself talking about 9/11.

"Sorry for the rambling," I said.

"No worries," he said. "Were you in the city?"

"Yeah, I was. I think everyone in the world knows where
they were that day. How about you?"

"I was in Madrid. I can't believe it's already been, what, six
years? I remember I was at school. Our driver came to pick me
up three hours ahead of time. At first, I thought that something had happened to my mother—she had been sick for a
while—but when I got in the car Federico told me about the
Twin Towers. My dad has government connections and there
was some sort of global alert."

"Is he a politician?"

"No, he's a businessman. But he has strong ties to the Par-
tido Popular. His father, my grandfather, was a minister with
Franco. Dad is very right-wing."

I took a last sip and finished a second bottle. It suddenly
became real that I was about to enter a world that I knew little
about. My memories were limited to the few years I had spent
living in Seville with my mother, and oftentimes those memories were also part of my dreams. Most of what I knew about
the country was through Chus. Growing up under the dicta-

torship and seeing it end had not provided him with any sense of closure, it had just made him even more vindictive.

I asked Jacobo about Zapatero, the current socialist president. The country was at the beginning of a recession with the highest unemployment rate in the European Union. His ratings were low.

"He's okay," he said, grinning. "Let me put it to you this way: He's a whole lot better than the opposition, but somehow still totally inept. I mean, at least he's kept his campaign promises. He withdrew our troops from Iraq and legalized gay marriage."

Chus had always made fun of how my gaydar was always off. When Jacobo had leaned over me to pull out my tray, used the words *Don't ask, don't tell*, an infamous LGBTQ military policy instituted, and mentioned gay marriage, he had acted with indifference. But I wondered.

"It's true that the poor guy doesn't know what the fuck he's doing with the economy," he continued, opening two more bottles.

"Yeah, that's what it seems. Unemployment is near twenty percent from what I read in the paper, not the best moment to move to Spain," I said, as if I had other options.

"Well, those are the official numbers, but Spain has a really developed underground economy, so it's hard to know. A lot of people work under the table while they're collecting unemployment."

Not knowing what to say, I smiled.

"It's a complicated situation," he continued. It was clear he was interested in politics. "I mean, not to oversimplify things, but in Spain, the right is good at making profits and the left is good at sharing those profits." He laughed noisily. Someone shushed us.

Then he might have felt the conversation was becoming too serious or boring, because he suggested playing a game.

"What's the craziest thing you've ever done?" he asked.

I was instantly uncomfortable with the premise, but in that moment, emboldened by alcohol, I managed to act as if this were something I actually enjoyed, because I knew he did. I might have made some kind of face, since he volunteered to go first.

"Okay. It's a little TMI but I feel comfortable sharing it with you. You seem open-minded enough."

My heart began to pound. "I *am* open-minded," I lied. "So, shoot."

"I once had sex for money."

Suddenly at a loss, I smiled to hide the realization that in the mere five hours we had spent together, I had developed feelings for him.

"That's cool," I managed to say. "Did you enjoy it?"

"Nah, I didn't. But I enjoyed giving the three hundred bucks to a homeless person afterward."

I pulled up the screen on my window halfway and noticed that, although it was still dark, a feeble light was beginning to outline a bed of clouds expanding into the horizon.

"We're almost there," I said, knowing it was my turn but too upset to keep playing.

He said nothing but looked crestfallen. I pulled the small blanket on top of me as if I were a corpse. The blinking plane had crossed most of the vast ocean made of blue pixels and was slowly approaching the coast of Portugal. I turned the screen off. The lack of sleep, the anxiety of the arrival, and all the talking and drinking had exhausted me. I had hoped the whiskey would push me into a light sleep. But I was wired.

Jacobo grabbed a small pillow, which had fallen in between us, and, folding it in two, placed it behind his right shoulder. He closed his eyes and shifted on his seat a couple of times. After staring at the living darkness outside my window for a while, I closed mine. His leg was touching my leg.

6

I woke to the smell of overheated plastic trays and burnt eggs. My nose was clogged, my throat parched. With my eyes still closed, I focused on the distant sounds: a loud yawn, trays being pulled out, a flushing toilet. Not knowing when I would be able to eat next, I pulled up the back of my seat. A dazzling morning light flooded the sleepy cabin. Jacobo was absorbed in a worn book, the pages barely holding together.

"What are you reading?"

"Engels," he said, smiling and showing the cover as if to prove it.

It was *The Condition of the Working Class in England*, which I read when I was twelve, and though I did not understand much of it, Engels's descriptions of the coal-black streams full of debris and filth meandering through industrial neighborhoods were unforgettable. Chus had promised me that if I finished the book, he would take me to Astroland, the amusement park on Coney Island. I had built up so many expectations during the long, dead hours sitting in front of the air-conditioning trying to make sense of the words that the rides themselves were a disappointment. But when the sun started to go down, the park turned into a giant party. Everyone gathered around the Himalaya ride and began dancing and roller-skating to the music. The crowd moved together as if it were one large body, everyone clapping and shaking their hips in unison. This was the first dance party I ever attended, the first of many, and the first time I saw Chus kissing another man. On the train ride back, he asked me if I wanted to talk about anything that could have upset me. I told him that nothing had upset me. It was true.

"So, once you're deported, you can't go back to the States?" Jacobo said, closing the book.

"Well, I haven't been *officially* deported," I confessed. "I did what's called a 'voluntary departure.'"

"Oh, I thought you said you had been deported."

"Sorry, no, that wasn't exactly true," I said. "That's just how I experienced it."

"No, I get that. I can't even imagine what it is to be illegal."

I wondered whether his use of the word *illegal* had been a slip of the tongue. Jacobo shifted in his seat and pulled down his underwear through his front pocket. "Is that how you say it?" he asked.

"No, it's not," I said instantly, as if the words were already in my mouth, waiting to be released. "It's undocumented."

"Oh, sorry about that. I should be paying more attention to the pervasive ways in which media shapes how we see the world," he said, using a tone that reminded me of Chus. "I've been studying that for the whole semester. 'Voluntary departure,' you said it's called? You have to be kidding me. What does that even mean?" he said, raising his voice.

"It means that you leave the country of your own will, so you avoid a criminal record."

"I see. It should be called voluntary-ish departure." He

laughed at his own joke. "Well, at least you'll be able to go back," he added, trying to sound cheerful.

I drank the orange juice for the vitamin C and did my best to eat the toxic-looking croissant, which became hard as a rock as soon as it cooled off.

"Are you okay?" Jacobo said.

"Why do you ask?"

"You look a little pale."

"Yeah. I feel like I'm getting a cold."

The shifting, glaring light coming through the windows filled the plane with the new day. I sneezed compulsively. My temples felt as if they were being drilled. I wondered if I was having some sort of allergic reaction to the high altitude, as if my body were not supposed to ever leave the ground.

The seat belt sign came on as the captain informed us we were approaching the final descent. We would be landing in Madrid in twenty-five minutes, where the temperature was eighty degrees Fahrenheit, twenty-six Celsius. The plane banked slightly to the left. My stomach cramped. I felt a sharp, piercing pain in my ears. As we descended through some clouds, a mild turbulence took over. Jacobo, his hands clutching the armrests, breathed heavily, his long, rhythmic exhalations making me nervous. Had I not been feeling so suddenly sick, I would have said something to comfort him, but my head was about to spin off my body. When we finally stabilized, endless flatlands in different shades of yellow extended over the horizon. The plane seemed to be chasing its shadow on a sea of waving barley. Down below, a group of stone houses blended with the golden color of the fields, and in the distance, the blades of a windmill turned lazily. I leaned my forehead on the window and remembered the raspy voice of Chus reciting the opening lines of *Don Quixote:* "En un lugar de la Mancha, de cuyo nombre no quiero acordarme, no ha mucho tiempo que vivía un hidalgo de los de lanza en astillero, adarga antigua, rocín flaco y galgo corredor."

JACOBO AND I EXITED the plane without saying a word, allowing the other passengers to walk in between us, neither of us making any effort to close our distance. I wasn't sure if there was a kind of plane etiquette that said one doesn't talk to one's seatmate after landing. All I knew was that it felt wrong not to say goodbye.

At times, it seemed as though he was slowing down. But it was hard to tell whether this was intentional or the result of being absorbed on his phone. The other passengers moved fluidly, with certainty, knowing that today they were here but tomorrow they could be somewhere else, and that somewhere else included the United States. They were used to moving in and out of countries effortlessly, walking through the glass hallway with ease. My steps were heavy and deliberate.

We entered the futuristic addition to the old airport where I had boarded my flight to New York sixteen years ago. Chus and I had caught a glimpse of this new, gleaming Terminal 4 in *Volver*, Almodóvar's latest film. It looked celestial on the screen and even more so in real life. The ceiling was clad in bamboo strips, and the early summer light, pouring through enormous skylights, bounced off a polished marble floor. I walked behind a couple from Long Island and listened to their conversation about museums and nearby towns that they were planning to visit, until we arrived at customs. The Americans were directed to wait in long, unruly lines with other foreigners. The EU line was short and moved quickly.

Jacobo was already at one of the booths. Staring at the screen of his phone, he handed his passport to the border patrol agent, who barely looked at it. He then put it back in his pocket and turned his head slightly, as if the thought of looking for me had entered his mind too late.

Standing behind the line marked on the floor, I was sweating profusely from what felt like a high fever. I was afraid of looking suspicious. When the agent motioned me to the booth, I felt my soaked shirt clinging to my chest, a cold gust of air making me shiver.

"Good morning, sir." I pushed my passport under the glass.

He glanced at it, uninterested. "Welcome home," he said, handing it back.

This moment, which I had imagined, asleep and awake, in varied ways and with different outcomes, was too short and perfunctory. In my most common nightmare, a border patrol agent refused my entry, and I was left suspended on a thick white line where I had to stay awake in order to not fall into the abyss. Alexis always knew when I was having that nightmare because my whole body moved from side to side, trying to keep my balance.

As I left the booth behind and officially stepped into Spain, my legs suddenly felt too weak to go on. I sat on a bench to blow my nose. Knowing that I still had a chance to catch Jacobo, I managed to pull myself together and rushed to the baggage claim. I anxiously scanned the lounge, full of yawning faces and tired, red eyes. Walking up to the belt, I stood next to a grandmother with a kid. Even though there was a screen with the flight number, I asked her in Spanish if this was the New York flight.

"Yes, it is. This is the best airport in Europe but the bags take forever. You always have to wait for too long," she said in English with a heavy Spanish accent.

"Oh, that's annoying."

"Are you on vacation?" she asked after a couple of seconds, when I had assumed the conversation had ended.

"Yes, I am."

"Oh, you'll love it here. It's the best country in Europe."

"I'm excited to see the Escorial and the Prado and have some tapas in Plaza Mayor," I said, repeating parts of the conversation that I had just overheard.

"Oh, you're going to love el Prado. It's the best museum in the world."

I nodded.

A billboard hung over us with two girls riding in a convertible down a winding road bordering a transparent, turquoise sea. Large bold type read *I need Spain*. They were laughing as if someone had just cracked a joke. Their arms were tan, their faces sun-kissed, their hair blowing in the wind. They didn't look like they needed anything, let alone a country. A beeping sound, as loud as a delivery truck backing up in the middle of the night, pierced my head, and soon after, the bags descended on the belt. I walked away from the woman, who was now complaining about the food on the plane to a young couple. As I turned my head to look for Jacobo one last time, someone touched my shoulder.

"Hey. How are you feeling?"

"Hi," I said, trying not to sound desperate.

"How's your cold?"

"Not so great. I think I have a fever."

He looked briefly into my eyes, as if asking for permission, then touched my forehead. "Yeah, you have a temperature."

I rested my head on his hand and closed my eyes. Even for a brief moment, his touch invigorated me. A couple of seconds went by, and then the thunderous noise of a golf bag falling onto the belt broke the spell. Jacobo grabbed it with two hands, put it on the floor, and tore off an orange priority label, as if embarrassed.

"Do you play golf?" I asked casually, as if I did.

"Are you kidding me? I hate golf. I can't think of a more despicable, bourgeois sport. I mean, if walking on grass can be called a sport. It's for my dad. He always needs to have the latest golf clubs. He's a terrible player, and it makes no difference."

I wondered if he had checked another bag or if we were just waiting for mine. Could it be possible that he was only traveling with the small backpack he had brought on the plane?

"I've never played golf. But it doesn't look like a lot of fun," I said.

He gave a disgusted look as he leaned over the moving belt, grabbed a worn-out military duffel bag, and ripped off the orange label again. I hoped mine would come soon so we could walk out together. We both stood uncomfortably for a couple of seconds, the bags in between us like barricades.

"Okay. I guess I should get going." He pulled out his phone. "Let's swap numbers."

"Sure." I nodded, then realized I didn't have one. "Wait. No, I don't have a number yet," I said, and laughed nervously, the earth opening underneath me.

Jacobo grabbed a pen from his pocket and wrote down his number on the back of his boarding pass.

"Call me if you need anything. Or if you want me to show you around."

I said I would. He gave me a hug that lasted a moment too long, then grabbed his bags and headed to the exit. I watched him, hoping he would turn back, and took tiny steps so that in case he did he would have a direct view of me. Walking steadily, he disappeared into the crowd, his head down, looking at his phone.

My bag came out soon after. But not soon enough to avoid thinking that it had been lost. It was hard to believe my life could fit in a Chinatown suitcase whose right wheel had begun to fail the moment I left the store. I put it on a trolley and, leaning heavily on it, pushed my way toward the exit. Two armed policemen asked me if I had anything to declare. I said I didn't. They let me pass and wished me a good day.

I entered my homeland through the sliding doors, expecting to experience something transcendental, a kind of revelation, but I only felt exhaustion. I followed the signs to the shuttle and roamed through a food court, trying to gather some strength. The smell of freshly ground coffee, which I usually found comforting, almost made me get sick. My fever was rising. I left the terminal and headed to a bus shelter, my head throbbing so intensely I had to close my eyes and lean against a pole. Although I was covered in sweat, the sun on my face was soothing.

SOMEONE GRABBED my arm. I opened my eyes and stared blankly at an old man in a dark blue uniform, his white, fleshy face under a peaked cap. Had I passed out? He handed me a small bottle of water. I took a sip, looked to my right, and realized that my suitcase had disappeared. I tried to remember the word in Spanish, but I was too feverish. Feeling dizzy, I noticed Jacobo putting my maleta in the trunk of a glistening black Jaguar, speaking in fast Spanish. He then helped me into the backseat, its leather momentarily cooling me off. As the car sped up, I closed my eyes. His leg was touching my leg.

7

I woke up in absolute darkness under heavy cotton sheets. I reached out, hoping to find a lamp, and found nothing. Holding my breath, I listened for sounds that could help me get a sense of the space. I extended my right leg toward the uncharted territory of the bed, traveling through cool pleats of cotton. A strong scent of fresh lavender filled the room. I turned over and realized I was naked.

I drifted in and out of sleep and woke again when a door cracked open. A frail light poured in and dimly illuminated the dark green wallpaper. There was an antique desk, an armchair upholstered in a floral fabric, and a massive carved dark wooden armoire that looked hundreds of years old. My suitcase, with a missing wheel, was next to the door. The clothes I had worn on the plane had been laid neatly folded on top. I wiped the corners of my mouth, fixed my hair, and sat up on the bed.

I heard dishes clanging in the distance, then a giggle and a floorboard creaking loudly. I looked down. A little girl with long blond curls held by a tie of silver stars was crawling into the room. I pulled the sheets and covered my chest.

"Hello," I said.

The girl stood up and ran out of the bedroom and through

what sounded like a long corridor. A door shut in the distance and shortly after, I heard it open, then steps coming down the hallway. I considered grabbing my clothes, but I was afraid of being caught naked midway.

Someone knocked on the door. "Good morning. I mean, evening," Jacobo said, the girl perched on his back. "I hope this devil didn't wake you up."

"I didn't!" she cried.

"No. I literally had just woken up," I said while he placed her on the bed.

"My name is Estrella."

"Nice to meet you, Estrella. I'm Demetrio."

"You are the American," she said.

"I'm glad you think so," I said, then grinned at Jacobo.

"You slept for fourteen hours," he said.

"What? I'm so sorry."

"No reason to be. How are you feeling?"

"Very rested." I tilted my head from side to side.

"Oh, good. You were passed out most of the way from the airport and had a really high fever."

"I barely remember anything."

Estrella began jumping on the bed. Jacobo asked her to stop, which made her bounce higher. He caught her midair and began tickling her. She laughed loudly, twisting her body maniacally. Soon, they were both rolling around on top of my legs. As she begged him to stop, he began roaring like a lion, pretending to bite her arm.

"Noooo!" she yelled. "Help, please, help!"

"Okay." Jacobo stood up and pulled her into his arms. "Now we're going to let my friend take a shower and get ready for dinner."

"That's the bathroom," he said, pointing at a double-pane door. "My bedroom is on the other side."

Before leaving, he turned on a switch. A massive chandelier of tiny, diamond-shaped crystals hanging from the ceiling illuminated the bedroom. When I heard them laughing down the hallway, I jumped out of bed and put on my clothes. They had been washed and ironed. Never in my life had I worn ironed underwear. I pulled open the long, thick, velvety drapes like stage curtains, not knowing what the city would look like. Maybe the buildings would be lower and not as well-kept, but the house across the street looked a bit like the heavy, ornate Upper East Side town house where Bloomberg lived. I opened the doors to the balcony and city noises flooded the room: mopeds, cars, kids shouting, and a metal awning being pulled down.

The bathroom was huge. It looked like the ones in the suites of the Peninsula Hotel that I had seen on the website, with a double sink, a large bathtub so deep that you could dive into it, and a separate shower. At first, I thought there were two toilets sitting next to each other, but then I realized one of them was a bidet. It made me laugh. I thought they only existed in France. A black toiletry bag stained with white toothpaste was sitting on top of the marble counter. I pulled the zipper open and looked at two amber pharmacy bottles. The labels were pretty faded, but I was still able to read the name of an antidepressant that Chus had taken for many years. I put them back stealthily and turned on the shower. I must have been under the hot water for a long time, because when I heard Jacobo opening the door, the glass shower was coated in steam.

I couldn't believe he had entered the bathroom while I was taking a shower. I shampooed my hair again, imagining for a second the door opening and Jacobo getting inside. Maybe I had just watched too much porn.

"So, are you ready to meet the García del Pinos?" he said in a voice loud enough to pierce the sound of the shower jet.

My whole body was trembling with excitement. I did my best to modulate my shaky voice. "Sure!"

"Get ready for some serious interrogation and quick judgment," he said. "They're not bad people, just old-fashioned. Okay, and a little fucked up."

Not knowing what to say, I waited for him to leave and washed my hair a third time. Still dripping, I put my underwear on, grabbed a towel big enough to cover two people, and began drying off. I couldn't believe where I was. For a quick second, feeling so out of place, I considered leaving. But the thought of dragging a suitcase with a missing wheel through the streets of Madrid looking for my motel was too much to bear.

Jacobo came back in wearing a towel wrapped around his waist. While he searched for the toothpaste, I observed him through the mirror. He had a yoga body, his skin was pale and had a bluish tone. He walked around the bathroom brushing his teeth, white foam dripping down the corners of his mouth, his towel progressively becoming looser. At one point, as it was about to fall, he fastened it again. I dried off my hair and inhaled deeply the strong chamomile smell that the conditioner had left.

"Listen, I don't want to impose . . . ," I said, not sure how to end the sentence, suddenly worried that I was wearing a pair of underwear with a hole in it.

"What do you mean?" he said after spitting the toothpaste into the sink.

"I'm just saying. I don't know. Maybe I should go? You've already done a lot."

"Come on, don't be so polite. Where are you going to go at this hour? Plus, my mother is excited to meet you."

"Okay, but I'll leave tomorrow morning."

"Tomorrow will be a different day," he said, and grinned.

I returned the smile and walked to my bedroom, leaving the door ajar.

I put on my nicest pants, the only button-down shirt in my suitcase, and sat on the bed waiting for him to get ready. The dusk light bathed the building across the street. I thought about the view from my Gansevoort apartment and looked up to the sky. There were no blinking lights of distant planes, nor the humming of air-conditioning compressors, sirens, or cars honking. Instead, there was a clear, blue sky and a feathery orange line dissolving quietly on the horizon. An absolute, comforting silence made the world seem miles away.

I wondered if the phone sitting on the nightstand could make international calls. At least in the States, you had to pay extra for the global plan, whose high rates were astronomical. Everyone I knew used phone cards that you bought at the deli, five dollars giving you enough time to run out of things to say. I pulled the handset from the console and considered dialing Chus, whose answering machine still had my twelve-year-old voice asking you to press one to leave a message for him and two for the Road Runner.

WHEN JACOBO PULLED the French doors open and we entered the living room, I was relieved to be wearing a button-down shirt, although it was a bit wrinkled. His mother, a tall, graceful woman with long, dark hair and piercing eyes, was formally dressed. Still, she didn't seem to mind Jacobo's ripped jeans and faded T-shirt stenciled with a portrait of Che Guevara. She was wearing a pleated silk skirt and a blouse with a subtle floral print, her shoulders covered with a silvery-gray shawl. The light colors of her clothes contrasted with the dark browns of the living room. Listening to Jacobo introduce me, I could tell he was proud of having me there, happy to bring home some palpable proof of his American life.

I extended my hand and then awkwardly pulled it back when his mother kissed me on both cheeks. She greeted me with fondness and familiarity.

"Lovely to meet you, dear. I'm Patricia. We're delighted to have you," she said in a British accent.

"Thank you."

Patricia apologized for her husband's tardiness and suggested that we start dining at ten regardless. As soon as we sat down, a maid wearing a uniform came into the living room. She was carrying a silver tray with a bottle of Tio Pepe—the same Spanish sherry we served at Le Bourrelet—glasses with golden rims, and a bowl full of what looked like Kalamata olives but smaller.

"Gabriela, this is my friend Demetrio," Jacobo said.

"Encantado," I said.

She walked up to me, and as I was about to kiss her, she extended her hand. "Bienvenido."

Jacobo asked her for a gin and tonic. By the expression in her eyes, I could tell she was happy to see him, and I wondered how long Gabriela had been working at the house. Jacobo spoke to her lovingly but also with a certain distance, as if he were talking to an old friend he had not seen in years. Sitting around a pale pink and gray marble table, we toasted to being back. I raised my glass with certainty and for a moment felt optimistic, the anxiety of the last few days fading away.

Estrella stormed into the room in footed Hello Kitty pajamas, her wet hair pulled back in a ponytail. She jumped onto Jacobo's lap, spilling part of his drink. A young girl whom I assumed to be the nanny ran after her and apologized.

"It's all right, Sarah. Would you care for a glass of wine before you put this monster to bed?" Patricia said.

The nanny couldn't have been more than sixteen years old.

"No, thank you," she said, grabbing Estrella's hand. "It's past nine, and girls who aren't already in bed never get married."

Estrella ran toward the door, stopping halfway to slide the last couple feet. We all said good night and Jacobo reminded her that if she clenched her fists in her sleep, she would dream of the Little Prince.

We moved to a dining room, and shortly after, as if she could see through the wall, Gabriela came in with some appetizers. Jacobo said we were about to have his favorite food: chorizo, manchego cheese, jamón ibérico, and a chilled white gazpacho with blanched almonds and green grapes. Though I knew a lot about ibérico, I let him speak. He explained that the jamón came from purebred black-footed ibérico pigs that roamed wild, foraging for acorns in the oak forests of La Mancha. Ibérico was not allowed into the United States because the slaughterhouses didn't meet FDA standards. I told them how ironic it was that a ham made of pigs that were fed organic food was prohibited, while most Americans living outside big cities ate GMO food that came in a box.

For the main dish, we had grilled bream with lemon slices, sprigs of parsley, and roasted garlic. The skin was expertly charred, the first layer of the flesh a light golden yellow. When I tried a small piece the flavor was fresh and pungent. I could almost taste the sea. For the past eight years, I had mostly eaten at Le Bourrelet, where every dish tended to be heavily seasoned and accompanied by creamy, rich sauces.

I had never met anyone like Patricia. Her elegance went beyond her clothes. Her manners were exquisite but not pretentious in any way. She cut her food in tiny bites, used her napkin before and after drinking, and refilled our glasses slightly but frequently, so that no matter how fast we drank, the wine always remained at the same level. The way she carried herself indicated that she was a woman of a certain upbringing. But what impressed me the most was her clear effort in making me feel at home, asking constantly about how I was feeling and whether I liked the food, though the more she asked, the more self-conscious I became.

I mimicked her manners and used my napkin more often than usual. When Gabriela entered the room to pick up the dirty plates, I acted as if I were used to having people serve me instead of having spent my life serving others. I wondered how much Jacobo had shared with Patricia about me and hoped he had not told her my reason for leaving the States.

He begged her to tell the story of a trip to New York that she had made with his father. While he was in meetings, Patricia toured the city, and one evening, she boarded an express train by mistake and found herself in the middle of the Bronx at night. While she narrated the events, I sipped my wine and looked at her big black eyes full of life, like the eyes of a child.

"Imagine her," Jacobo said, unable to contain his laughter. "Imagine her, dressed for a gala in the middle of Pelham Bay at midnight."

"I was not dressed for a gala and it was not midnight, darling." She laughed. "You exaggerate."

"Whatever, Mom. You're always decked out and wearing jewelry. Even when you play golf."

"I'm not always wearing jewelry, and that's not a proper thing to say in front of your mate."

I couldn't refrain from glancing at her gleaming necklace and the vintage watch she wore with the face down.

"And, by the way, I stopped playing golf long ago. I realized I despise it. Get with the program, darling. Is that how you say it in America?"

We all exploded in laughter.

Jacobo lit the long, black candles of an aged silver candelabra. I noticed Patricia's cheeks turning pink like rose petals and wondered whether this was caused by the two bottles of Ribeiro we had drunk or by her proximity to the flickering flames.

"My mom has a beautiful voice."

"I know, it really is," I said.

"No, I mean her singing voice."

We laughed again.

"I'm tired, darling. I would rather not sing tonight."

"Okay, okay. Although it's my first day back, and we get to do what I want." Jacobo smiled mischievously, turning into a little kid.

When the meal was over, we went back to the living room. Patricia lit a cigarette and Jacobo excused himself for a moment.

"I'm glad Jake brought you."

"Me too. I don't know what I would've done without him." My brain was soaked in wine.

"Have you rung your uncle?"

I froze. That she knew about Chus implied that Jacobo had shared my story.

"No, I haven't yet. I'll call him tomorrow."

"I admire your courage," Patricia said. "Jacobo told me what you've been through."

I didn't know how to respond. I now felt as if I had been standing naked in front of her during the entire meal, trying to give the impression I was someone else.

"I want you to know that we're here for you."

"Thank you." Even though her words were meant to comfort me, my pride was wounded. I began to perspire. Maybe the fever wasn't completely gone.

Jacobo walked back into the living room, drying his hands on the back of his jeans. "Here, let me show you the best part of the house."

Thankful for an escape, I followed him to what I thought was a balcony, defeated, like an impostor who had just been exposed. Jacobo opened the doors and flipped a switch. A string of lights illuminated a lush garden suspended over the city. I stepped onto the spongy grass, momentarily feeling lighter, and noticed a variety of plants in terra cotta pots lay neatly arranged, the patina on the clay betraying their years under the open sky. I recognized a bush of calendulas, having once used their petals to make ice cream. We walked across to the edge and leaned on a railing covered in ivy. A long, wide avenue stretched below us like a river of floating lights.

"It's crazy."

"Friday night. Isn't it insane? I kid you not, the traffic jam lasts until dawn," he said, putting an arm around my shoulder. I could feel not only his arm but also his chest attached to it, his heart underneath beating excitedly.

"So crazy. What's the name of the avenue?" I said, wanting to prolong the moment.

"That's Gran Vía. It's kind of the Broadway of Madrid. Are you ready to go?" He tightened his arm around me.

"Sure," I said, wanting to stay there, feeling our bodies connected, my eyes hypnotized by the flickering lights.

By the time we went back inside, there were no signs of Patricia. The table was clean, the ashtrays emptied, our immediate past already erased. Jacobo went to his room to grab his wallet. I sat down on the sofa and listened closely for signs that would indicate her whereabouts. The only sound I heard was his phone beeping intermittently.

THE HEAVY IRON GATE shutting behind us, and the blinking red light of the security camera hanging above, made clear that Jacobo's home was galaxies away from the street where we now stood. Walking on a narrow and crowded sidewalk full of kids running around, I couldn't stop thinking about Patricia and what she meant by "we're here for you." I imagined her leaning on the balustrade, perched above the city, smoking one last cigarette, then entering the living room covered with Persian carpets.

Jacobo flagged down a cab while he talked excitedly about the night ahead and the friends he had not seen since Christmas. His phone was constantly chirping. I wanted to tell him how grateful I was to him for taking care of me while I was sick, for welcoming me into his home and introducing me to his family. But I said nothing.

Jacobo interacted with the cabdriver in a cordial but deferential tone, similar to the way he talked to Gabriela. I wondered if this was due to their age difference or because they held menial jobs. We were moving very slowly, and at the end of the avenue we came to a halt next to a beautifully lit fountain, a massive marble sculpture of a Greek goddess riding a chariot pulled by lions. The sound of the water momentarily pushed back the murmur of idle engines around us. I thought of Patricia again and wished her words had not caught me by surprise. I regretted not being able to say something eloquent instead of succumbing to the deadly silence. People walking on the sidewalk were moving faster than us. The meter, going up quickly, was making me nervous. Jacobo was engrossed looking out the window, as if seeing the streets for the first time.

"You know, it's funny. I love this city, but since moving to New York, I haven't missed it one bit," he said, as if this were the result of serious consideration. "There's just nothing here for me."

Then he turned his head.

"I mean, Madrid is a great city. Don't get me wrong," he added apologetically.

"Well, I'm excited to see what it's about," I said, as if I also had the alternative of going back to New York.

"Let's get the fuck out. This is insane." He opened the door, handed a twenty-euro bill to the driver, and didn't ask for change. The meter read twelve fifty.

I was amazed at the liveliness of the street. Most people walked in big groups and spoke loudly, not only the teenagers who were passing around big Coca-Cola bottles full of what looked like red wine. There was something profoundly distinct about Madrid. An intense, festive energy pouring in and out of bars and extending through the sidewalks, an energy that I had only experienced on New Year's Eve.

"Is it always like this?"

"Like what?" he said.

"Everyone drinking on the streets, shouting. I don't know, the whole thing."

"Yes," he said. By his tone I could tell he was proud.

We went down a dark, narrow alley that ran parallel to the Gran Vía. Groups of kids hung around on the sidewalks, leaning on the hoods of parked cars, smoking hashish. Jacobo stopped in front of a heavy door whose gilded plaque had the number sixteen engraved on it. Shortly after Jacobo rang the bell, the face of a man appeared behind a tiny window. He greeted Jacobo by name, unlocked the door, and ushered us into a bar that looked untouched since the 1930s. Two enormous fans hung from the ceiling, moving slowly, with effort, as if too tired to keep going. The waiters, blending in with the décor, seemed the same age as the Art Deco sconces hanging on the walls. Most of the customers looked like old Brooklyn hipsters, gathered around antique Singer sewing machine tables and drinking cocktails from vintage glasses.

"This place is one of the best-kept secrets in Madrid. We love coming here for the first drink," Jacobo said. It was nearly one in the morning.

His friends were sitting in the farthest corner of the bar, near the bathroom. When we approached the table, they stood up to greet him. I was introduced as a friend from New York. Excited to start practicing my Spanish, I assumed that being from there would provide me with a certain allure. But after the warm welcome and a short, polite interaction, the group got into a serious conversation about politics. Their strong local accent, and their fast-paced talking over one another, made it impossible for me to follow.

Jacobo seemed uninterested in me. I could tell that he had been happy to bring me along but was now somewhat uncomfortable. He acted differently in front of his friends. He made jokes and racy comments that were welcomed with loud guffaws. Even his body language had changed. Most of them were having gin martinis, which I found odd because in New York it was a cocktail for older people. His friends went to the bathroom often and discreetly at first, but as the night wore on, they began going in pairs and then groups, and it became clear that they were all snorting coke.

I avoided thinking about what I needed to do, like opening a bank account, finding an apartment, buying a cell phone, and reaching out to Matías, a friend of Chef's who ran El Lucernario, a Michelin-starred restaurant. I mostly talked to one of Jacobo's friends, Adolfo. He liked to speak in English and added the word *cool* to most of his sentences. A law student who had been sober for a couple of years, he was about to start at his dad's firm. At one point in the conversation, he mentioned that his uncle had been the first president of Spain after Franco. It took me a while to fully absorb the information. I acted normally, but I was completely baffled. Looking at Jacobo's friends, I wondered if their lack of interest in me was because they sensed I did not belong.

Adolfo excused himself early and said that he was leaving for the beach the next day. As soon as he left the table, Jacobo came over and sat next to me. His jaw was moving so much that it was hard for him to enunciate.

"You do blow, right?"

"Sure." I hadn't done coke in years. The last two times, it had made me so paranoid that I had stopped altogether.

"Let's go." He pointed to the bathroom.

We locked ourselves in the only open stall. Jacobo cut two lines on top of his wallet. Someone sniffed loudly next to us, flushed, and banged the door.

"I haven't done blow in forever."

"I wish I could say the same," he said, and then retracted. "Don't get me wrong, I don't do it *that* often."

He rolled up a bill, snorted the longer, thicker line, and handed me the wallet. The moment the coke entered my nostril, I felt an instant numbness in my mouth and a bitter taste go down my throat. Jacobo wet his finger and cleaned the wallet.

"Wait. Is this five hundred euros?" I said, unrolling the bill.

"Yes." He put it back in his wallet. "They're called Bin Ladens. Get it? Bin Ladens because they exist but no one ever sees them." He laughed.

Jacobo pulled down his zipper. I turned around, feeling my blood starting to heat up, a mix of panic and excitement pushing me out of the stall as his stream hit the bowl. Instead of going back to the table, I walked up to the bar. Hyperaware and with a tingling throat, I noticed the rows of martini glasses perfectly laid out, the vivid red color of the cherries, and an unpolished silver tray of fresh lemon wedges. The movements of the bartender shaking a cocktail seemed to be choreographed to the beat of "I Wanna Be Sedated" by the Ramones coming through the speakers. I sat down on a stool next to a tall woman in a red dress who was explaining the differences between American and European economics.

"The main difference is that the United States has the option of printing money, and we don't. It's that simple," she said, gesticulating nervously, her long fingers underlining the last sentence.

A guy in a plaid suit nodded his head tensely, his eyes widening like an owl's. I looked around the bar and realized that most people were on coke. Now that I was high, I entered a parallel world that had been taking place right next to me.

Jacobo joined me at the bar and ordered two shots. We toasted to the future, and as the tequila went down our throats, I banged the glass against the bar to distract from the burning. The coke made me enjoy the taste of the tequila, the alcohol momentarily appeasing my speedy heart. Jacobo put his arm around my shoulder, and this time, I put mine around his.

We left the bar without saying goodbye. As we stepped out onto the sidewalk, the lampposts turned off and the sun was beginning to rise. I enjoyed not having to decide on a destination, letting myself drift through unknown streets, unaware of whether we were getting closer or farther away from the house.

A water truck went through the narrow street, brushing the cars parked on both sides with its mirrors. Two men wearing green, waterproof jumpsuits were coming toward us, hosing the sidewalks. I inhaled deeply some of the remaining coke left in my nostrils, my heart racing again. As we began to get wet, we took an alley that descended into a square. By the erratic trace of his steps and the carefree swinging of his arms, I could tell Jacobo had drunk too much. The plaza was almost empty except for a group of homeless white kids bathing in a fountain. One of them, who had to be our age, was struggling to zip up a rolling suitcase. His hair, a thick mess of matted dreadlocks, was drawn back by a bandana with the colors of the Ethiopian flag. He noticed I was staring at him and, as we crossed paths, asked for a cigarette and said something about paying a viewing fee.

I had assumed that we were drifting through the streets. But at one point, I found myself going through a cobblestone alley, a faint smell of bittersweet chocolate becoming more and more present. We had walked in silence since leaving the bar and the silence had turned corporeal, like someone walking between us. I asked where we were going and Jacobo just pointed to a green door.

The chocolatería was a quaint little coffee shop whose waiters were dressed in dark uniforms and black ties with busy looks on their faces. The day had barely begun but the place was already crowded. Most people were kids, who had clearly just left the clubs, and older couples reading the paper. Jacobo grabbed the only available table while I made my way to the counter, where an ancient waiter was making churros with his bare hands. He cut the long, deep-fried donut coiled like a serpent and sprinkled confectioners' sugar on top. I ordered a dozen of them and two hot chocolates even though my stomach was sealed like a Ziploc bag.

"Wow, this place is amazing," I said back at the table.

"Right? I knew you would love it," he said, flipping through the pages of a newspaper that someone had left on the table. "It's the oldest chocolatería in Madrid."

Before dipping the churro in hot chocolate, I took a bite to savor it. The olive oil, with a low percentage of acidity, made me think of an article that I had read a long time ago in the *New York Times*. Spain had over two hundred and fifty varieties of olives and produced the most varied olive oils in the world. Even some of the so-called Italian ones came from Extremadura, but because it was bought in bulk and then bottled in Italy, companies were able to market it as such, which sold at a higher price. I took another bite of the churro and wondered where this particular oil was from, and whether after living here for a while, I would eventually be able to identify its origin by taste.

"These churros are ridiculous."

"Wait until you try the chocolate," Jacobo said. "Isn't that how you are supposed to eat them, señor chef?"

"Yes, it's how you're supposed to eat them. But not how you savor the pastry itself," I said, grinning. As I dipped the churro in the sauce, he slapped the back of my head, making me spill some on the saucer. His most fleeting touch woke up my entire body.

8

Although he had his own bedroom, I woke up with Jacobo sleeping next to me in his underwear, an arm wrapped around my neck. My mouth was parched, my nose dry, a dark, menacing cloud loomed over me. I lay with my eyes open thinking about the previous night and made an effort to remember getting ready for bed, but all I could recall was lying on top of the covers and hearing the bells of a nearby church calling eight o'clock. His almost naked, beautiful, and fragile body next to mine, which would have elicited some untamable urge in a different situation, had no effect. The need to find a job, a place to live, and a phone to call Chus was all I could think of. I slipped out from under his arm and sat up on the bed looking at his face, a light and patchy stubble covering his chin. A wet circle near his mouth had darkened the flowers embroidered on the pillowcase. I extended my hand and laid it on his chest, feeling the cadence of his breathing through the blanket. The house was silent. Only faint, indistinguishable sounds of the street below permeated the double-paned window. A copper sunlight entered through an opening in the curtains, the crystals of the chandelier projecting a fleeting rainbow on the wall.

I took a quick shower and got dressed, putting on the same underwear I had slept in. The door to his bedroom was slightly open. I pushed it with my shoulder and went in. The walls were covered with large black-and-white photos that had been taken through what appeared to be a thick and porous fog of a hidden cove, a scorched black tree with its trunk split in two and a lighthouse that made the mist whiter than white. Something about the images felt indelibly Jacobo.

His watch was sitting on the nightstand. I put it on and moved my arm up and down, marveling at its extraordinary weight. I walked in front of a full-length mirror, looked at my wrist wrapped in eighteen-karat yellow gold. My white shirt, dark gray jeans, and worn-out sneakers suddenly looked like expensive designer clothes. Without taking it off, I opened the door of his closet, just to experience how it would feel performing an ordinary task with the watch on. I was surprised to see so many button-down shirts, dress pants, and suits, clothes that I couldn't imagine him wearing. I placed the watch back where I had found it and left the room.

At the end of the long corridor, on top of a credenza, there was a photo of a high-ranking soldier looking defiantly into the camera. The long strip of medals on his uniform made me think he was the fascist grandfather Jacobo had mentioned on the plane. In another photo, looking much older, the soldier was in the desert riding a horse into an army of men wearing turbans with long sabers dangling from their waists. From the *1975* inscribed on the frame, I deduced they were Moroccans and the picture, whose corners had begun to fade, had been taken during the Green March. I only knew this because Chus had considered fleeing to Tangier before going to Paris and was obsessed with the history of the Spanish protectorate in Morocco.

I walked into the kitchen and picked up the phone hanging on the wall. I dialed Chus's number just to stop the dial tone from drilling into my ear. As I was getting ready to leave a message, half hoping he wouldn't be home, he answered.

"Hello?"

"Hi, Chus."

"Deme! I've been waiting to hear from you for two days. Are you okay?"

"Yes, of course. Sorry for not calling you sooner, but I got really sick on the plane, like a twenty-four-hour flu or something."

"It was probably psychosomatic."

"God, you're so new age–y."

"Well, there are studies that say—"

"Okay, okay. I don't want to get into that now. I can't talk for too long because I'm using someone else's phone. It's a long story but I met someone."

"What?"

"Yes. We sat together on the flight. He's very cute, model cute, and charming, and we kind of hit it off. But he's also a hot mess and might have a drug or a sex addiction problem. Or both? I'm not sure. I just think we might be too different, you know? Like our values are not the same? I feel kind of paralyzed. Because he's also super rich, like car-with-chauffeur rich."

"Deme, you're rambling. Slow down."

I took a breath.

"So you met a cute guy that you clearly like and he happens

to be from a different socioeconomic background? Welcome to the serendipity of life. It sounds wonderful, if you ask me. Very old Hollywood."

I cracked up. "What does that even mean?"

"Is he from Madrid? How old is he?"

"Yes. My age. Maybe a year younger."

"Is he gay-gay, or Richard-gay?"

"I can't tell for sure. You know I've never had a gaydar."

"That goes without saying. Have you had big-boy sex yet?"

"Chus!"

"Sorry! But that would shed some light into his sexuality as far as I'm concerned."

"No sex yet."

"Okay. Well. Just take it one day at a time. You have a lot going on right now. What else? How's the motel?"

"I never made it there. I'm staying at this guy's house."

"Does this guy have a name?"

"Yeah, Jacobo."

"That's such a posh name."

"Is it?" It suddenly occurred to me that Chus understood certain subtleties of the country in ways that I might never. "I mean, I told you about the chauffeur. . . . Anyway, I should go. I'll call you as soon as I buy a phone. I just didn't want to worry you. Madrid is, I don't know, very different from New York."

"I'm sure it's changed so much," he said hesitantly. "I miss you and love you."

"Love you too."

I regretted the conversation as soon as I hung up. There were so many things I wanted to talk to him about and I had ended up spending all the time talking about Jacobo.

Without Patricia, the dark brown color of the walls, the Persian rugs, and the heavy furniture made the space cold and unwelcoming. On the low table where the previous night we had drinks, there was a note from her. She hoped we had a good time and hadn't come home too late. They were having lunch at a friend's house and Gabriela had the day off but had left food in the fridge in case we were hungry. At the bottom of the page, in the same handwriting but slightly rushed, as if it had been an afterthought, Patricia wrote that there was a set of keys for me inside the vase by the entrance.

Stepping out on the street and hearing the heavy metal door shutting behind me, I questioned whether going for a walk and leaving my host behind was an appropriate thing to do. I did not want to get lost, so I took the previous night's route through the Paseo de la Castellana. But after a couple of blocks a strong desire to leave my own footprint on the city pushed me in a different direction, as parts of the blue sky were beginning to turn a fiery orange. This was the first time since I had arrived in Madrid that Jacobo was not by my side. I drifted through the streets and, knowing that no one was watching me, I suddenly felt an intoxicating sense of freedom. I had finally arrived at my destination, which was, strangely enough, also the beginning of a new journey.

The city was bursting. I was convinced that the stores in Spain were not open on weekends, but the sidewalks were full of people with shopping bags slung on their arms. Compared to the fast-paced, solitary individuals of New York, everyone here seemed to walk leisurely in groups. I noticed many families, the kids sprinting back and forth, their parents stopping from time to time to greet acquaintances.

Pulled along by the urban tide, I arrived near the gates of the Parque del Retiro. It was hard to visualize its scale from the street, but once inside, I was surprised by the size. Multiple paths meandered into the lush gardens, where plants and trees seemed to have been planted thousands of years ago following an ancient master plan. Groups of teenagers lay on the grass, passing around large bottles of beer. I was shocked at how freely they burned small rocks of hashish that were then mixed with tobacco and rolled into a joint. Although the park was crowded and there were many families with small children, the parents didn't seem bothered by it. I leaned on a marble balustrade that circled a man-made lake and noticed a young guy selling drugs on the steps. A police car driving by made me realize I hadn't grabbed my passport. I walked to one of the lawns from which there was an open view of the lake. Rickety rowboats floated on the water, their painted red numbers beginning to fade. As I lay down on the grass, a flock of ducks bathing under the shimmering light took flight, the flapping wings briefly muffling the sound of cars and mopeds. In the distance, a group of barking dogs feverishly ran after a soccer ball.

I MUST HAVE fallen asleep for a while because when I got up, the sun had set. Retracing my steps, I arrived at the Castellana but I couldn't figure out what direction to take after that. A half hour later, I realized I had gone in the wrong direction. I hailed a cab and repeated the address twice to ensure the cabdriver, a man with long, thick, unkempt eyebrows, had understood me. The moment he stepped on the gas, I got dizzy. He spoke in a pronounced, almost unintelligible accent and was determined to make conversation about the coach of the Real Madrid soccer team or a new player they had just signed up. After my boring, one-word responses, he retaliated by turning up the volume on the radio. I instantly became absorbed in the harsh voices flowing into the car. Agitated journalists, at the point of yelling at each other, were discussing the precarious condition of the European stock market. The raspy voice of an outraged reporter made me think of the woman in the red dress. I remembered what she had said about the ability of the Fed to print money at will. The cabdriver, bothered by my refusal to engage in conversation, yelled, "¡Putos Yanquis!" to the air, expecting me to react. I did not.

The key went in smoothly, but the lock did not move. I turned the knob and pushed the hefty metal door with my shoulder. It was locked. I slid the key several times and turned it to the left. A rush of anxiety flooded my body. I rang the bell, counted to ten, then rang again. I took a couple of steps back and looked at the gold numbers above the door. My hands were trembling. I went back and repeated the same motion, forcing and shaking the doorknob, pushing the door with my shoulder, then stopped when a man walked by with his dog and gave me a strange look.

I sat on a bench and tried not to panic. I had little money on me and no form of identification. A police car rushed by, illuminating the front of the building with blue lights. My heart was racing. I waited until it had disappeared, then inspected my pockets, hoping to find Jacobo's boarding pass, where he had written his phone number. Closing my eyes, I remembered seeing it on the desk in my room, next to my passport. I considered trying the door again but was scared that someone would call the police. I looked at my watch. It was nine o'clock. If I wanted to find a place to spend the night, it was time to start looking.

The same welcoming streets that I had walked with Jacobo the previous night now seemed entirely different. Instead of the well-dressed, happy families and loud party kids, I noticed many homeless people and drug dealers. Going down a cobblestone street, a young kid came out from behind a recycling container and unwrapped a watch from a colorful scarf.

"Barato, barato," he muttered. "Where are you from, amigo?"

Pulling my shoulders back, I puffed up my chest and walked to the square. The bars at the Plaza del Dos de Mayo were so crowded that people spilled onto the sidewalks, the tables so close to one another it was impossible to know which bar they belonged to. I sat at one of them with a direct view of a statue of two soldiers with swords pointing at the sky, their white marble muscles illuminated by halogen lights. Most people were gathered in large groups, some of them barely teenagers, drinking beers and smoking hashish. Two nuns in brown habits, crucifixes dangling from their necks, crossed the square with rushed steps, their downward gazes implying disapproval. I counted my cash several times, as if moving the bills from hand to hand would multiply them. Would forty-four euros be enough for a hostel?

A group of American tourists sat down a couple of feet away. Craving to hear English, I moved next to their table. I watched them closely and listened to their conversation, their voices instantly making me feel less stranded. Most of their talk revolved around classes they could barely follow, food, and nightlife. They were a group of students in an exchange program. One of them, a stunning woman with long, jet-black hair and full lips, kept glancing at me, and when our eyes met, she grinned confidently. I overheard her ordering drinks. She spoke Spanish without an American accent. I sipped my beer in silence and feigned being engrossed in the kids playing on the swings. Their parents yelled at them from afar and when they grew tired of being ignored, they rushed to the playground, taking their drinks with them.

I enjoyed listening to the Americans. Even though we probably had little in common apart from speaking the same language, hearing their voices intertwined with the sounds of the square was soothing. I closed my eyes and focused on their words, familiar and comforting.

"Excuse me." The proximity of the voice startled me. "Are you okay?"

I opened my eyes and saw the woman with the long hair kneeling next to my chair.

"Yes, I am, just a bit jet-lagged."

"I knew you were American."

"You did? How so?"

"I don't know. I just did," she said, blushing. "My mother is from New Jersey but I'm from here."

I wondered what she meant by "here." Spain, Madrid, this square?

"Oh, that's why your English is perfect," I said.

"Thanks, yours too." She made a face as if to acknowledge how predictable her joke was.

We laughed. I motioned for her to sit.

Using my best Spanish accent, I ordered two beers from a waiter cleaning the table next to us. He said that I would have to wait because he was busy. I was shocked at the response and wondered if I had misunderstood him.

"Very nice accent," she said, paying back my compliment.

"Oh, thank you."

"Where in the U.S. are you from?"

"New York."

"Very cool."

"What do you do?" I asked.

"You Americans, that's *always* the first thing out of your mouth."

"I know. I'm sorry."

"Don't worry, I'm used to it."

I could see her friends settling the bill.

"I'm an English teacher," she said.

"Triana, are you ready?" her friend yelled. Blond, muscular, wearing clothes one size too big, a frat boy.

"Yup, I'll be right there!" She rolled her eyes.

"It was great meeting you, Triana. I'm Demetrio." She bent over and we kissed twice. Her smooth skin made me think of Jacobo's chin covered by feathery stubble.

"When do you head back?"

I didn't respond.

"To the States, I mean."

"I'm not heading back," I finally said. "I'm staying. I just moved here."

"Oh, fantastic!" Her face lit up.

The excitement in her words made me forget my temporary homelessness. "Yeah, I'm thrilled."

"Let's swap numbers."

I told her I didn't have one yet and wrote down hers on a paper coaster. We said goodbye as a kid tried to run over a flock of pigeons on his bicycle.

. . .

I DECIDED NOT to look for a room and return to the house instead. Sitting on a bench in front of Jacobo's building, I watched a lone man walk up the street, his tight black overcoat buttoned to the neck. He looked back from time to time as if he were being followed. It was strange to see a man dressed in winter clothes in the middle of summer. And though I had seen much stranger things on the streets of New York, I didn't expect it in this neighborhood.

The wild energy of the city was slowly fading out. The music from the bar at the corner had stopped a while ago, and now the gate was being pulled down and the neon sign turned off, its buzzing, electric murmur gone for the night. With the absence of sound came a terrifying sense of loneliness. Glancing back at the imposing oversized metal door with its shiny brass lock, I wondered if Jacobo and Patricia had ever existed, if it all had just been part of a dream.

The street was completely deserted. Certain that no one would be observing me now, unable to stop thinking about how smoothly the key had gone into the lock, I walked up to the door of the building. I slid in the key one more time and turned it to the left. Nothing. As I turned the key to the right, convinced I had tried that before, the lock released. I stepped onto the red carpet that lay over the white marble steps of the entry foyer, my legs shaking uncontrollably. After so many hours wandering cobblestone streets and uneven sidewalks, I enjoyed the springy feeling of soft fabric under my feet. I opened the metal gate of the elevator and pushed the wooden double doors. Closing them behind me, I pressed the PH button inside the brass box with deliberation, leaving my anxiety below.

When I entered the apartment, the lights in the vestibule

were on, the silence amplified by the glowing light from the chandelier. As I walked stealthily through the long corridor under the menacing look of the soldier in the photograph, I wondered if Jacobo's grandfather was still alive.

The door of my room was ajar. I pushed it open and promised myself that I would never leave the apartment again without Jacobo. My bed was neatly made. There were no signs of him. I took off my shirt and hung it on the back of the chair. I lay down quietly and inhaled the clean, fresh smell of the sheets.

Staring at the ceiling, unable to sleep, I went to the bathroom. His door was wide open. I stood in the doorway, trying to make out his body in the darkness. The silence was heavy, and in the absolute stillness, I sensed his eyes looking at me, I wanted to go in and explain what had happened. Instead I walked up to the sink and glanced at myself in the mirror. I touched his wet towel, then washed my hands, rubbing the soap bar until I erased the fear of not having a roof over my head.

I took off my pants and lay on top of the covers, thinking about his body curled up against mine. I got up, crossed the bathroom, and stopped at the door.

"Are you there?" I whispered.

"Yeah," he finally said after a long silence.

I could sense his leg moving under the sheets.

"Come in." He spoke distantly, as if the words had been traveling from far away.

I heard Jacobo adjusting the pillows and imagined him sitting up. Hesitantly, I crawled onto the bed. I wanted to get under the sheets with him, feel his body, but I sat on the edge closest to the door and made sure our knees didn't touch.

"You won't believe what happened."

"You're right. I won't." His tone was flat and dry.

"I couldn't open the door." I realized how dumb it sounded.

My eyes had adjusted to the lack of light, and I could now see his contour. He looked smaller and farther away from me.

"Sure," he said.

"In the States, the locks open to the left, not to the right," I said, stating a fact he probably knew. "I guess I should have tried to turn the key the other way, but I panicked."

He didn't respond.

"Are you okay?" I said.

I waited for him to break the silence. But he didn't.

"You think I'm lying?" I said, not allowing him to answer. "You think I'm lying."

The sound of a moped traveled in the distance.

"Where did you go?" He lifted his head and stared into my face.

"I wanted to buy a cell phone, but the stores were closed. So I went to the Retiro, and when I got back, I couldn't get into the building."

"Why didn't you call me? I gave you my number," he said.

"I didn't have it on me."

My words, scattered through another long and uncomfortable silence, made me feel like an impostor. I considered going back to my room, packing my suitcase, and leaving the apartment. I had to find my own place sooner or later, and from the conversation, it seemed that the time had arrived. Before standing up, I extended my leg until it touched his. The darkness was being replaced by a frail, eerie light, and now I could almost see his face. Wishing him good night without looking into his eyes, I left the bedroom. He didn't respond. The thought of leaving in the middle of the night dissipated as I got under the covers and listened to another moped going up and down the street. That night, I dreamed of giant mosquitoes buzzing through the streets of Madrid while I ran hysterically, looking for a bottle of Off!

9

Drawn to the smell of frying dough, I ventured through the long corridor toward the kitchen while a voice crying from pain grew more shrill. I pushed the door open. Flamenco music blasting on the radio, Gabriela was giving quick shakes to a frying pan that was occasionally catching on fire. After lowering the heat, she moved to the deep fryer, where a dozen or so donuts were turning a dark golden brown.

I observed her from a distance. Not using measuring cups, she merely pinched spices from old enamel containers and threw them into the pans as she sang along. Her voice was light and honeyed. She moved around spontaneously, unburdened and free, a stark contrast with the experience I had had of a kitchen, where everyone's movements were cerebral, planned and exact, the scrutinizing gaze of Chef and his unwavering demand for excellence turning our daily jobs into a constant competition.

The voice on the radio became a long, deep sob, as if streaming from the afterlife. It was a familiar sound, though I couldn't remember where I had heard it before. When the music ended, a momentary calm took over the kitchen, revealing only the murmur of scalding oil and the rhythmic chopping on the cutting board. Gabriela kept humming the chorus, prolonging the life of the lyrics she didn't want to end. The radio host, who spoke so softly his words seemed to slip from his mouth, revealed the name of the song: "Como el Agua" by Camarón de la Isla, one of Chus's favorite singers.

As the host praised Camarón's vocal technique, I imagined the words turning into electromagnetic waves, moving through space, oblivious to borders and physical demarcations. I wished I could become one of those waves and travel across the ocean to our old apartment, where, given the six-hour difference, Chus would be engaged in his morning ritual, drinking café con leche and listening to *Morning Edition* on NPR.

"Buenos días, Gabriela," I finally said.

"¡Virgen santa!" she yelled, turning around. "Casi me matas."

"Sorry, I didn't mean to scare you."

She looked shocked and uncomfortable. Was there some unspoken rule about guests' not entering the kitchen?

"Dios santo." She touched her chest.

I enjoyed her exaggerated tone and hyperbolic gestures. "What are you making, or should I say, what are you not making?"

She smiled. "Bacalao y patatas con espinacas. Sopa de mejillones. Y de postre, donuts."

I stepped closer to the stove and saw a whole cod on a bed of garlic cloves and thick lemon slices nestled in long sprigs of rosemary. Next to it, simmering in a big copper pot, was a vegetable soup whose smell of cinnamon and ginger reminded me of a Moroccan chickpea and lentil soup Chef liked to make in winter for family meal.

"Jacobito told me that you're a pastelero." She lifted the lid and threw in a bunch of fresh thyme.

I laughed. That was what the washers at Le Bourrelet called me behind my back. I noticed a pound of bittersweet chocolate sitting on the counter. "Are you making a chocolate sauce for the donuts?"

"Yes."

"Do you have fresh mint? I make a killer sauce."

Gabriela looked puzzled. For a moment, I wasn't sure if she had understood me. Then, without uttering a word but with a slight smile on her face, she opened the fridge and handed me a bunch of mint.

I melted the chocolate on the stove and filled a kettle to make instant coffee. Gabriela observed me closely. As I started chopping the mint, moving the knife with dexterity, she gave me a playful look, a mix between awe and disbelief. As usually happened when I cooked, time seemed to stop. Making sure the sauce obtained the right consistency, I stirred it frequently until the anxiety that I had woken up with slowly melted away.

She knew most of the songs playing on Radiolé. Every now and then she spoon-fed me what she was cooking. The flavors were rich and sharp. I was unsure whether to give her my opinion or not, so I simply made a pleased sound that she welcomed with a smile. The few times she spoke, a strong accent that I assumed was from Andalucía buried the shape of her words. I wondered what Gabriela thought of Jacobo and his family, what she thought about me. Her high spirits were clear evidence she was happy and proud of her job. I observed her gentle movements and constant humming and wondered what my mom would have looked like now. Even though Chus and I had no secrets, and I shared with him my most private thoughts, we avoided talking about her. I knew the reason she had sent me to live with him was because she had learned her hepatitis was incurable. It was later, during my teens, when the kids from the neighborhood began toying with heroin, that Chus sat me down and confessed she had been an addict. That kept me away from doing hard drugs during a time when many kids disappeared from the streets of our neighborhood and turned up years later pushing shopping carts around Times Square, their eyes vacant, devoid of life.

I PUT THE DONUTS in the oven and covered them with aluminum foil. Dreading going back to the bedroom and facing Jacobo, I looked for chores to do in the kitchen. Against her will, I washed the pots and pans, and scrubbed the wood cutting board until it became a lighter shade. While I was wiping the counters for a second time, I heard Jacobo's voice in the hallway. Suddenly, all the anxiety I had managed to keep at bay returned.

"So how do you make the bacalao?" I asked her, so he would catch me in conversation.

"It smells amazing!" Jacobo pushed the door open and hung up the phone. "Look at you, the A-Team." In his words there were no traces of the conversation from the previous night.

"It's all Gabriela. I'm only making a sauce for the donuts."

She smiled and grabbed a newspaper from a shopping bag.

"Gracias." He gave her a coin that she put in the front pocket of her apron. "I'm starving," he said. "Have you had breakfast?"

"Not yet," I said, though I had been nibbling on small pieces of chocolate all morning.

"Gabriela, can you please make coffee, toast with ham and tomato, and orange juice?"

Before giving her a chance to answer, he thanked her and

motioned me to follow, the connection that Gabriela and I had carefully nurtured instantly destroyed. I walked to the garden feeling remorse for how quickly I had returned to the role of guest.

Jacobo sat at the long wood table and began reading *El País*. The sun was high in the sky and though it was sizzling hot, the heat was dry. I walked into the shade and looked at the clock tower with Roman numerals across the street. It was twelve thirty. I took my sneakers off. The grass, moist and fine, tickled the soles of my feet. I walked up to the railing. Down below, two old ladies who looked like sisters wearing long black dresses sat on a bench feeding pigeons, and a mother walked with a kid dressed in a school uniform, holding his tiny hand. I thought how different this world was from where I grew up. I remembered Chus's taking me to the East Side Community High School in the mornings, walking north on Avenue C, the rats feasting from overflowing trash cans. And how during my lunchtime, I ventured out to Tompkins Square Park, where the ground was littered with used condoms and syringes.

I unrolled a green hose attached to the wall and turned the faucet on. The water painted a translucent rainbow through which I could see Jacobo immersed in the newspaper. I pointed the sprayer at my feet and enjoyed the water hitting my skin. Bits of our night conversation filtered into my head, and despite feeling less anxious, I knew it was time to look for an apartment. Lost in my thoughts, making sure the grass was being watered evenly, I didn't notice Gabriela setting breakfast on the table or Jacobo walking up to me. It was only when I stepped backward onto his foot and lost my balance that I realized he was behind me.

"Sorry," I said, his hands grabbing my elbows. I let myself sink a little deeper, prolonging our contact, and felt his muscles flaring up.

"No worries. Are you enjoying yourself?"

"Yeah, I love it," I said, pointing the sprayer toward his perfectly manicured feet.

"I used to spend hours here," he said in a nostalgic tone, still holding one of my arms. It sounded as if he was going to elaborate. Instead, he let my arm go and walked back to the table. Every time we were next to each other, I felt an undertow pushing us closer. Every time, one of us pulled away.

I rolled up the hose as neatly as I had found it and joined Jacobo at the table. Immersed in the newspaper, reading an article on gay marriage, he served me coffee, barely lifting his eyes from the page. I spread finely chopped garlic on the toast and poured a deep-yellow olive oil on top, richer and more viscous than the one we used at Le Bourrelet. The pungent taste of fresh garlic blended seamlessly with the smooth, extra-virgin scent. Maybe because I had been educated in a strict French culinary tradition, I was particularly drawn to these simple flavors, which seemed, at least to me, utterly Spanish.

As the sun climbed behind the church tower, he took off his shirt. I suspected Patricia had bought for him the anchor-print pajama bottoms he had on but never wore in bed. I marveled at how domestic this moment felt and wondered if I could ever let myself fall for someone like him, a beautiful rich kid who had been given everything and had a special interest in sabotaging his body.

His phone rang. We both sat there watching it ring. I stole a glance at the screen and thought perhaps the caller was the same person with whom he texted often.

"Aren't you going to pick up?" I said casually, masking my interest.

"No."

"Today, I'm calling Matías at El Lucernario, looking for an apartment, and getting a cell phone." I made it sound inevitable.

He looked at me, smiled, and asked for the milk.

HAD I BEEN alone in Madrid, by then I would have had a place to live and a phone, but every time I mentioned I needed to begin crossing things off my list, Jacobo said that lists were for grown-ups and found ways to delay me. I couldn't recognize my own lack of drive and reminded myself that both Chus and Richard would have been happy to see me relax. This week felt like the first real vacation I had had since I started at Le Bourrelet.

The evenings were for going out, the mornings for sleeping in. After I insisted too many times, Jacobo finally agreed to help me find an apartment. He assured me that, compared to New York, it wouldn't be difficult, especially if we looked in the Lavapiés neighborhood, which he thought would be a great area for me to live in because it was mostly populated by hipsters, immigrants, and young couples who couldn't afford other, more centrally located neighborhoods.

We went up and down its main street, Calle de Zurita, several times. The narrow sidewalks made people constantly spill onto the pavement, forcing cars to move slowly, carefully, often making them come to a halt. Passersby seemed to have the right of way, even if they walked in big groups, holding one-liter beers in their hands. The streets were steep, and the low tenements with laundry hanging on long cords gave the area a rural feel. I noticed many police cars, more than in any other neighborhood we had visited, but Jacobo swore it was safe. He said that they only made themselves visible to dissuade gangs from taking control of the area.

We had already visited three apartments when we climbed five flights up to a small attic with views of El Rastro, a famous flea market. The real estate agent was on the phone and signaled us to go ahead and look around. The apartment smelled of fresh paint and the sun reflected off the bright white walls. As I entered, I imagined myself waking up every morning to the sounds from the nearby playground. I opened the windows that ran the length of the room and the distinct aroma of fresh sardines being grilled poured in. I looked at the red tile roofs across the street stabbed by TV antennas and listened to the shouts of kids playing soccer.

I inspected the kitchen, which had an old stainless-steel gas stove and limited counter space. There was the same IKEA rolling cart from my Gansevoort apartment, though this had been used to chop strawberries and not cleaned afterward, the wood stained a deep brownish red. I walked into the bathroom and discovered that it had not only a window, but a window with a treetop view.

Jacobo called from the bedroom. His tone was serious and matter-of-fact. He pointed at a green folding cot and a vintage suitcase next to it used as a night table.

"They come with the apartment," he whispered. "Aren't they cool?"

"Very," I said. "I love the place. Is seven hundred euros a good price?"

"Yeah. It's a good deal. We should take it."

Giving him the thumbs-up was the most spontaneous way

to conceal that his use of *we* had not come as a complete shock. Jacobo walked out of the bedroom with a businesslike look on his face. I glanced at a skylight framing a square of the radiant blue sky and listened to their conversation.

"Not to make any assumptions, but I just want to say that there are many gay couples moving into the neighborhood," she said.

Before she could go on, Jacobo said: "Oh, we're not gay, but thank you for the information. It's always a good sign when the gays move in."

I took a deep breath to drown my laugh.

"So, I was wondering," Jacobo continued. "If we gave you six months cash, would it be possible to avoid getting bank references to speed up things?"

"Of course. Cash always makes things faster." The sound of these last words was different, lighter, as if they had escaped through the corners of her mouth.

Borrowing such a large sum made me uncomfortable. It felt weird to become even more dependent on him. I called Chef from Jacobo's cell phone to ensure that I would be getting my money soon. He had talked to his bank, and they assured him that, once he gave them my account information, the transfer would only take forty-eight hours. He was happy to hear my voice and wanted to talk more, but I kept the conversation short and promised to call him back later in the week. It felt awkward to be cutting Chef off. Before we hung up, he asked me if I had talked to Matías and was surprised I hadn't. Feeling embarrassed, I turned the fever of the first day into a long cold and told him I would reach out to him the next day.

Shortly after we left the apartment, Jacobo handed me the keys.

"Here you go."

"When did you get them?"

"You were busy looking at the kids playing ball. I gave her a couple of Bin Ladens."

"So, it's done? I can sleep there tonight?"

"What's the rush?" he said, then handed me a piece of paper.

"No rush. Just thrilled it worked out so easily." I looked at the receipt, her handwriting acknowledging she had received forty-two hundred euros. I couldn't believe he had been wandering the streets with that much money in his pocket.

I walked Jacobo to the nearest subway station, the keys to my new home rubbing against my thigh. At the top of the stairs, we hugged as if we weren't going to see each other again, even though we had made plans for dinner later that evening. I got the sense that he enjoyed his position of power, deciding where I would live, prolonging my dependence on him.

AS THE SUN LOWERED and the dry June heat receded, I decided to venture into the neighborhood on my own. Stopping to greet acquaintances and engaging in long, animated conversations, my new neighbors relished their time outside. Although it was rush hour most passersby didn't seem to be in any kind of hurry. During my stroll, I began encountering the same faces going in and out of bars, fruit stores, and small supermarkets the size of a New York deli. The shops of Lavapiés catered to the people who actually lived there, unlike the Meatpacking District, overpopulated with designer shops and overpriced wine bars geared to tourists and the wealthy. There was a working-class barrio feeling in this part of the city that reminded me of the Loisaida I grew up in.

Listening to the Arabic techno music permeating the streets, looking at the buildings and the faces I passed, I suddenly felt like a foreigner walking the streets of a place that was supposed to feel like home. Nothing around me was familiar, welcoming, or friendly. Without Jacobo by my side, Madrid was just a city I had no attachment to, the capital of a country my passport insisted was my homeland.

I scanned the surrounding sidewalks near my building, hoping to maybe find a piece of furniture for my new apartment. I thought about the midcentury-modern coffee table that I had rescued in front of a building on Fifth Avenue and the vintage sofa that Chus had found near Washington Square that I had helped carry for thirteen blocks, and which he still napped on in the afternoons. But unlike the streets of Manhattan, what had been discarded on the sidewalks of Lavapiés was real junk, a yellowed mattress showing its springs, an old fridge with a missing door, the black hood of a portable barbecue.

Jacobo had repeatedly praised how diverse this part of the city was compared to other areas. In his opinion, this made Lavapiés the most thriving neighborhood in Madrid and the place where I would feel most at home. In fact, I wouldn't have minded the Barrio de Salamanca, where he lived, with quieter streets, grand limestone buildings, and wide sidewalks free of trash. But I was grateful to have a place I could call my own.

As I looked for the closest laundromat, supermarket, and gym, my original impression of the neighborhood changed. There were even more bars than I had originally noticed, though people preferred to drink outdoors, sitting on stoops and park benches. The festive energy was palpable. After a lifetime of not being able to carry open containers of alcohol on the street, it was shocking to see people enjoying themselves without the fear of being caught.

I stumbled upon the Mercado de San Miguel, an upscale market full of stands selling delicacies. It looked like the Spanish version of Chelsea Market, only a thousand years older. I spent a good ten minutes trying cheeses while the young attendant, who clearly wanted to practice her English, explained to me in detail their different origins and processes. I assumed the man at the cash register was her father, because he looked proud watching her speak in front of other customers whom he called by their first names.

After tasting too many cheeses in no particular order, I decided on a Valdeón, a sheep cheese from Castilla y León wrapped in chestnut leaves, which had a strong blue cheese flavor, although not as sharp and salty as the Cabrales. She cut a big piece, enough for a family of four, which I found a reasonable way to charge me for her time. When her father was not looking, she snuck a sample of cheese from Zamora that I had liked into the plastic bag, a furtive smile slipping across her face.

Going up the hill to my place, crossing Plaza de Tirso de Molina, I heard the familiar clatter of skateboard wheels. I looked up and saw two teenagers, yelling and laughing, sliding in between cars, against traffic. One was wearing an oversized Lakers shirt and the other a New York Mets hat. Just seeing these pieces of Americana in the street filled me with momentary joy.

I went through the list I had made and looked for a place where I could get some necessities like linens, towels, and cleaning products. The stores had already closed. Although the sky was darkening, it still held the pink silvery light of a long summer day refusing to depart. Despite its being a Monday night, the street was full of people. Crossing through a park, I noticed a large group of men wearing djellabas. They seemed middle-aged, but their constant laughter and body language made them look much younger. Some of them were holding hands. I wondered if they were gay and undocumented, if they had fled Morocco and asked for asylum, if they had crossed the Strait of Gibraltar on rickety dinghies like I had seen in *El País*. I wondered when I had started to think like a person with papeles.

On my sixteenth birthday, I had just blown out the candles on a frosted cake from Veniero's, the smoke still hovering in the air, when Chus handed me an envelope. I tore it carefully and pulled out a Social Security card. I looked at him, incredulous. He said that though it wasn't official, it was official-looking enough to apply for a job. Staring at my name next to the foreign numbers that seemed to have been typed on an old typewriter, I repeated them like a mantra. I remember pedaling up Park Avenue, unstoppable, the pavement sliding smoothly under my wheels. With the card secured in the inner pocket of my bomber jacket, I visited the most famous restaurants in the city: La Grenouille, Jean-Georges, Le Cirque. After locking my bike, I would pull out the card and glance at the numbers to make sure they hadn't disappeared. None of them were hiring, but, too excited to let defeat enter my mind, I stopped by Le Bourrelet before returning home. A younger Chef, already pasty-faced and strong tempered, gave me a harsh look and a trial period.

Now, as I arrived at my building, an ancient-looking woman was sweeping the stoop. Wearing a black dress and a net over her hair, she reminded me of the widows I had seen in the

Fellini movies that Chus watched repeatedly. I wished the door wasn't open, so I could use my key and prove that I belonged there. With a nervous smile, I went in, expecting to be stopped, but she smiled back and kept on caressing the stone with her broom.

Entering the apartment, I closed the door behind me but didn't switch on the light. I stood in the foyer and peered into the living room. The walls were thick and covered with many coats of paint, the wood beams whole tree trunks that had once been part of a forest and now supported the roof.

I finally turned the light on and walked into the living room. The sound of my steps and the opening and closing of cabinets made the present feel more real. In the night, the space looked smaller but also cozier, even more welcoming. Time seemed to slow down and the afternoon felt long ago, longer than the four hours that had gone by. I put the cheeses on the kitchen counter and went to my new bedroom.

Taped to the inside pane of the closet door was an old, faded map of the city. I looked for Jacobo's street and, with a blue pen, traced the path to my building through the Castellana and Calle de Zurita. Then I tried to remember every walk, every excursion, every night out, and began drawing lines, some of the streets becoming a thick blue, as I tended to take the same routes to avoid getting lost. By the time I finished, I realized that most of my walks had taken place in a small part of the map, and the city, its limits vast, remained mostly unexplored.

THAT EVENING, Jacobo, taking advantage of the fact that his parents had gone to Mallorca, turned our dinner into a get-together at his house. After hearing the stories he had shared about his friends, I was fascinated by them. With the exception of the kid I talked to on my first night out, the law student, most of them hadn't worked a day in their lives and spent their youth in boarding schools, and in and out of rehab. One of them, the son of one of the most aristocratic families in Spain, owned enough land to travel from Madrid to Seville through his territories. Another one, shortly after inheriting money from his grandmother, spent it on a drug binge that lasted for weeks and ended up blowing his head off with a rifle. Jacobo spoke about them lovingly but also in a way that was judgmental and with great detachment, as if wanting to reinforce he was not like them.

I realized I still had my set of keys and suddenly dreaded giving them back. I had been looking forward to getting my own space, but the prospect of losing the shelter and comfort of his place made me anxious. That didn't stop me from wanting to demonstrate my recently gained independence, so instead of letting myself into the building, I rang the intercom. Going up the stairs, as the sound of distant music and people yelling became more audible, I thought about how getting my own place marked a true beginning. The apartment was so crowded that it felt like I was in a bar. Walking into the kitchen, I found a sea of opened bottles and ice bags in puddles of water. I made myself a tequila soda while a drunken kid read aloud a sangria recipe as he poured two bottles of red wine into a big glass bowl.

Outside, thick clouds of smoke floated in the air. The roar of Vampire Weekend coming from a speaker made people shout to hear one another. Even though I had been staying at the house for more than a week and all my belongings were still in the bedroom, I felt like an intruder. I walked around the garden taking big gulps from my drink, looking for Jacobo and becoming increasingly uncomfortable.

I went back to the kitchen for a refill. Pushing the glass against the ice maker, I noticed two vaguely familiar faces. I tried to remember where I could have possibly known them from and considered places I frequented in New York. Grabbing a bottle of Don Julio, I was so absorbed fighting with my memory that I poured myself a glass of tequila and left no room for soda. I crossed in front of them, and when I heard them speak in English, I could barely contain myself. They made no signs of recognizing me. As I was gathering enough courage to go introduce myself, they grabbed their drinks and walked out of the kitchen.

The apartment, taken over by strangers, had become an entirely different place. Maybe because I felt isolated and awkward, I suddenly became proprietary. I toured the living room full of young couples too busy making out to notice my presence or look for a coaster to put their glasses on. The long hallways, which had been so silent that you could hear the creaking of the parquet floors, were now conduits of jumbled voices and sporadic shouts that only added to my sense of loss. The strangers, emboldened by alcohol, came in and out of bathrooms in groups. I felt compelled to open every door and inspect every room, which I had not dared to do before. The apartment was much bigger than I had thought. It occupied an entire floor of the building. The service quarters were modest and had the only bathroom with no window and a shower instead of a soaking tub.

I was making my way back to the kitchen, crossing the dining room, when someone yelled, "Americano." I turned my head and saw the girl whom I had met at the square sitting on the other side of the room. She was wearing a red skirt with a matching top. Her hair, slicked back into a bun, was held by a tiara.

"Hola," I said, not producing any sound but moving my lips exaggeratedly instead, so she could understand me from afar.

She was sitting at a table with the same two friends I had seen her with when we met. I walked over to them, happy to have a momentary destination.

"What's up, guys?" I said, playing up my American self and kissing Triana on both cheeks.

"I told you it was him," the girl said.

"I saw you guys in the kitchen. I was trying to figure out where I knew you from."

"From the terrace," she said.

"No, I know." I looked at Triana and sipped air from my already empty drink. The jock refused to make eye contact. It was clear he disliked me. We stood there without talking, uncomfortably waiting for someone to break the silence. When the first chords of a new song came on, Triana said: "I love Mercedes," and walked in the direction of the music.

I followed her with my eyes through the living room and, before she vanished, ran after her. The song was "Todo cambia" by Mercedes Sosa. I didn't expect to hear the voice of a communist singer in a party of the Spanish elite.

"I can't stand that guy. He's such a fucking niñato," she said, lighting a cigarette.

I assumed that the term *niñato* had the same derogatory meaning for Spaniards as it had for the Nuyoricans that I grew up with.

"How did you end up here? Who do you know?" she asked.

"Jacobo."

"Oh." She seemed surprised. "How?"

"It's a long story. We met on the plane. I've been staying here since I arrived."

"Shut up. You have?"

I told her about getting sick on arrival and being rescued by him.

"And you, who do you know?"

"I taught Jacobo for years," she said, touching her hair and adjusting her skirt.

"Taught what?"

"English. I teach at a high school in the suburbs and also give private lessons."

"That's right. I forgot you were an English teacher."

"Have you met his parents?"

"Only his mother."

From the way she glanced at me, I could tell that what she was about to say next was meant to be shocking.

"Do you know anything about them?" she asked, and then continued without allowing me time to respond. "His father is one of the most famous businessmen in Spain, the president of Endesa."

"Yeah, he mentioned that on the plane. I haven't met him yet."

"And Patricia is a countess, but very progressive."

She pronounced the words in a different tone, expecting a reaction. Learning that Patricia was an aristocrat caught me off guard, though it made sense. I smiled slightly as if to make believe I already knew. I wasn't sure why this information made me feel tricked.

"What's Endesa?" I asked, faking interest.

"How could I explain it?" She made a long pause and moved

her head up as if the answer were climbing through the bougainvillea. "Endesa is like the Con Edison of Spain," she said, proud of her comparison. "The main difference is that the CEO is appointed by the government. So, it's a very political position. Like, *very* political."

As I replayed bits of my conversation with Patricia, Jacobo came into view, wearing the same faded Che Guevara T-shirt and ripped jeans. Leaning on the balustrade, he was holding hands with a young, petite woman. She stared at him in silence while Jacobo looked absentmindedly at the city lights. They seemed to be having an argument.

"That's Jacobo's girlfriend," Triana said. "Well, I'm not sure if they're still together."

"Wait, what?" I began to shake my glass full of ice like a maraca.

"He's not gay if that's what you're thinking. I can assure you of that," she said with a smirk.

"Oh, I wasn't thinking that. I don't think so literally," I said, hoping the words would cover my shock. Then, not being able to restrain myself, I blurted: "Was he good?"

"I have no complaints," she said, proud to confirm her position of power.

I tried to visualize them having sex but couldn't.

Triana's friends returned with their hands full of drinks. She handed me a plastic glass of sangria with unevenly cut pieces of fruit floating on top. I thanked her and asked her to remind me of her name again.

10

The party was slowly coming to an end, but the people who remained kept talking animatedly and either were unaware of the time or refused to be pushed out by the first light of the day. Jacobo's girlfriend left soon after I saw her, and we spent the remainder of the night together. The few conversations we managed to have in private, most of them about feeling torn between two countries, were interrupted by his friends, who kept coming over to ask about his year abroad. They wanted to know the music he was listening to, which were the hottest clubs, and if he had seen any famous people. Jacobo delivered the answers effortlessly, as if he had rehearsed them. The clubs he mentioned were straight, bottle service, and exclusive, catering to celebrities and rich kids who liked to dance and do blow without being bothered, where phones didn't get signals and photos were strictly forbidden. The few times I went because Bondi was bartending, I found them dull and sterile, though the music was unquestionably better than what played at mainstream clubs. Observing him interact with his friends, I noticed what seemed a studied masculinity, as if he was putting on an act. What couldn't be denied was that he was socially gifted and well-liked. And that he preferred me over his old circle. Throughout the night, we acted out our foreignness in front of them, and that foreignness was a place that only we could inhabit, our own private country.

"Let's go," Jacobo said after one of his friends grabbed his iPod from the dock.

The silence made the morning light even more menacing as the last group began gathering their stuff.

"Let's fucking go," he repeated.

"Go where?"

"Out of the city. The beach isn't far. If we leave now, we can be there by lunch."

The excitement of having my own place, now that I was back at Jacobo's, had turned into a strange sense of loneliness. As the night wore on, I began dreading the moment of returning to my apartment and fantasized about sleeping here for one more night.

"I wish I could. But I need to meet this chef who might have good leads for me, he might even offer me a job."

"Come on." Jacobo stuck his tongue out. "You know you want to."

"I do. But I can't."

"Come on, you just got an apartment. And thanks to who?" he said in a sassy tone.

I didn't mind the emotional blackmail; quite the opposite. I loved feeling wanted.

"Okay," I finally said, because I wanted to prolong our time together but also to see his face light up. "Two days."

"Yay!"

Although Jacobo had drunk as much as me or more, it was hard to tell. Given the many times he had excused himself to the bathroom, and how often he pinched his nose, I suspected he had been doing bumps. But as we went to pack our bags, I studied him closely and he seemed sober enough to drive.

WE TOOK the elevator down, walked to the back of the building through a courtyard, and entered a small garage. Most of the cars had dark tinted glass. I recognized the Jaguar that had picked us up from the airport and assumed we would be taking it to the beach. Jacobo unlocked the doors of a deep-blue vintage Mercedes instead. It was older than us but in great shape. The light brown leather seats were evenly worn and lightly cracked, the wood dashboard shined with polish. We put our bags in the trunk and got in.

"It was my grandfather's."

"I love this model," I said, as if I were into cars.

"He was the British ambassador to Spain in the sixties. This car used to have diplomatic plates."

"Wait. I thought your grandfather was in the military."

"That's on my dad's side, the shitty part of the family. Mom's half British."

Jacobo maneuvered the car out of the garage with ease. We drove through the courtyard, listening to the sound of crunching gravel. An old man dressed in green overalls came out to open the gate, rubbing his eyes. He lifted his hand effusively and walked toward us. Jacobo rolled down the window. They hugged each other awkwardly and exchanged some words. I noticed Jacobo's tone again, the same tone that he had used with Gabriela and the cabdriver.

The city was almost deserted. On the bench in front of the building, the wood bench that some nights ago I had contemplated using as a cot, a homeless man lay with eyes wide open, listening to a radio. When the gate closed and the car crossed the sidewalk, he turned and looked at me, enthralled by the sound of the old diesel engine.

We stopped at a traffic light. The street was quiet, the sidewalk almost empty. Just an old woman with a dachshund, who was so energetic and was pulling so hard on the leash that the dog seemed to be walking her instead. Across the street a large truck was parked in front of a kiosk and a man unloaded piles of bundled newspapers. He was wearing one of those elastic belts that protects the lower back, and every time he bent over, his face tensed with pain.

I turned to Jacobo. "Are you okay to drive?"

He nodded. We fastened our seat belts and drove down, passing taxis with green roof lights going in the opposite direction. At the end of the Castellana, we merged into the right lane, which turned into a curve and then a tunnel. Jacobo stepped on the gas until we reached one hundred kilometers per hour, the speed limit. Before long, the road began to twist and turn. We entered an area of endless curves in an oppressive maze of weathered concrete, not quite able to fully escape the city's confines.

When we finally left downtown, and I began to sober up, the novelty of prolonging the night was wearing off as I worried about everything I needed to do. Jacobo turned on the radio. Soothing instrumental music flooded the car, its tempo accompanying the constant rattling of the engine. For the next fifty miles, we passed deteriorated commuter towns of gray industrial complexes and tall jail-like buildings, a testament to a different Spain, to other lives whose existence wasn't protected by the limestone façades of the Barrio de Salamanca. What would have happened had my mother not put me on a plane? Now, seeing these ghostly buildings, some of them boarded up, in desolate industrial areas full of abandoned cars and junk, I felt even luckier.

We drove south in silence and finally the last traces of Madrid disappeared behind us. Jacobo, with his eyes on the road, glared at the speed limit signs while smoothly operating the gearshift. Every time he noticed I was looking at him, he gave me a quick glance and stuck out his tongue.

I couldn't shake off the disappointment in Chef's voice when he heard I had not contacted Matías yet. My thoughts were a mix of regret for abandoning my obligations and pure excitement to be on an open road. The steady hum of the engine was strangely comforting knowing we were heading to a new destination. Distant specks slowly morphed into recognizable shapes, gas stations, car dealerships, a tractor working a field, a group of cyclists in the shape of a bullet defying the wind.

The only road trip I had ever taken was in the summer of 1996, right after I turned thirteen. It was the middle of July; Ben and Chus had borrowed a car from a friend to see Niagara Falls. I remember it being an endless drive. We played games, told stories, played more games. After I fell asleep and woke up several times, we finally arrived. We were trying to decide the best spot to explore the falls. The attendant at the boat tour stand assured us that it was on the Canadian side. Chus became annoyed. I thought that he was upset about forgetting our passports, but after listening to him and Ben talk in code for a while, I suspected there was more to it. The discussion escalated. When I asked Chus what was wrong, even though Ben implored him not to tell me, he said that if we exited the country, we would not be able to go back home. Sitting on a bench from where we could see Canada across the river, he repeated what I had once overheard him say to my middle school principal: We didn't have papeles. At first, I hadn't grasped what that meant. Then I understood that we were undocumented, and that being undocumented made us different, limited.

I ran back to the car and refused to go on the tour the next day to see the falls from the American side. I was so frightened of being next to the border that I begged them to drive back to New York right then. After they failed to convince me otherwise, we drove the four hundred miles back to the city, only stopping to refuel. Every time we saw a border patrol or police car, I was gripped with terror. Once we arrived home, I locked myself in my bedroom for days. I spent most of that summer in the apartment or playing pelota in the projects on Avenue D, where, back then, the police didn't dare enter.

Now, crossing my foreign homeland, letting the hot, dry air blow through my hair, and admiring new, unknown landscapes, I felt I could finally relax for the first time since my arrival. After an hour of driving, a sign informed us that we were entering the Comunidad de Castilla–La Mancha. We had been silent for most of the journey, and when I began reciting the opening lines of *Don Quixote* with the over-the-top intonation that Chus always employed, Jacobo burst out laughing, then joined me. I stopped after the first couple of lines, which were all I knew. He recited the whole first paragraph by heart. Throughout the early morning, those black, fragile hours that are slowly defeated by the first light of day, the music kept coming, the signs kept pointing straight ahead, and the landscape continued to change.

At one point, the road split in two and most of the traffic veered west, toward Córdoba.

"Twenty kilometers down that road is where I went to rehab."

I didn't respond right away. Jacobo had a sudden way of sharing intimate information that I found unnerving. Maybe it was due to our cultural differences, but I wondered at times if he enjoyed offering the most shocking parts of his past to provoke a reaction.

"How long ago was that?"

"A couple of years ago. I didn't really need it. Just a way for my dad to punish me for being a rebel."

We crossed through an area with strip clubs on both sides of the road, run-down, weathered buildings and lonely parking lots with names like Paradiso, Sofía's, and Belleza Tropical. Jacobo said that this highway had the biggest concentration of roadside brothels in the country. He considered it to be an interesting sociological phenomenon. I just found it odd.

"Have you ever been to one?" He put the blinker on and released the gas pedal. I fixed my gaze on a sign with the word *Heaven* written in fluorescent-pink neon and considered the possibility that his slowing down the car meant we were going in.

"No, never. Have you?"

"Yeah, I have." He gave a theatrical pause. "A long time ago."

I wondered, given our age, how long ago it could have possibly been.

"Does your girlfriend know?" I blurted out, not allowing myself enough time to evaluate the potential effect of my words.

"Who?" He sounded offended.

"Your girlfriend," I repeated casually. "Triana pointed her out at the party. She's cute!"

I'm not sure why I enjoyed putting him on the spot, why I thought this was not a dangerous game to play. Maybe it was because I had been given an excuse to not pursue him and act on an attraction I couldn't justify to myself. Deep down, I knew I could never be with a rich kid who had been given everything and was willing to have sex for money just because he could.

"That was my *ex*-girlfriend," he said, punching me lightly on the arm.

We took a service road that ran parallel to the highway, leaving behind the brothel to our right with its depressing, empty parking lot, and pulled into a gas station. Next to it there were a restaurant and a convenience store whose windows were covered with signs advertising cheeses from La Mancha and lottery tickets. A minibus with a large white decal on its side that read *Discover Andalucía* was parked out front. I thought of the words *I need Spain* on the poster at the airport and how we had become a version of the two girls riding in the convertible.

Shortly after we stopped, a middle-aged man came out wearing a red and gray uniform three sizes too big. He had on rubber boots even though it was the middle of summer and the radio had announced the temperature was going to reach thirty-five degrees, which Jacobo converted to ninety-five degrees Fahrenheit.

"Can you please fill it up with diesel?" Jacobo asked as he headed to the store. "I'll be right back."

I got out of the car to stretch my legs.

"It's going to be a hot day," the man said.

I nodded and walked to the side of the road to avoid getting into the conversation he clearly wanted to start. Despite being only eleven in the morning, the sun was strong. The freeway had light traffic and at times, the silence was so absolute that I could hear the cars in the distance way before my eyes were able to spot them. In this quietness, the irresponsibility of leaving the city a day after getting an apartment became louder and louder. I headed back to the car as the attendant squeezed the last drops.

"Thirty-six," he said, hanging up the hose.

"Give me a second."

I got in the car and opened the glove compartment as if looking for my wallet, which was in my back pocket. When the man started checking his phone, I grabbed a pair of shorts from my bag and went to the bathroom.

Managing not to touch the dirty floors, I stepped into my shorts and stayed by the window until Jacobo came out of the store carrying a bottle of water in one hand and a plastic bag in the other. I waited until he paid the attendant and I saw the red taillight go on and the white exhaust blowing into the air. By the time I left the bathroom, Jacobo had parked in front of the restaurant.

"Oh, you've changed." He shut the door of the car, an old map in his hand.

"Yeah. I feel so much better."

"Those are nice shorts," he said, staring at my crotch.

"These? They're pretty old," I said, blushing, aware the elastic lining had loosened, the mesh no longer black but a faded gray.

"I'm dying for a cold beer," he said.

"Yeah, me too."

"This is by far the best place to have a bite on the autovía."

The bar was old. It had not been made to look old, like so many New York establishments. You could tell by the paint on the walls, which had begun to peel off, the turn-of-the-century three-group espresso machine, and the faded color of the posters advertising bullfights in Seville. And there was something else, something indescribable about the space that conveyed the passage of time, something that no interior designer could replicate, like a patina formed by the steam of infinite coffees, cigarette smoke, and something else.

A thin layer of olive pits, shrimp shells, and crumpled paper napkins crunched under our feet as we made our way to the bar. A big flat-screen TV was playing Bugs Bunny, who, instead of speaking with a mix of Brooklyn and Bronx accents, pronounced the words in heavy Castilian Spanish, which made him actually funny. A group of kids sat absorbed with Coke bottles in their hands, guffawing loudly. Jacobo ordered two cañas. The bartender expertly poured the beer in short glasses, leaving just the right amount of head, then brought them along with two pieces of toast with a slice of tomato and thick white anchovies on top.

"I love these pinchos," Jacobo said, grabbing one. "Isn't it crazy that they give you free tapas with each caña?"

"Yeah. I don't even know how they make any money."

A midsized truck parked next to our car and a group of men got off the back of it, most of them wearing blue overalls and boots, their faces damp with sweat, moving slowly, as if they were about to collapse from exhaustion. As they entered the restaurant, one of the workers, a young guy wearing a tracksuit, locked eyes with Jacobo. When Jacobo realized I had noticed the exchange, he looked away, out the window beyond our car and up onto the hillside covered with deep yellow shrubs. I wondered if he was attracted to guys wearing athletic clothes or who simply looked like they were from a working-class background. I wondered if it was some kind of kink and considered whether mine was skinny rich kids with beautiful green eyes who wore my salary on their wrist.

"So, where are we heading to?"

He grabbed the road map, which looked as old as the car, from his back pocket and unfolded it on the table.

"We're here. And we're going to Cabo de Gata." He placed a finger with a bloody cuticle on a thick blue line, then slid it to a cape in the Mediterranean, leaving a light orange smudge across the map. "It's one of my favorite places in the whole world."

The two points were pretty distant from each other. Seeing our placement on the map, and how far we were from Madrid and how much farther we were going to travel, made my stomach churn.

"I don't think I can take so much time off, Jake. I need a job soon. I just rented an apartment, remember? I need money." I made it sound as if I were cracking a joke, then laughed to hide the anxiety behind my words.

"Oh, don't worry about money. Money is the last thing you need to worry about."

His words were intended to comfort me, and though I had become accustomed to his constant generosity and found his empathy soothing, I was overwhelmed. Stranded at a roadside bar halfway down the Iberian Peninsula, I worried about the prospect of continuing this dependency and risking the best chance at getting a job.

"What's today, Thursday?" he said, ordering two more beers with his hand.

"No, Tuesday."

He burst out laughing. "I'm such a mess."

I nodded.

"Hey. Let's just play it by ear. Okay? Don't worry about the money." He grabbed the back of my neck.

Feeling his hand on my nape, I wished I had not changed

into my gym shorts, whose mesh lining couldn't hide my excitement. Or that at least I had kept my underwear on.

"Seriously." He gulped his beer and went to speak with the bartender.

I put the map on my lap. It struck me that I felt the same as I had when he disappeared in the crowd at the airport. I wondered if this uneasiness was caused by my attraction to him or pure dependence.

Jacobo came back with a handful of crumpled bills.

"So, what do you think?" He grabbed the map and carefully folded it into a rectangle.

I didn't respond immediately. I made it seem as if I were considering the option of going back, although we both knew that option didn't exist.

"Fuck it," I said, faking the excitement he was looking for. "Let's do it!" A nervous happiness made my stomach flutter. I knew it was another attempt to keep the relationship going, to create the illusion that our lives were similar.

Back in the car, listening to him talk on the phone, I noticed again how masculine his Spanish mannerisms were, a masculinity he lacked when speaking in English. As he hung up and switched languages, he began explaining where we were, his soft intonation so different another persona seemed to have emerged, one that was more like the Jacobo I had met on the plane: freer, happier, more at ease with himself.

Absorbed in the shifting colors of the landscape, I tried to stay awake. But after contemplating the silent fields before me, engulfed in a mix of sun heat, beer torpor, and the steady, light rocking of the car, I succumbed to sleep and dreamed vividly. I was traveling on a high-speed train through infinite wheat fields. The train car had only two seats: the one I was sitting in and an empty one directly across from me facing the opposite direction. It was difficult to know whether we were moving forward or backward. Every few minutes the ticket collector tapped my shoulder. I opened my wallet fearing to be caught without a ticket, but each time, I was relieved to find a new one. The man was rapidly aging. The skin from his face, turning into big folds, had begun to cover his eyes. I decided to get off the train, grabbed a large FedEx package from the overhead compartment, and dragged it with difficulty toward the doors. By the time I stepped out, the high-speed train had turned into the shuttle that goes to Times Square and I found myself underground.

THE SOUND OF the hinges as Jacobo opened the door of the car brought me back. I kept my eyes closed and inhaled the salty, humid air that hinted we were near the sea. In my teenage years, during the period when Chus was translating the dreams of Georges Perec into Spanish, I began recording mine in a blue spiral notebook that sat on my night table. Every morning, I would diligently write down all I could remember. Soon, it became not only a daily ritual but also a way to notice certain patterns that helped me understand some of my deepest fears.

When I heard Jacobo walking on the gravel, I opened my eyes and was dazzled by the lunar landscape surrounding us. The earth was a charcoal gray, the color of ashes, and there was no vegetation except for some ancient cacti spreading over the hills. Jacobo was climbing a rock. The radio had lost its signal and a light static sound was coming through the speakers. The sun was low. I looked at the clock embedded in the dashboard. It was almost five. I had slept for three hours.

A strong sea smell increased as the breeze picked up, carrying with it the distant murmur of a car. I walked up to him and caught my first sight of the Mediterranean. The expansiveness of the view and the arid, volcanic landscape against the bright blue of the water was an incredible sight. My only experience of the sea had been the Atlantic Ocean, whose color was no match. This vivid blue reminded me of a postcard Ben had sent me from Puerto Rico that had hung over my bed for years.

"Sorry I slept for so long. This is gorgeous."

Jacobo didn't move as I climbed up the rock.

"Isn't it?" He rubbed his eyes and kept looking straight ahead. Had he been crying?

In the distance, I could see small towns near the sea, tiny drops of white on a massive gray canvas, and a blue line crossing the horizon. A winding road meandered on the vast landscape toward the sea, dividing it in two. A car moved through the curves, the sun turning the windshield into a momentary mirror. I wasn't used to seeing so much open space before me. Because I had grown up in Manhattan, my eyes were used to a limited depth of field, and the expansiveness of this view had a hypnotic effect on me. As I admired the landscape before me, time seemed to have stopped. I suddenly had all the time in the world, all the time to contemplate where I had arrived.

11

The following morning, having breakfast on a hotel terrace facing the sea, after a night of flimsy dreams, I thought about Patricia. I had refrained from asking Jacobo about her because I didn't want to appear nosy. But I had never met an aristocrat before and was curious. Did she go to a finishing school? Or a special college? Wasn't she supposed to have married another aristocrat? Was her husband one? Even though we hadn't spoken for long and the conversation had been steered by Jacobo, I was fascinated by her. The candor of her words *I admire your courage* and the gravity of her tone had made a lasting impression on me.

Jacobo read in *El País* that the temperature was supposed to reach the nineties. He was obsessed with the newspaper. Chus, born right after the Civil War, had explained to me that Spain was still a nation of glaring political divisions. The military dictatorship that ruled the country for thirty-six years had inflicted deep wounds and made carrying one newspaper versus another a political act to this day.

His devotion to *El País* reminded me of Chus and his sacred Sunday morning ritual when he read the *New York Times* from front to back. They both saved their preferred sections for last and tore out certain articles, a similarity I found endearing. I imagined them having coffee together at the Hungarian Pastry Shop, where Chus usually met his students and worked for hours on poems that he scribbled on small scraps of paper, on the back of an envelope, or at the bottom of a utility bill, when Jacobo asked for the check. It suddenly dawned on me that he would be going back to New York at the end of the summer, and soon I would be left alone.

He went to settle the bill and I headed up to the room. Climbing up the stairs, I thought about whether his insistence on paying for everything gave him pleasure, or if money was just something he didn't think about because it had no significance for him. One thing was clear: He enjoyed my company. Maybe, spending time together, he felt less Spanish, less connected to a past he clearly despised. As for me, being with him was a way to latch on to the very last remnant of America and avoid the inevitability of looking for a job and settling in a country that had the unfair responsibility of becoming my home. Up until now, I had considered myself to have two countries of origin, and the notion that I could always establish myself in my other homeland had reinforced the belief that I was inhabiting the space voluntarily. That was no longer the case.

Shutting the door behind me, I stared at the room. The turquoise spread that had been so neatly laid over the queen-sized bed when we first entered was now on the floor crumpled into a ball. The room had a smell. A musty smell that told the story of the night. I walked up to the window, parted the curtains, and opened the door to the balcony. A fresh sea breeze quickly erased the traces of our stale selves.

After trying different combinations of nines and zeros, I managed to dial Chus but got the answering machine.

"Hi, it's me. Sorry I missed you. Everything is good. You won't believe this, but I'm on a road trip! We're in . . . Cabo de Gata. Spain is so incredibly beautiful, it's overwhelming. Anyway, I'm trying to relax about the guy, and about everything. I think you'd be proud. I'll call you again when I get back to Madrid. I love you. I love you a lot. Wait! I got an apartment. I haven't slept there yet but the bathroom has a window. It's pretty neat. I'll send you photos when I get back. Okay. Bye for now."

I took a long, hot shower despite the high temperature outside and changed into trunks that I had last used in the pool of the YMCA on Fourteenth Street. They still had a faint smell of chlorine.

When I got out of the bathroom, Jacobo was kneeling down in the middle of the room cutting off the legs of his jeans.

"What are you doing?"

"What do you think? I'm making a pair of shorts."

"Well, don't quit your day job," I said, noticing the unevenness of the cut.

"Okay, señor artista." He handed me the scissors. "Let's see how good you are."

I kneeled down in front of him. Pushing the blade into the denim, I felt the fabric tear open. As the metal touched his flesh, Jacobo gasped.

I pulled back the scissors. "Did I hurt you?"

We locked eyes.

"No, they're just cold," he said. "Keep going. But be gentle."

SINCE WE HAD ARRIVED late at night, we had seen little of the town, which consisted of a main street with a pharmacy, a supermarket, and a restaurant, Casa Pepe. Stray dogs lounged in the shade, and as we walked by, Jacobo spoke to them in baby talk. They acknowledged his words by wagging their tails, though they were not excited enough to get up, as if the heat were a massive stone that lay on top of them. Dirt roads curved up into the hills, where white stucco houses sat in lush, mani-cured gardens with blue water pockets. I wondered if such a quaint and unpretentious beach town like this could exist in the United States, where the houses were newer and bigger, at least the ones on Long Island and the Jersey Shore.

"This is the last town before we enter the Cabo de Gata Natural Park. It's been designated a Biosphere Reserve by UNESCO."

"Is that where we're going?"

"Yeah. To a cove called San Pedro. Trust me, you won't regret it. It's a long hike through volcanic hills but the view of the sea at dusk is out of this world."

"Sounds dreamy."

"How do you feel about spending a night or two sleeping on the beach?" he asked as we entered the small supermarket.

"The real question is not how I feel about it, but if you can survive without reading the newspaper for two days."

He laughed.

We walked leisurely through the aisles and, at one point, took separate ways. I went to the back, where behind a glass counter, an old man armed with a long, narrow knife was labo-riously slicing a leg of jamón serrano. I observed the move-ment of his finely veined hands, how expertly he swiveled the leg to produce slices thinner than the wax paper on which he was carefully arranging them. He focused with intensity on the course of the knife, and though he had not yet acknowledged me, he explained out loud the importance of cutting from the bottom up so the meat wouldn't dry out too soon. As he peeled the flesh away, the leg began to sweat, and the bone underneath emerged with the sheen of a massive pearl.

I stood there in silence, feeling weightless. A motley group of young, loud German guys with dreadlocks and faces cracked by the sun lined up behind me. They smelled like skunk. Without lifting his eyes, the man asked who was next, and I ordered half a kilo of ham just because I wanted to keep watching him. I should have gotten chorizo because it also looked good and was much cheaper.

DRIVING UP a dirt road, inhaling a fine layer of dust that filtered through the vents, turning the dashboard a light gray, we arrived at an esplanade that served as a parking lot. We left the car next to a van hand-painted with peace signs and I asked Jacobo if this was a safe place to leave it. He said it was, but then went back and locked the wood steering wheel to the pedal with one of those bright yellow metal bars that I hadn't seen since the Tompkins Square riots, which I watched on TV.

Jacobo took the lead and hiked ahead of me. He was wearing my gym shorts, and the worn-out mesh tight on his butt glistening in the sun made it hard to look anywhere else. We had put all the food and supplies in a large backpack that he refused to let me carry, making me grab a light straw tote bag with two beach towels, bug spray, and a bottle of tequila he had insisted on buying. We walked through an immense rock formation that seemed sculpted by Gaudí. Its shape, Jacobo said, was the result of volcanic explosions that had happened millions of years ago and the constant effects of the tramontana, a northern air current from the Mediterranean Sea. The winding trail along the coastline made the turquoise water come in and out of view and, against the ocher and red colors of the hills, gave the landscape an eerie quality. Not having seen a single tree since we entered the park, I thought about the stray dogs back in town, sprawled on the side of the road, lounging in the cool shade.

We walked silently and Jacobo seemed to be immersed in deep thought, only coming back to the present when he exchanged short greetings with other hikers going in the opposite direction. At one point, when we had reached the highest elevation, the trail came into the flank of the hill, and when it came out again, the ruins of a castle perched on a cliff appeared in the distance. It had a magnificent tower with a large oval window, but most of the rectangular adjoining structure had collapsed to the ground. The only standing wall was covered in ivy so thick and uniform that you couldn't see the stone underneath.

"That's the castle of San Pedro." Jacobo peeled off his backpack and leaned it against a rock. The back of his shirt was soaked in sweat. "Isn't it splendid?"

"Yeah. Spectacular."

He fished a water bottle out of the bag. I noticed we were almost out.

"It's sad to see it in such bad shape. The tower dates from the Moors, but the fortress was built by the Reyes Católicos after the Reconquista."

Chus had taught me Spanish history during our summers at the beach, and I knew that the Reconquista was when Isabel and Fernando had taken over Granada in the fifteenth century. I began formulating a thought that would show my knowledge of history, but not fast enough.

"I always wonder what would have become of Spain had the Muslims not been forced out of the peninsula. The world would be a completely different place." He took another sip of water. "Or not."

As Jacobo turned his back to the wind to light a cigarette, I grabbed the backpack. Its green cloth was drenched. I hung it from my shoulders and enjoyed feeling his sweat against my back. By the time he noticed, I was already a couple of feet away, marching toward the beach.

The sand was not fine and yellow. The sand was the color of ashes. It was a ghostly sight: the dark gray, charred beach against the vivid crystal color of the water. I remembered the photos hanging in Jacobo's room and wondered if they had been taken here. The line between the sea and the sky was missing, the horizon casting infinite shades of blue. At the end of the beach, there was a massive rock formation and, at the bottom, a string of caves had been turned into summer shelters. I spotted the Germans from the supermarket, tending a fire. They were naked. I wondered if this was a nude beach, or whether the freedom to be naked was another Spanish civil right, like drinking alcohol on the streets.

Next to the sea, a breeze picked up and the heat lessened. I was itching to go into the water to rinse off the brown layer of dust that covered my body. Jacobo insisted on looking for a place to settle. He was adamant about securing a territory before more people arrived. From the moment we had decided to camp, a different part of him, more sensible and organized, had emerged. Amid a clutter of tents, we were able to find a spot that was, if not secluded, at least separated enough from others by a short but steep walk over a rock covered with tiny mussels that could easily slice open the soles of your feet. We unpacked our bags and spread their contents out, covering as much terrain as possible. That way, Jacobo said, people wouldn't try to squat in. He unfurled the sleeping bags even though it was only four in the afternoon. I set the cookware and utensils near a circle of rocks blackened by flames. I was surprised to see how much camping gear was in the bag. After getting settled, Jacobo rolled a thick joint.

I didn't want to go into the water anymore. We lay next to each other on a rock listening to the sea. Random thoughts entered my mind and left quickly, some merging into other thoughts, like the waves below us. I looked up at the sky. A line of wispy clouds floated against the blue. Searching for a plane, all I could see was a vanishing white trail without a clear beginning or end. For a moment, I thought of the New York skyline and the constant crossing of planes, and how sometimes police helicopters floated above the city, combing the streets with powerful halogen lights. Then bits of conversation from the couple at the airport about the different places and monuments they were planning on visiting played in my head.

"What's El Valle de los Caídos?" My voice came out flat.

Jacobo took a long time to respond. "Why are you asking?" he finally said, as if the words had gotten lost in the air.

I made myself a pillow with a towel. We were silent for a long time. I knew it was long because when I woke up, the rock had made marks on my arms and Jacobo wasn't by my side. I walked around the camp and inspected the food, which we had put in a plastic bag and hung from the limb of a tall cactus. I waited and waited for him to return, and when the sun started to set, I decided to walk down to the beach. I opened a side pocket in the backpack to leave my keys and found a sketchbook, its faded green cover roughened by seawater. Jacobo's name was carefully written in black capital letters.

The first pages had been left blank, but then a series of disquieting drawings began to emerge. They looked like the illustrations of human bodies in anatomy posters. The most disturbing one was of a man in black tights standing in a pool of dripping blood. He was flexing his arm, his biceps exploded into broken muscles and chunks of cartilage, his head covered with a black rubber mask. The contrast between the detailed, anatomical depiction of his body and his erased face was chilling. Despite it being a drawing, I instantly thought of the sadomasochistic Polaroids of Robert Mapplethorpe. Chus was a big admirer of his work. In response to Mapplethorpe's obscenity trial in the early nineties, he had written a piece for a now longforgotten downtown art magazine. The article centered around how the First Amendment guaranteed freedom of expression for all citizens, and "all citizens" included homosexuals. The conceit was that the general public could find certain art morally repugnant or degenerate but that didn't mean that it should be banned. His words created an uproar and were used as part of the defense strategy. Months after the trial, to celebrate the verdict, Chus was invited to a party in the back room of an S & M club in the West Village that no longer existed. At one point during the night, an androgynous model, dressed in black leather studded shorts, climbed a ladder, pulled his zipper down, and began peeing over a tower of champagne cups. Everyone celebrated the performance and the unruliest drank from the glasses. Chus produced a sonorous guffaw, most likely to alleviate the shock it could give an eight-year-old boy. I remember leaving the party upset. Years later, we talked about that night, and Chus defended himself by saying that those moments had been crucial for my education, freeing my sexuality from social constructs. I did not agree.

A sound of guitar chords blended with the crashing of the waves and became more audible as I climbed down to the beach. I squinted, trying to spot Jacobo in the water, but all I could see was a boat sailing away, its white hull slowly rocking back and forth. I walked up to a group of people sitting around a bonfire. Most of them looked like European travelers who had been living on the beach, their skin dark brown from the sun. The Germans from the supermarket were part of the circle and there was also a young woman singing flamenco who reminded me of Triana. I could spot the few Spanish by the dexterity of their hands and the deep sound of their palms. An old man was playing the guitar and moved its neck from side to side, as if catching gusts of wind to propel the music forward.

I sat down, enthralled, and filled my lungs with a mix of hashish, burning wood, and the salty breeze. The girl, who could not have been older than sixteen, sang with her eyes closed. Her voice seemed to originate in the depths of a wound, and as it left her body, her feet moved sporadically, creating furrows in the sand. Some people celebrated these spasms, shifting the tempo of their clapping as if to fill a space that had been torn open with the intensity of her voice. These moments were accompanied by shouts from the guitar player acknowledging her trance. When the song ended, the clapping stopped, and a thick silence wrapped around us, the only sound the fire crackling, making its own music. Then everyone burst into a roaring applause.

The beach wasn't long. I walked to the end and glanced at

the sea, trying to spot Jacobo in the water. During the hike, he had mentioned a natural spring where we could refill our bottles. I looked up to the hill and saw a lush patch of green in stark contrast with the gray sand, and a narrow path that went to the beach, people in colorful swimsuits going up and down.

I climbed up slowly, taking my time, pushing away the image of the biceps with its torn muscles like snapped guitar strings. It was hard to believe that those dark, gory images could live behind his big, green eyes. By the time I made it to the top of the hill, my shirt was soaked in sweat again. I didn't know what I was expecting the spring to be like, but I was disappointed to discover an oxidized pipe through which the water came, and a long line of people waiting to refill all sorts of plastic containers. Jacobo was talking animatedly and sharing a joint with an older man wearing tracksuit pants, his arms covered with stick-and-poke tattoos, his earlobes deformed by thick wood plugs. He would have never suspected that this barefoot guy in shorts was the son of one of the most powerful businessmen in Spain and a British countess. Spying on them from behind the bushes, I sensed that the farther away he got from his house, the freer and more at ease Jacobo was.

BY THE TIME he got back to our camp, I had prepared a simple dinner of sandwiches with jamón serrano, manchego, sliced tomato, and a paste that I had improvised using local figs, olives, and garlic. For dessert, I made a basic ganache, melting dark chocolate in heavy cream, that I poured over raspberries.

We ate in silence. The drawings were so vivid that every

time I looked at his face, I caught myself thinking about the man hooded in rubber. The moonlight reflecting off the sea illuminated the sky, and though we had readied a gas lantern, we didn't need to turn it on. After dinner, I went to the sea to wash the metal plates while Jacobo made a fire. Rinsing off the utensils, thinking about the implied domesticity in the unspoken division of tasks, filled me with an inexplicable joy.

Sitting by the fire, we drank and smoked hash until our throats became sandy and our words began to slur. Jacobo, quieter than usual, took long gulps from the tequila bottle as if wanting to drown some interior voice.

"I want to live in this moment forever," he finally said.

"Yeah. It's totally magical."

By now, a luminous amber moon hung low on the horizon, casting a sparkling line over the sea. Jacobo lay down and put his head on my thigh. I could sense his eyes staring at me. Facing the sea, I squinted, trying to make believe I had spotted something in the water. He grabbed my neck and pulled me toward him. I tried to think but my brain was full of smoke. He forced my face down until our lips touched. I pulled myself back. He grabbed my head again.

"Stop it, Jake!"

His face tensed. He closed his eyes with force and, holding on to my legs, struggled to sit up.

"I thought you liked me." He was slurring his words.

A flapping swarm of bats materialized in front of us, their black wings a fleeting shadow against the fiery orange sky.

"Of course I like you. But let's take it easy."

"You could at least be brave and say it. It's okay if you're not into me. Or are you going to tell me you're not gay?" He raised his voice. The black swarm fled in the opposite direction and entered a small cave.

"I don't think in those terms," I said, using the first thought that had materialized in my head, a sentence Chus used often and which bothered me immensely.

His face was lit by flares of fire, his eyes open wide. A spark landed on his shorts, and he let it burn out on its own, singeing them slightly.

"You know what?" He stood up. "Fuck you."

The sound of the crackling fire became unnervingly louder.

"I'm sorry," I said, trying to lower the temperature.

He staggered toward the edge of the rock, away from me.

"I'm sorry," I repeated much louder, afraid of losing the only person I had.

I walked up to him and put an arm around his shoulders. He took a step forward and left my arm dangling, then turned around, furious.

"Tell me you don't want to fuck me." His tears were full of rage.

"I don't want to fuck you, Jake. I'm sorry. You know I like you."

"Don't fucking belittle me!" he shouted.

He stormed toward me and pushed my chest, knocking me down to the ground. I fell on a sharp rock barely two feet away from the fire. My lower back hurt but I swallowed my scream before it came out. As I lay on the ground, trying to grasp what had happened, Jacobo jumped on top of me. We began to wrestle. He was much stronger than I had expected. I was scared we would roll into the fire. I struggled to push in the opposite direction, even though we were approaching the edge of the rock. He tried to punch me in the face, but I managed to catch his fist before it hit me. I dodged his second punch and then knocked his chin as hard as I could, splitting his lip. Blood dripped all over my face.

"Stop, please!" I yelled. Our faces were inches apart. I turned my head to prevent his blood from entering my mouth.

He dug his fingers into my neck. I felt his nails scratching my throat. He hit my right temple with his elbow, and taking advantage of my momentary daze, he punched me twice. I covered my face. Then I pushed with all my strength and managed to turn him over. I sat on his stomach. His back was now against the rock. I held his neck with my left hand and punched him repeatedly.

"Stop!" I cried, the order directed at me. I clasped both of his wrists to the rock. He was writhing and screaming, trying to escape my grasp. He looked possessed. Slowly, as he realized that he was immobilized, he stopped fighting back.

A weak breeze tickled the embers and illuminated his face. It was covered in blood. I freed his arms. Sitting up on the lower part of his stomach, I felt his hard cock. He covered his eyes and started to cry. I lay next to him with my back on the rock, looking at the moon. The sea had woken again, and the sound of the crushing waves flowed underneath his sobbing. Tears began running down my cheeks. I looked at my hands, splattered with blood. The skin on my knuckles had peeled off. I explored with my fingers a harrowing pain on the right side of my face and discovered I was also bleeding. Pressing with my shirt, I tried to stop the flow of blood.

Jacobo lay next to me in silence. He had stopped sobbing. I turned around and looked at him. His right eye had swollen so much I wasn't sure he was able to see me. I extended my arm and laid it on his chest. His heart was racing. He opened his arms and we fused into a hug. The wind carried the distant sound of guitar chords. I closed my eyes and fell asleep free-falling through the rift the singer had opened with her voice.

12

I woke up sweating. A foggy light not fully formed grew thicker and brighter as the sun climbed from behind the horizon line. Jacobo was sleeping next to me. His right eye had turned black, a long cut on his cheek was covered with dried blood, his lip swollen. I couldn't bear to look at him.

I hadn't noticed him getting into my sleeping bag during the night, our bodies now wrapped in polyester sweat. I opened the zipper quietly. My lower back ached. I walked to the edge of the rock. A flock of ducks were flying in V formation until they became thin black lines that disappeared into the distance. Down on the beach, the campers were still in their tents. It was quiet except for the rhythmic sound of the surf breaking on the shore. I thought about the moment I had him pinned down, each punch disfiguring his angelic face, and wondered where my rage had come from, a rage I had to yell at myself to control.

I was afraid of being left alone in this faraway place, miles away from the nearest city, but I was even more afraid of having destroyed our friendship. I wished I had taken my suitcase to the new apartment, as everything I owned was sitting in a home where I was no longer welcome. While I watched the sea, I thought about my new empty living room waiting to be inhabited.

I WENT DOWN to the beach and sat on the sand. The sun was now perched just above the horizon line. The heat was rising fast. I had gotten used to Jacobo's converting the temperature for me. I guessed it out loud: ninety-eight Fahrenheit, thirty-two Celsius. I stripped down to my underwear and balled up my clothes. Looking at both sides of the beach, not seeing anyone, I got naked and walked slowly into the sea.

The water was much warmer than I had expected. The color, the transparency, even the density was different from the Atlantic Ocean. As soon as I dove in, my face began to burn. My skin was covered in scratches. After the stinging lessened, I took long, steady strokes into colder, darker water.

Swimming had been the only sport I practiced growing up, maybe because I learned late. Ben had been an avid swimmer and belonged to the diving team at Dartmouth. When he heard I didn't know how to swim, he took it upon himself to teach me during a summer in my early teens. For two months, we would wake up early and walk from Cherry Grove to the Pines through the beach, avoiding the "meat rack," a group of dunes where men cruised around the clock. I only found out about it when I read an article about the AIDS crisis that described Fire Island as one of the main points of infection from which the virus spread to other parts of the world. It presented the Pines as an international gay vacation resort, which I found odd as, for me, it was just another beach on Long Island, one that helped forge some of my happiest memories.

In the mornings, we went to the pool of one of Ben's friends, a fashion photographer who owned a modern home with so much glass it was difficult to change into my bathing suit without feeling spied on. Sometimes we were there so early the owners were still draining their last cocktails and made insinuating jokes about my long board shorts. I missed those summers and thought about them often as an adult. I wondered what Ben would think about my reckless departure from the States, my abandoning Chus.

I lost track of time. The rhythmic movement of the strokes, the physicality of having to be active in order to stay afloat, occupied my mind. I could swim for hours at a time. At one point, I stopped and let myself drift. Playing dead, I looked at the clear sky, the salty water creeping through the corners of my eyes. Then I slowly began to swim back to shore and, struggling to fight the strong undertow pulling me in, I realized how out of shape I was.

The beach appeared slowly in the distance. People moved around their camps. Remembering that I was naked, I started to swim faster, hoping to make it back before more campers came out of their tents. I took long strokes but stopped often to see if I could touch the bottom. Almost out of breath, I finally felt the ground and began walking. Someone was sitting next to my clothes. I waited. When it was clear that whoever it was had no intention of leaving, I stepped out of the water, taking long strides to look confident and hide my embarrassment. Near the shore, I recognized Jacobo, his gaze fixed on the sea. He didn't look at me once. Not wanting him to think I was self-conscious, I fought the urge to put my underwear on and sat next to him. Since we had arrived in Madrid, he had looked for every chance to see me naked. And now, I found myself wanting to fulfill that desire, though I hated the feeling of my butt touching the sand.

He kept staring at the sea. Knowing that I had caused his black eye and all his cuts and bruises filled me with an overwhelming sadness. He pulled a bent cigarette from his pocket and straightened it out with his fingers for a long time. When he finally lit it, he shrugged to protect it from the wind and groaned. The slightest movement of his shoulders seemed to cause him pain. He took a long, hasty drag and gave me a defiant look.

A thick, white puff came out of his nostrils and floated around us, refusing to vanish. We spoke no words. Our fingers touched as he passed me the cigarette. I pulled it toward my lips and noticed a red rim of blood around the filter, like lipstick. I took a drag, inundating my lungs with sooty air, then smashed the cigarette into the sand. Jacobo gave me an annoyed look. I lay down to expose my body. As I faced the clear sky, I sensed his eyes staring at my cock. To fight back the urge of my expanding groin, I translated the chemical formula of sugar into Spanish.

THE DRIVE BACK was long and uncomfortable. Not just because the first hundred or so miles we didn't utter a single word. My shoulders were sunburned and my underwear, soaked in a mix of salty water and sand, irritated my skin. I looked out the window, Jacobo was fixated on the road, neither of us brave enough to make permanent the thoughts passing through our heads. From time to time, I used the excuse of his shifting the gears to look at his hand, then his arm and chest, before stealing a quick glance at his torn-up face, hoping the swelling would have decreased. It hadn't.

No longer feeling I could ask Jacobo for his phone, I wished I had my own to call Chus. Now more than ever, I wanted to be more like him, or Richard, open-minded, progressive, comfortable with dating others with addictions to sex, drugs, or both. Not having any real reasons to believe that Jacobo was an addict of any kind, I couldn't help but question whether my inability to act on my attraction was not based so much on his bad-boy quality as on an ingrained and toxic envy, an envy of a life that required no effort.

"Can I say something?" Jacobo muttered at last, his words barely audible.

I smiled because of what I imagined was a willingness to begin rebuilding our friendship. "Please."

Jacobo took his time. He didn't start speaking right away, and by how long he took to gather his thoughts, I knew the words were the consequence of profound deliberation.

"I think you lack balls," he said, then stopped.

I felt stupid for having smiled, expecting this was going to be some sort of apology, or at least an attempt at reconciliation.

"You're scared shitless that I'm a fuckup. That's why you don't want to pursue me," he continued, and then made another pause. "I've seen how you look at me. You've been wanting to get in my pants since the moment you saw me on the plane. The problem is you feel both superior and inferior to me. And there's nothing I can do about that because that's all in your little head. You complain about America but as fucked up as it sounds, you believe in a different version of American exceptionalism; you believe you're better than me.

Because I'm not self-made like you, because I haven't suffered what you have."

I could not believe his words, the razor-sharp comments, how close to home they felt. I stared at his face as he spoke, looking at his broken lip moving up and down. I hoped he was done but after a short pause he continued with the same sober intonation.

"I told you about how I had sex for money five hours into meeting you, not because I wanted to play a game. I wanted to show you how I am, how broken I sometimes feel. I thought you, of all people, would understand given what you've gone through. But you're like every other fucking gay I know, obsessed with meeting the perfect person, a person that only exists in your imagination."

After a couple of seconds of trying to say something, anything, I stopped staring at him and looked out the window. He turned on the radio. I was grateful to hear a voice, any voice other than his.

WE ENTERED THE CITY as the sun was setting. The traffic moved fluidly. I had been impatiently waiting for the end of the journey but now it felt overwhelming.

"We'll pick up your bag, then I'll drop you off at your place." His tone was flat.

"I can take a cab from your place. You've driven enough."

"I don't mind."

When we arrived at the gate, he stopped the car and asked me to wait. He made it sound as if it was more efficient for me to not go up, which was probably true, but it was hard not to interpret it as a way of punishing me. A way of saying I was no longer welcome.

After so many hours sitting down, I stepped out to stretch my legs. The hinges made a squeaking sound, the door complaining about too many decades doing the same job. As I leaned on the hood, someone passing by congratulated me on the car and asked about its age. I thanked him and said I didn't know.

Jacobo crossed the patio dragging my cheap suitcase, its missing wheel making a groove in the gravel. "What did he want?"

"He wanted to know the year of the car."

These were our conversations now, made of words not looking to convey anything other than what they meant on the surface.

We didn't say anything else until he pulled over in front of my building.

"Thanks for driving," I said. "And for everything else."

"You're welcome. And I'm sorry about the fight. I started it."

"And I continued it."

He turned off the engine. I looked at his skin, the swelling had started to go down. His sun-kissed face made his green eyes look brighter. I patted his lap, then opened the door and got out of the car. He began to cry. Some of the dried blood on his face turned into a lighter red.

"What now?" he said.

"I have no idea, Jake." My eyes became moist as I leaned through the window. I rubbed my eyes with my fists and pushed my tears back in.

"Do you need money?"

"No, I think I'm good."

13

⌒

When I opened the door after dragging my suitcase up five flights of stairs, sand still in my shoes, a rotten smell almost knocked me to the floor. At first, I thought a mouse had died in the middle of the apartment and begun to decay. But as soon as I entered the kitchen, I noticed the cheeses I had bought in the mercado sitting on the counter, the plastic bag no longer white but a patchy and moldy yellow.

As the distant church bells rang midnight, I dragged the military cot from the bedroom to the middle of the living room. Lying down, I observed the low buildings of Lavapiés, their roofs covered with TV antennas and laundry cords full of clothes waving like flags. I thought of Chus, still inhabiting the same apartment I grew up in, a fixture in a city that no longer existed. Everything else around him had changed. Our friends and neighbors had fled to deep pockets of Queens, pushed out by hipsters and rich kids whose rent was paid by trust funds, most small businesses replaced by bars where they could drink away their sweat-free money. I wondered whether Lavapiés would gentrify too, and if so, how long it would take before I was forced out.

After dragging the military cot from the bedroom to the

middle of the living room, I lay down and observed the low buildings of Lavapiés, their roofs covered with TV antennas and laundry cords full of clothes waving like flags. Waiting for sleep to come, the beach towel spread out over my legs, I thought about what I wanted to get accomplished the next day. I had been so looking forward to getting my own place that I expected a rush of happiness, or, at least, to feel something other than disappointment. It was almost completely dark, and all I could see was the blinking clock on the oven, flashing zeros in an endless loop. My inability to track the passing of time only heightened the sense of loss that kept me up, until the morning light brought in sounds of the garbage truck and dumpsters being dragged.

WALKING AROUND MY new neighborhood in the early morning, I went to the bank and a supermarket where the fresh produce was stored in wooden boxes piled on the floor. At a cell phone store, I was expecting to see different models, more European looking, but they were mostly the same. I grabbed a black Motorola Razr, flipped it open a couple of times, and put it in my pocket to feel how sleek it was. I wished I had accepted the money Jacobo had offered me, because until I received the bank transfer, I couldn't justify buying anything other than the standard Nokia that only teenagers and old people used in the States.

Macondo was an Internet café where one could make international phone calls and surf the web on computers older than those in my high school. The partitions of the booths were so thin you could hear not only the conversations people were having with families back home, but also the noise they made as they typed. I emailed Chef the number of my bank account but didn't have the energy to go through my inbox, taken over by spam. I only responded to an email from Richard, giving him an update and sending him my new cell phone number. Then I typed "Chef Matías" in the search bar and clicked on a link that showed a picture of him standing in front of El Lucernario the day after it was awarded two Michelin stars. I copied and pasted the address of the restaurant and Jacobo's house. They weren't far from each other. Then I switched to Street View and played with the arrow going up and down the street. The images had been taken on a cloudy winter day, and the lush trees in front of the house looked like telephone poles. In one of them the black Jaguar was waiting at the front of the building with its brake lights turned on.

I opened a currency converter and entered $6,000, the amount Chef was supposed to send me. It was 4,797.22 euros. On another site, the difference was three hundred euros. I hoped that Chef would find the best exchange rate possible. After some calculations, I realized that in either case, I would have enough to survive for three or four months. And, in the unlikely case that it took more time to find a job, both Chus and Richard had offered to lend me money.

Closing the windows on my screen, I wondered if the kid who ran the cybercafé, with whom I had locked eyes several times, was monitoring my searches. And if the traces I left on the Internet were being watched by the USCIS to ensure I wasn't planning my return to America. Before leaving, even though it was six in the morning in New York, I entered one of the rickety booths and called Richard.

"Hello?"

"Hey. It's me. Sorry it's so early."

"What's up, bud? No worries. I was getting ready for bed. How are you?"

"I'm good. Just responded to your email."

"You don't sound good. What's wrong?"

"I'm having a complicated time."

"Looking for work?"

"No. I met this guy I really like and have been hanging out with, and I just got into a fight with him."

"Oh, that's okay, buddy. It happens."

"I mean we got into a fistfight."

"Wait. What?"

"Yeah, you heard right."

"Get out! You got into a *fistfight*? Are you a teenager now?"

"I don't know, man. It's hard to explain. We kind of really like each other but—"

"So you beat the shit out of each other?"

"Come on, don't be an ass. We were kind of wasted and got into an argument. Next thing I know, my face was bleeding."

"Oh, man, that sounds super intense. I'm sorry, buddy."

"I don't know, it's very confusing. He's also über-rich. I've been staying at his crib. They have a driver, a cook, the whole nine yards. That might be part of the problem."

"Well, that shouldn't be a problem."

"I don't know, I feel kind of inferior or something."

"You? Inferior?"

"Not sure how to better describe it. He's also a party animal."

"I mean, you're no Mother Teresa either."

"No, I know. But he might have an addiction problem. It's hard to know. Anyway, enough of the guy. I got a cute apartment. You should come visit."

"Would love that. Listen, I'm going to hit the sack. I'm dead. But let's talk again soon."

"Sounds good. Love you."

"Love you too, bud."

TRUDGING AROUND my neighborhood for a while, eerily quiet as most people were probably at work or enjoying a siesta, I wandered into Bar Jamón. I ordered a caña that the bartender poured in short intervals, hitting the bottom of the glass against the counter several times and with such force that I worried it would break. The bubbles rushing to the top created a thick layer of compact foam that crowned the glass. Taking my time to decide, I stared at the tapas sitting behind a glass until the bartender lost his patience and proceeded to name and describe each one of them with the speed and annoyance of someone who is tired of doing the same thing over and over. I ordered the patatas bravas and the boquerones en vinagre with my index finger. The aioli was made with expertly emul-sified olive oil and just the right amount of garlic, the crispy potatoes a beautiful golden color. As I savored the flavors, I marveled at how the taste of tapas constantly changed depend-ing on the order in which you ate them, something I had been fascinated with since my time working as a busboy at Rio Mar. Then I ordered another caña and paid the bill. It was so cheap I had to look at it twice.

EL LUCERNARIO SAT at the end of a pedestrian cul-de-sac behind the Prado Museum. The main dining room, a repurposed greenhouse with lush plants and square tables, had about one hundred seats and a gigantic fireplace filled with moss. In the back, a thick, bright pink bougainvillea climbed to the ceiling, opening up like a gigantic umbrella. In contrast with the rustic setting, the tables were readied for a formal five-course meal with gleaming wine glasses and European water goblets, and old sterling silver flatware. Waiting by the entrance while the hostess went to look for Chef Matías, I followed the waiter with my eyes. Leaning forward with his head down, he was serving vichyssoise with a bronze ladle. He poured the soup with rehearsed care, as if it were the most deliberate and important act of his day. Something about him reminded me of Gabriela and the waiter at the churrería. There was a strange quality about them, a radiating peace that seemed a mix of both pride and respect for their work.

Chef Matías looked like a young version of Chef, only taller and in better shape. He also wore a dark suit, but even dressed so formally, he seemed younger than forty-five. I noticed him crossing the dining room with agile, decisive steps, observing the servers on the floor as if making mental notes. Given his uncanny resemblance to Chef, by the time we shook hands I had the strange sense I knew him.

"Demetrio!" His tone was friendly.

Happy he knew who I was, I relaxed. "Hello, Chef. It's great to meet you."

"We already met. At Le Bourrelet! Arnaud introduced us."

"That's right. I remember now!" His face was not familiar.

He spoke briefly about Chef and expressed his admiration for what he was doing at the restaurant. While we walked to the back, he remarked he had been expecting me for a week.

His comment could have sounded like a reproach but didn't. Suddenly becoming aware of my tan, I acted as if I had not heard it.

"What happened to your face?"

"What do you mean?" I said, knowing exactly what he meant. "Oh, the scratches. Believe it or not, it was my friend's cat. I call her La Pantera now."

Chef appeared content with my answer. He offered a short laugh, and my guess was he didn't find my joke funny but was trying to be polite. I followed him to the service area thinking about the image of Jacobo's swollen eye. It occurred to me then that his family would also have asked him what happened to his face and I hoped he had not told them the truth.

The kitchen had the same layout as traditional New York restaurants, an enormous Bonnet Maestro stove at the center. The cooks were diligently running their stations in starched white uniforms, their skin tightened by flames. No one acknowledged my presence, but they sharpened their movements as Chef made his way through the prep area. One of the sous-chefs, plating a red sea bream on the spotless stainless-steel table, became visibly nervous. I could sense the tension that Chef generated, and it became clear he ran a tight kitchen. The lunch shift was almost over, and even though the cooks had probably prepared more than a hundred and fifty meals, the counters and the doors of the lowboy refrigerators, the telescoping heat lamps, and all the gaskets and handles were immaculately clean.

Matías introduced me to the sous-chefs, who stopped briefly to greet me in English. One of them looked hungover. His face was fluorescent white. His yellow, uneven teeth reminded me of Dominic, a cook at Le Bourrelet, who used our ten-minute breaks to chain-smoke on the loading dock no matter how cold the weather was. They both shared the same caffeinated, worried look. I suddenly felt the anxiety that came with those days when we arrived with barely enough time to prep, Chef breathing down our necks and following us attentively, waiting to call out the tiniest mistake.

After touring the kitchen, we went to the bar and drank a homemade liqueur made from blackthorn berries.

"It's called pacharán. We make it ourselves."

"It's so good," I said, nodding effusively and worried I looked drunk.

A young woman walked toward us, stumbling on her stilettos.

"Pardon me for a second," Matías said.

Gesticulating wildly, she whispered sentences into his ear that seemed to have no end. At one point, as it was clearly a conversation to have not in the dining room but behind closed doors, Chef stepped back and spoke to her in a tone that was louder than needed, his words aiming at the clients eavesdropping.

"Okay. That's wonderful. I'll be right there," he said diminishingly.

The woman turned around on the verge of tears.

"By the way, Úrsula," Chef said, grabbing her elbow, "I want you to meet Demetrio. He's from New York."

His need to legitimize me by saying where I came from was odd.

"Encantada," she mumbled, then left hurriedly.

"Excuse me." Chef took a sip from his drink. "Give me five minutes." He walked to the back of the restaurant and stopped briefly at some tables with a forced smile.

Left alone, I tried to understand why I was feeling estranged from a world that had brought me so much comfort for almost a decade. I had become an adult in a twenty-six-by-fourteen-foot kitchen among aggressive, type A chefs and cooks who yelled the first chance they got. While my friends spent their teenage years skating on the streets of the Lower East Side, I learned to surf the heat waves radiating from convection ovens. Growing up among boiling pots and scalding pans, by the time I was eighteen, my arms were scarred from four-hundred-degree trays. More often than not, a workday would turn into an eighteen-hour shift, my only reward knowing that I was contributing to making Le Bourrelet a world destination. I was proud of my meteoric rise to pastry chef after two years as an apprentice, a fact that Chef used to measure the talent of other employees. Pastries had been my companions, my saviors. While kids from my neighborhood inked their arms and necks with symbols of the gangs they belonged to, I had $C_{12}H_{22}O_{11}$, the molecular formula for sucrose, tattooed on my upper back. But now, after being in a kitchen for less than ten minutes, the idea of returning to a windowless life, even if it would mean I was the luckiest person on earth for having landed a job so easily, weighed heavily on me.

The bartender poured me another pacharán and served himself a shot. We clinked our glasses with the camaraderie of those who work in the industry. While he kneeled down to gulp his so the customers wouldn't see him, I swiveled on the stool. The dining room was at full capacity. As opposed to the stiff clientele of Le Bourrelet, who seemed more interested in being seen at a luxury restaurant than eating the extraordinary culinary creations of Chef, the atmosphere here was relaxed and had a festive spirit, even though men wore suits and ties, and most women were buried in gold.

I was trying to find words that would buy me some time with Chef when Patricia entered the restaurant. She was wearing a light floral dress and big tortoiseshell sunglasses that covered most of her face. A young guy, tall and fit, and so muscular he made his suit look like armor, walked behind her. He was a little older than me. They went to the back of the dining room, away from the windows. As soon as they sat down, the maître d' came to greet them and grabbed a *Reserved* sign from the table. The proper, distant, and rehearsed way in which they behaved suggested they could be lovers.

"So, what do you think?" Matías said, gently tapping my shoulder. "Good, huh?"

"Oh, yeah. Awesome stuff." I took another sip and gave him a thumbs-up.

"Listen, can we talk some other time? I'm having a bit of a crisis with a food critic who showed up unannounced."

"Of course," I said too quickly. "Thanks for the tour and the pacharán."

I suddenly felt I hadn't been eager enough, hadn't shown enough interest. I didn't know what I had been thinking but one thing was clear: I needed a job. And I needed it soon. Following Chef as he walked to the entrance, I turned my head slightly to steal one more look at Patricia.

"I love the restaurant, Chef. It's a very special place," I said, noticing the few steps left to the door. "And it seems that business is going well. How many shifts do you do per lunch?"

"No more than two. We hate rushing people out. It's a very different culture."

"Yeah, no, I get it. It's the way it's supposed to be, an experience, not a transaction."

"That's exactly right."

I was aware my face revealed a glimmer of anticipation for having redirected the conversation.

"Here, take one." Chef opened a leather folder and pulled out a menu. "I'd like to hear your thoughts. Can you come back on Tuesday?"

"Tuesday's great," I said, holding the paper as if it were made of fine glass.

He patted my shoulder once again. I thanked him for his time and walked out of the restaurant. Stumbling lightly through the alley, not quite sure whether my instability was caused by the two glasses of pacharán or the unevenness of the cobblestones, I felt optimistic.

FOR THE NEXT couple of days, I roamed the streets without a destination. Every morning I stepped out of the building and walked in a different direction. Following the sun or a random passerby, I encountered palaces, monuments, and parks that evoked the Madrid of a different era. Among my favorite unexpected discoveries were two royal gates: the Puerta de Toledo and the Puerta de Alcalá, a breathtaking granite gate built in the eighteenth century that once marked the boundary of the city. The Templo de Debod, a second-century BC Egyptian temple rebuilt near the Parque del Oeste, looked like it had come out of a fairy tale. Strolling through its gardens at sunset, when the reflecting pool surrounding the temple clung to the fiery light of long summer days, filled me with joy. I was so enthralled walking without a map that after hours of drifting in the radiant July sunlight I had no other way to return home but by metro, which was clean and quiet by New York standards. And without rats. I descended into the underworld and traversed the city in efficient air-conditioned lines. Sometimes, exhausted from walking for most of the day, I fell asleep and missed the Lavapiés stop, finding myself in a working-class neighborhood on the other side of the Río Manzanares that I knew about because it was home to the biggest prison in Spain.

One day, I took the subway and headed to Carabanchel, which had been built by political prisoners after the Spanish Civil War, and shut for almost a decade. Those who were considered a threat to the Franco regime, among them communists, union leaders, intellectuals, and left-wing sympathizers, were kept in the sixth gallery and tortured on a regular basis. The ones with questionable sexual orientations were confined in El Palomar, where rapes under the surveillance of prison guards were common practice. In the 1980s, that section of the prison became an AIDS swamp. Having to serve time there was an unspoken death sentence. I knew the history well because Chus spent two months behind bars, accused of being a student activist, and it was right after getting out that he fled the country forever. He still had nightmares about his time in the prison, but he refused to talk about it with anyone. Not even with Ben.

I had seen pictures of its walls covered in graffiti on the blog of a young colleague of Chus's who used photography to document patterns of human movement and socioeconomic processes. Though I had an idea of its scale and monstrosity, nothing compared to the eeriness of the space, the concrete walls soaked in decades of tears and pain.

Through an opening in the wire netting, I entered the premises, which contained thousands of cells and long, interminable corridors. The walls were in a severe state of disrepair and parts of the ceiling had collapsed on the floor. Wandering through the inmate patio, under basketball hoops with rusted rings, I couldn't imagine Chus living behind the massive brick walls crowned with barbed wire.

I avoided eye contact with the squatters and the heroin dealers selling their merchandise in the open, and, walking into the main building, I climbed up the stairs to the watchtower. Late afternoon sunlight filtered through the broken mesh glass windows, tinting the graffiti with a gilded patina. The walls of the corridors had been turned into colorful murals. Some of the art reminded me of Mark, a high school friend and talented graffiti artist who turned to crack at the end of the nineties, but whose work still survived in the tunnels of the abandoned Eighteenth Street subway station.

I snapped some pictures for Chus that didn't do justice to the abandonment and decay, an irrefutable testament that those days were long gone, hoping they might provide him with a sense of closure. After walking around and getting lost in the interminable corridors looking for El Palomar, I noticed two men following me. I became nervous struggling to find my way back through the concrete labyrinth. By the time I got out through the hole in the wire netting, the summer daylight was turning to dusk.

TUESDAY WAS STILL days away. The hours went by slowly, and though I gradually began to enjoy my solitude and the streets were becoming more familiar, I still did not feel at home. Near the Lavapiés subway station, a couple of blocks

south of my apartment, stood a ramshackle hotel with a grand
and lavish-sounding name: El Real. The antithesis of royal, the
old four-story tenement building had a façade encrusted with
grime and layers of posters in various states of decay. Every
time I passed by, I peered through the window into the rickety
carpeted lobby full of suitcases and people in transit.

One early morning, unable to decide which route to take
for my daily stroll, I went into the hotel and sat confidently on
a sofa at the entrance, pretending to be a guest. I observed a
group of tourists readying for their excursions, looking at maps
and flipping through guides while I listened to their conversations. Then a young couple got out of the elevator. Not quite
sure why I was drawn to them in particular, I stood up and
rushed behind them as they exited the lobby. I followed them
down Zurita and soon found myself becoming their shadow as
they made a right on Santa Isabel toward Atocha.

I couldn't make out their distant voices, but because I had
first seen them at a hotel, I presumed they weren't Spanish or,
at least, not from Madrid. They walked with the determination
of people sure of a destination and only hesitated at a confusing
intersection, where they momentarily looked bewildered. The
woman seemed to be in charge and quickly pulled out a small
guide that she studied attentively. It was apparent they had an
address, a promise of a place. As I walked behind them at a
safe distance, I remembered the screen on the plane that laid
out my journey, the blinking light that I stared at in anxious
anticipation, not quite knowing what the endpoint would actually look like.

The couple took the Paseo del Prado so I assumed they were
going to the museum, but they passed the entrance and kept
walking to the Plaza de la Lealtad, leaving the long line of

visitors behind. A huge, waving banner showed a man kneeling down, his face taken over by terror, a firing squad pointing rifles at him. It was a Goya exhibition. At another time I would have gone in, but after so many days adrift, I enjoyed having a destination.

Shortly after leaving the Prado behind, the couple veered to the right, toward the Parque del Retiro, and entered the roundabout of the Ritz hotel. A wide array of luxury cars, most of them German, all of them black, were parked at the front, the chauffeurs leaning on their doors. The couple walked up to the main entrance and was greeted by a smiling doorman who pushed the revolving door for them.

The lobby had highly polished pink marble floors and columns, and was crowned by a massive chandelier hanging over a round table with an opulent arrangement of fresh flowers. The couple sat down on a matching pair of beige antique chairs, acting as if they were guests. I wondered if I had been discovered, if their actions were a way of telling me, *We know you're following us.* I walked around the lobby and almost tripped over the corner of an Oriental rug. Instantly feeling the menacing stare of two security guards, black wires like spiders coming out of their ears, I rushed out the door and disappeared into the morning.

14

Slowly, almost without my noticing it, people in my neighborhood began to acknowledge my presence, even those whom I never exchanged words with. The first person was the woman at the flower stand one scorching afternoon. On the deserted square, all you could hear was the cooing of pigeons and Arabic rock music coming from a double-parked car in front of Bar Jamón. I was crossing the street carrying groceries when she stepped out of the stand to pour a bucket of water onto the sidewalk. She gave me a toothy smile, and realizing that I was unsure if it was directed at me, she waved her hand. I looked behind me, and seeing the empty street, I raised my hand, pulling up the bags as if lifting a dumbbell. Then it was the man at the newspaper kiosk where I bought *El País* in the mornings to improve my Spanish, the lady in the black uniform compulsively sweeping the entrance of my building, and an old fragile-looking couple who every evening, when the sun was setting, pulled out folding beach chairs to sit on the sidewalk. The woman was always knitting, while her husband held a portable radio next to his ear, looking up at the sky as though in communication with the hereafter.

The menu from El Lucernario went from the kitchen counter to the night table to the bathroom floor, where it lay under
a pile of dirty clothes. On Sunday night, I studied the dishes.
The menu was heavy on meat, with lots of charcuterie, two different types of steak, and a suckling pig served with potatoes-
three-ways in a Jerez wine reduction. There were only two fish
dishes: dorada grilled with preserved lemon and Manzanilla
olives, and a salt-crusted whole róbalo served with a sweet fig
and rosemary vinaigrette. Fish was the most delicate and difficult food to prepare and what most critics based their reviews
on, so I found it strange that there were only two options on
the menu. Using a Spanish-English dictionary I had bought
ten years ago at a flea market, I deconstructed the dishes. All
the flavors were on the rich side. The desserts, unless Matías
wanted a defibrillator under each table, had to be on the light
side: fruit, foams, granitas, or sorbets.

I decided to make a marigold ice cream, inspired by Patricia's flowers, with paper-thin slices of candied yuzu to break
through the sharp taste of the petals. I wondered if I would be
able to find yuzu in Madrid. Having developed an appreciation
for less complex flavors like Gabriela's donuts and the churros
from the Chocolatería de San Ginés, I began creating simpler
desserts, a significant departure from what I had done at Le
Bourrelet. As I considered different options I felt as if Chef
were in the room, challenging me on each one of them. Since
I had learned how to bake, every dessert I had made was with
him in mind, and turning off his voice, attempting to exercise my new freedom, proved to be more difficult than I had
predicted.

I spent most of the afternoon and part of the evening thinking about the menu, writing down rough ideas, quantities and

temperatures that were approximations I would eventually need to test. Even though Matías had only asked for thoughts, I assumed he was expecting to see potential desserts. By the end of the day, I had five more I was excited about. Three of them were fruit based: lychee jelly parfait with chia seeds, raw cream, and tapioca pearls; a roasted red plum with a mascarpone purée of endrinas; and a churro apple tart served with apple butter and a cup of hot spiced apple cider. The other two were slight variations of desserts that I had created at Le Bourrelet, a bittersweet chocolate biscuit with hazelnut cream, apricot sorbet, and crushed praline, and a butterscotch coulant with chocolate soup, fleur de sel, and milk granita.

After working for so many hours without pause, I could no longer think straight and put down the notebook. Had I been in New York, I would have gone for a long bike ride along the Hudson to the George Washington Bridge, then crossed to New Jersey, all the way to Nyack. In the summer, I liked taking the Manhattan Bridge to Brooklyn and biking along the water to the Rockaways. During biting-cold New York winters, when the streets were icy and unwelcoming, I walked to the Barnes & Noble in Astor Place, where I would order hot chocolate and sit on the floor flipping through art and fashion magazines, the glossy images slowly freeing me from my momentary paralysis.

I paced the apartment and walked up to the window. The schoolyard was empty. Looking at the basketball hoops with their bright white nets swaying in the air, I wondered what Jacobo was doing at the moment. Even though I had promised myself I wouldn't initiate contact, I almost sent him a text message. His accurate description of what had been on my mind had made me angry. But I was also grateful because I would have never had the courage to share how I really felt. Not having refuted any of it had made it all true.

Spending the day working on recipes and reliving my days in New York made me feel blando. I kept thinking about the conversation with Patricia and caught myself obsessively repeating her words, *I admire your courage.* I wasn't sure that the young man I had seen her with at the restaurant was her lover. But as I readied for bed, thinking about the floral dress that accentuated her cleavage, I concluded she had dressed for him.

I had fallen asleep to NPR for years. Now, lying on the mattress in the pitch dark, at midnight, listening on my laptop to *All Things Considered,* a show I had on the radio at Le Bourrelet, was another reminder of being so far away from home that even time ran on a different clock. Convinced that the sound of the buzzer came from the motorbike I was riding in my dream, I finally woke to the voice of Melissa Block still streaming into the living room. I couldn't have been sleeping for more than an hour. Wide-awake, I realized that the low-pitched noise was nothing like an engine. I remained still, waiting for the person ringing the bell in the middle of the night to go away. After four long and electrifying rings, it finally stopped. I walked quietly to the bathroom, and as I was flushing the toilet, someone knocked on the door.

I stood still for a while on the old wood floor. The image of Philippe Petit, the French high-wire artist, suspended on a tightrope between the Twin Towers, entered my mind. My leg was slowly falling asleep. I imagined the intruder standing outside, hiding in the silence, attentively listening for signs that would alert him to my presence. Someone turned on a faucet in the apartment above. Pipes rattled. I could hear the hazy, muffled sound of water traveling through the walls. Then silence again. When I was beginning to question whether the intruder had been a figment of my imagination, the bell rang again. I pictured Jacobo's face full of cuts and bruises and considered opening the door. An envelope was pushed underneath. The messenger trampled down the stairs. Only when the front door of the building shut in the distance did I walk to the entrance to grab the package.

There was no addressee. The flap was tightly glued. I placed the envelope on the kitchen counter, and after convincing myself not to open it until the morning, I searched for a knife. I pulled out a stack of black-and-white photographs. The first image had been taken the morning we left for Cabo de Gata. The Mercedes was coming out of the garage, and though it was still pretty dark, our faces behind the windshield were clear. The photographer, standing across the street, also captured the bench in front of the building but not the homeless man who had been lying on it. In another photo, the car slipped through the arid, flat landscape of La Mancha. I remembered seeing a tractor work the fields but not the high-speed train that the shutter caught. The next photo was of my right hand massaging the wind, a road sign above us indicating 327 kilometers to Almería.

There were many moments immortalized, moments that included buying supplies, rolling joints, hiking over the cove, and sleeping next to a dying fire with our bodies tightly intertwined. Most of the photos, taken in daylight, were of Jacobo and me together; some were only of him on his excursion to the spring. The long lens used by the photographer exposed fleeting, intimate behaviors that were never supposed to be made permanent. In one of them, Jacobo was crying helplessly in the camp the morning after the fight, his swollen face covered with blood. The pain drawn on his face, honest and raw, made my legs tremble. I looked inside the envelope and found a written report that detailed our journey, from the moment we left the house until he returned the car to the garage.

REPORT

Day 1. Tuesday, July 17, 2007

5:47 subjects leave 92 Lagasta in a Mercedes 450 SEL. Plates M-2081-AF.

6:25 subjects take the E-5 toward Jaén.

9:57 subjects stop at a Repsol gas station (Km 235).

9:59 subject A goes into the mini market.

10:02 subject B walks toward the highway.

10:05 subject B has a short conversation with the attendant and enters the vehicle.

10:07 subject B walks away from the car toward the bathroom, carrying a pair of shorts.

10:09 subject A walks back to the car carrying a plastic bag. He pays the gas station attendant.

10:12 subject A and subject B enter the car and drive to the restaurant.

10:31 both subjects get in the car and head to Almería.

13:43 subject A makes a phone call.

16:42 subject A stops the car on the side of the road and goes for a walk.

16:45 subject B joins subject A. They smoke what appears to be hashish.

18:02 subjects enter the car.

19:03 subjects arrive in the town of Las Negras.

19:09 subjects stop in front of the Hotel La Torrecilla.

19:13 subjects leave the Hotel La Torrecilla.

19:21 subjects stop in front of the Hotel Buendía.

19:34 subjects leave the Hotel Buendía.

19:45 subjects check into the Hotel Miramar.

I walked to the window and, for the first time, pulled down the white blinds, their plastic yellowed by sunlight. Sitting on the floor with my back against the stove, I read every line in the report and searched for the corresponding images in the stack of photographs. I looked at the visual slices of time, now covering the kitchen tiles, and couldn't identify with them. The words were an acute, objective rendering of our journey, but the photos created a somewhat deceptive way of telling a story. Capturing certain moments and choosing to ignore others proved that the person behind the camera had a preconceived idea of what that story should be. This visual narrative on the floor informed my experience of the trip in a simplistic way. The images, far from capturing the closeness we felt for one another, seemed to establish an insurmountable distance between us and didn't resemble any of my memories. I questioned whether the effects of the fight and how it had strangely brought us closer were just all in my head.

I was anxious to know the identity of both the photographer and the messenger, and whether they were the same person. By the time I was able to calm down and fall asleep, the night had slipped away, and the edges of the blinds were illuminated by bright morning light.

. . .

IT ONLY TOOK two text messages for Jacobo to acknowledge that he had been the midnight messenger. His delay in
responding and his language indicated that he was either not
paying attention or trying to act distant. After texting back and
forth several times, we agreed to meet at the Café de Oriente, a
coffee shop where I had spent long afternoons after my expedi-
tions through the Parque del Oeste.

I left the house with ample time. Knowing that we had been
followed for days, I now couldn't shake the fear. I stopped several times at street corners, behind columns and dumpsters,
hoping to catch the person who had been spying on us. The
familiar, lurking anxiety that I had experienced growing up
when New York undercover police flashed their badges was
triggered as I crossed the city, the images on the kitchen floor
coming in and out of my mind.

WHEN I ENTERED the Plaza de Oriente, I spotted Jacobo sitting on the terrace of the café under the scorching sun wearing
jeans, a faded Strand T-shirt with cut-off sleeves, and green
aviators. I made my way through pigeons who were determined
to continue picking at debris caught in between the cobblestones. Halfway through the square, a couple asked me to take
their picture. I focused the lens on Jacobo and zoomed in as
the waiter poured some Beefeater into a glass. I shifted focus
back to the couple, who had been posing for a while, no longer
smiling, and pressed the shutter button.

I walked to the café and remembered its modest décor had a
sense of dignity, of wanting to preserve its traditional origins,
refusing fleeting trends. The wood of the doors had cracked

and was filled with multiple coats of varnish; the mirrored walls, with their glass darkened by time, turned the sunlight into smoky, muted light. The grout between the tiles, once white, was now black and eroded from having been swept countless times.

As I neared the table, Jacobo stood up. He shook my hand like he would a stranger's.

"I was about to call you," he said.

"Sorry I'm late. How is it going?" I tried to sound calm.

Jacobo motioned to the waiter.

Even though I had only had an espresso for breakfast, I ordered a gin and tonic.

He looked distracted. "I'm good," he said, clenching his jaw.

The waiter came over and poured a generous drink, leaving a small stainless-steel ice bucket that instantly began to sweat. I grabbed the tongs and put two more cubes into my glass.

"Sorry I dragged you into this," he said, taking a long gulp from his drink.

I noticed that some of the scratches on his face had disappeared and others had turned light pink.

"My dad hired a private detective to follow me. It's not the first time. He prefers to ask others what he doesn't want to hear from me."

He took another sip that made the ice cubes splash on his nose, then dried his cheek with the back of his hand.

"I'm sorry, Jake," I said. "I can't even imagine how you feel."

"I'm okay. You know he's a public figure." His tone was icy and dry. "I guess he wants to know what I'm up to before others find out. My mom knows about the detective. She's furious." Jacobo lit a cigarette, and the remaining words took the shape of white smoke that hung above us for a while, then vanished into the thick heat. I wondered if his mother was also being followed.

"If he's so controlling, how does he allow you to be in New York? Does he also have people spying on you there?"

Jacobo took a long time to respond. "He might. I don't know. He probably doesn't care because I'm thousands of miles away. It was his idea that I study abroad." His phone beeped. "Anyway, how're you liking Madrid? How's the job hunt? What else is going on? Wait. Let me run to the bathroom. I'll be right back."

"Should we move inside?" My armpits were dampening.

He left without answering. I looked at the digital clock on the square and took a sip of my drink. The heat was rising. As August approached, the city was slowly emptying, and most of the people left were fearless tourists defying the asphyxiating, dry air. On the midday news I usually watched at Bar Jamón, the white sandy beaches were slowly disappearing under colorful towels and bare flesh. Their capacity appeared to be of national interest, and given that the country was now on the cusp of an economic crisis, tourism seemed an industry carefully monitored by the media.

"Ninety-three Fahrenheit," Jacobo said, sitting down.

I turned around and saw a thermometer on top of a billboard across the street marking thirty-four degrees Celsius.

He gestured to the waiter for another round.

"I'm okay, Jake," I said, feeling light-headed after just two sips.

He pulled his hair back and put on a faded Yankees hat, his shiny forehead slowly breaking into a sweat. I noticed his jaw clenching intensely.

"You're doing blow." I looked at my watch even though I knew the time. "You're doing blow at twelve-thirty in the afternoon and in this heat. Are you insane?"

He pinched his nose and stayed silent.

"I went out last night. Just got out of the Space."

He lit another cigarette. His hands were shaking. I assumed the Space was an after-hours. The waiter poured him a fresh drink. He left a new ice bucket and dumped the melted ice on a nearby tree.

"I'm done with the bag, but I can get more."

"Fuck, Jake," I said. "Partying is not going to fix anything. So you find out your dad is spying on you and decide to get fucked up?"

"Well, next time I come to your apartment, open the fucking door!"

He scratched a mosquito bite on his right elbow until it began to bleed. I handed him a paper napkin. As he pressed it against his skin, his fatigue became more visible. He said something through big yawns, the unintelligible sounds like lyrics on a record playing backward.

WE DIDN'T DISCUSS him coming over to my place. I paid the bill, slipped my arm over his neck when we stood up, and helped him cross the square, taking tiny steps. He was so exhausted he almost fell asleep getting into a taxi. The moment I shut the door, he rested his chest on my legs, instantly passing out. I ran my fingers through his hair and caressed the marblelike pink marks on his face as if it were a sculpture. I was beginning to accept that being next to him, even when he was deep asleep, made me more complete. I looked out the window and smiled at the thought that a little over a month ago, I had been the one passed out in the back of a car. I couldn't help but wonder if he had done the same. If he had also taken advantage of that moment to act on how he truly felt. If he had caressed my head all the way home.

Having the shutters closed kept the apartment cool; a faint luminescence underlined the edges of the windows. As soon as Jacobo entered the living room and saw the pictures laid out on the kitchen floor, he became teary-eyed and began to undress carefully, absentmindedly, laying the clothes down as if they were origami. The coins in his pocket spilled out, rolling away to the lonely bedroom, where my open suitcase lay empty in the middle of the floor. He walked to the bathroom in his underwear. His lower back was covered with mosquito bites that seemed to continue under his briefs. It took him a long time to pee. I heard his jet going intermittently, as if he couldn't focus. Coming into the living room, he moved to the cot, sat briefly, and lay down.

The notebook sitting on the kitchen counter now seemed unimportant, expendable. I stood still in the middle of the room, waiting for his breathing to deepen. Shortly after curling into a ball, he began snoring, a soft, high-pitched whistle, his legs twitching as if he were dreaming of playing soccer. He was mumbling words impossible to understand, the pillowcase quickly dampening around his mouth. Having Jacobo sleeping on my cot the day before the interview was unsettling. Even though it had felt right at the time, bringing him home made me lose the little focus I had managed to gather. I was nervous about presenting my ideas to Matías without having rehearsed the desserts and was now even more doubtful about some of the flavor combinations.

I grabbed the notebook quietly, went into the bedroom, and shut the door. I had planned on spending the evening working on the names and practicing their pronunciation. Now, lying on the floor of an empty room knowing that he was sleeping in his underwear behind a wall I wished were made of glass, I couldn't stop wondering what would have become of us had we met in other circumstances—on a dance floor, at the gym, or at MoMA, following each other through different rooms until finally one of us made a move. The fact that he had literally picked me up after I passed out on a sidewalk and brought me back to life seemed to have steered our relationship in one very specific direction. Caring for him now felt like a way to balance things out.

THE NEXT DAY, I woke up in a haze of anxiety, my neck stiff from sleeping on the floor, a folded towel for a pillow. Despite the heat permeating the walls and closed windows, Jacobo slept soundly. I took a cold shower, dressed quietly, wrote him a note, and left the apartment with the notebook tucked under my arm. I walked through the neighborhood, dormant even at noon, the sleepy buildings with their wooden shutters pulled down like eyelids. Hanging on the door of Bar Jamón, by then my usual breakfast spot, a sign indicated it would be closed for the month. After drifting for several blocks, I found an open cafeteria, where I drank my first mediocre coffee since arriving in Spain. As I leafed through a scrawny *El País* someone had left behind, it was clear that August, with the Senate and Congress adjourned for the summer, was a month of little news. The most prominent article on the front cover was about the royal family, who had arrived at the Palacio de Marivent in

Palma de Mallorca, where they would reside until the end of August.

I decided to splurge on a cab because I was already tired and did not want to show up at El Lucernario drenched in sweat. When I arrived the main door was closed. Peering through the windows, I saw the dining room, neatly tucked in, with clean tables and overturned chairs. I walked to the end of the alley, where a man dressed in blue overalls was hosing down the cobblestones and a delivery truck was pulling into the loading dock. One of the sous-chefs was sitting on a milk crate smoking a cigarette.

"Hey, man." He shook my hand as if we had known each other for a long time.

"What's up?" I said, shocked to hear myself acting American again. "Is Chef around?"

"Yeah, he's in the office." He pointed at a window below. "Down the stairs, first door to the left."

The floors were spotless. The morning light poured through the back door, bouncing off the stainless-steel counters, the perfectly polished intake hoods, and the slightly scratched mixing bowls. It was quiet. I could only hear the low murmur of the walk-in freezers and, farther in the distance, the faint, rhythmic sound of carrots being peeled. As I walked through the kitchen, I discovered the morning prep cook silently labeling and storing the produce that had just arrived, crossing items off a list. He seemed annoyed at a foreign presence disrupting his morning routine.

Before heading downstairs, I kneeled by a wood crate full of tomatoes covered with a thin layer of soil. I inhaled their smell, then rubbed my fingers with dirt. The other sous-chef, whose name I couldn't remember, stepped out from a walk-in freezer and greeted me amicably. Even though I barely knew Matías and had spent little time in this kitchen, I sensed that El Lucernario was the kind of restaurant where familial bonds were easily forged.

Matías was writing an email in his office, his back to the door. The ceiling was low, its damp patches looked like storm clouds. A portable plastic fan droned, the deafening sound mismatched with the puny breeze coming from it. On a metal desk, covered with invoices, there was a photograph of Matías with the king of Spain. It was almost identical to one I had seen at the entrance of Jacobo's apartment where his father, also with his head slightly bent, was shaking hands with Juan Carlos I. The composition, even the outfits, looked exactly the same.

I knocked on the open door.

"Come in," Matías said without turning around, continuing to type furiously with his index fingers.

I stood by a tall corkboard papered with dozens of reviews and magazine cutouts. Most of the articles were in Spanish but some were in English and French. There was an op-ed by Frank Bruni, the chief restaurant critic of the *New York Times*, which I did not expect to see there. His photograph, along with those of other food critics, was taped on the kitchen wall at Le Bourrelet to keep their faces fresh in the minds of the less experienced servers. Standing in silence, waiting for Matías to stop banging the keyboard, I wondered if the food reviewers from *El País* held as much power as the ones from the *New York Times*.

"How are you?"

"I'm good, Chef. Thanks for taking the time."

The sound of an incoming email made him turn his head

back to the screen. I used the opportunity to open the note-book and glance at the name of the first dessert.

"Sorry. It's been an insane summer." He shut down the computer. "We're fully booked through October. It's crazy."

"Wow." Despite not feeling intimidated by him, I was at a loss for words. I followed him up the stairs, telling myself to be friendlier. As we crossed the kitchen, quickly entering prep mode, Matías said good morning to everyone, addressing them by their first name. I simply smiled. Like Chef, he was personal, had a strong presence and self-confidence.

Once we sat in the empty dining room, I took Matías through the desserts while he sipped a double espresso. He seemed distant and unmoved.

"They're good," he finally said. "The ones that I'm not convinced about are the churros and the marigold ice cream. Too easy."

"Okay." I tried to disguise my defeat and hoped he meant they were too simple, not too easy. I wondered what he thought of the molten chocolate cake variations that were on most New York City menus and had proven to be the most successful dessert over the years.

"Do you want to come up with a couple more options?" he asked. "I like the general direction, but I want to see more complex stuff, closer to what you did at Le Bourrelet."

"Sure, I can do that," I said, happy he wasn't American and couldn't identify the tinge of mockery in my tone.

"In the meantime, send me the list of the ingredients you need. I'll make sure Aitor orders them for you." He handed me his business card. "Do you want to meet next Wednesday? We're closed, but I have a lot of paperwork to do."

"Wednesday's great."

I followed him to the exit and admired the loneliness of an empty dining room in the pre-hours, the echoing silence amplified by the lack of voices and drunken giggles. As we crossed the kitchen again, I remembered the short breaks at Le Bourrelet, catching parts of muffled conversations through the ventilation system that for a while I captured in a small, blue spiral notebook.

Chef walked me to the loading dock, and though he appeared to have genuinely liked what I had come up with, it was clear the position wasn't mine yet. If I wanted a real chance at getting the job, I needed to find a place to rehearse the desserts.

"Good job, Demetrio." He pinched my shoulder.

I was still getting used to hearing my name pronounced in Castilian Spanish, the harsh and severe sound of the last syllable, a strange echo that connected to an old, faint memory.

"Thanks, Chef. I appreciate the opportunity," I said, and walked out into the stifling August morning.

15

Madrid was desolate. The wide avenues, congested a week ago, now looked like empty airport runways. In the same way I enjoyed walking bundled up through a New York blizzard, the city paralyzed by snow and frigid temperatures, I loved strolling through Madrid wearing skimpy running shorts and a sleeveless shirt, slicing through the heat as if inside a convection oven, all parts of my body heating evenly.

Going up Serrano, a street of regal buildings, I stopped in front of a posh store with bulletproof windows as a security guard pushed a glass door open and a tall woman with tortoiseshell sunglasses stepped onto the sidewalk. The lightness and poise with which she moved, her inborn sway, reminded me of Patricia. Before she could notice my presence or feel the fiery breeze that had just picked up, she vanished into the back of a gray Audi that rushed down the street, quickly disappearing under fleeting green and amber lights.

Jacobo was keen to show me the Reina Sofía, an old hospital turned modern art museum and the home of *Guernica*, Chus's favorite painting. Like him, the canvas had fled Spain during the Franco years and Picasso had instructed that it was not to return until the dictator was six feet under. Taking temporary shelter at MoMA, *Guernica* ended up on display for more than forty years.

At the corner of Serrano and Diego de León, I found myself in front of the American embassy, a concrete building wrapped by a high black fence crowned with video cameras. I crossed the street so that I would pass by the long line of people waiting at the door, their hands busy with documents to prove their legitimacy. They all appeared to be light-skinned, young, and well-dressed. Upscale immigrants. You could see they were nervous, their bodies taken over by anticipation. Two grim officers stood next to the entrance holding submachine guns. As people reached the front of the line they were instructed to leave their cell phones outside the building, check that all forms had been signed, and have their passports ready for inspection.

I listened to the officers speaking in a loud, condescending tone, clearly enjoying their position of power. I walked up to them and stared insolently, the only civilian not standing in line. As soon as they noticed me, I was asked to line up or otherwise keep walking. When I didn't move, a younger officer began talking into his radio, alerting others of a possible situation, the situation being my unwillingness to obey his American orders.

As I heard through the walkie-talkies the imminent dispatch of a unit, I gave the officers one last look of contempt and strolled down the street to the Castellana. Most people waiting glanced at me approvingly for challenging authority and acting out what was on their minds, the officers now speaking in a more respectful way.

I took the subway to Atocha, and as I emerged from underground through the escalators, my forehead broke into an immediate sweat. Following the shade as I crossed the square, I headed to the entrance of the museum, marveling at two breathtaking elevator towers made of glass and steel that were attached to the old façade of the building.

Jacobo was sitting on the steps. He was wearing my faded NPR T-shirt whose sleeves I had cut off to turn it into a tank top, and the same tight denim shorts that made it impossible not to look at his crotch.

"You can borrow it anytime," I said, kissing his cheek.

"Oh, sorry. I wanted to put on something clean after showering the other day."

"I'm kidding. It's totally fine."

"I have to say, didn't expect you'd own such a faggy-intellectual piece of clothing."

Jacobo's wit always caught me off guard. He also tended to end his jokes by sticking his tongue out, a childlike gesture that made him look much younger and my heart flutter.

"It's faggy because you're wearing it. Otherwise, it's actually kinda butch." This time it was me who stuck my tongue out.

He cracked up.

"Did you also steal my underwear?"

"I didn't."

From his tone, I could tell he was excited I had taken the conversation there.

"But I have to say your jockstraps are hot."

I was suddenly out of air.

"Oh my god. You're blushing right now."

"Stop," I said, laughing nervously.

"I can't. It's too cute."

Taking advantage of Jacobo's walking in front of me to the counter, I dried my armpits with the palms of my hands and rubbed the sweat on my shorts. He flashed his student ID and paid for both tickets. When he handed me mine, the word *adult*, printed in capital letters, felt like a taunt. He put his purple NYU card back into his wallet and I was reminded that the fall semester was beginning in a couple of weeks.

"Before looking for *Guernica,* I want to go up in the elevator," I said right after we showed our tickets to the security guard.

"You're such a little kid sometimes."

"Me?"

"Yeah. It's pretty adorable."

After riding the glass elevator up and down a couple of times, I experienced a mild sense of vertigo.

"The idea of attaching the elevators to the façade is pretty neat. Who did it?"

He paused and clacked his teeth, trying to remember. "Jean Nouvel, I think. The architect in charge of the extension."

We reached the top floor, the square far below us.

"It's a little scary, isn't it?" he said.

"Nah. You're just being a baby."

We toured the first-floor cloister looking for *Guernica* and I wondered what the space had been like before, when it was the Hospital de San Carlos, with its operating rooms and doctors rushing though hallways. The interior courtyard now held a massive standing Calder mobile with yellow and red metal blades that moved slightly in the breeze. I imagined the patients sitting in the sun, the bravest holding on to their walkers, venturing through the gardens as they regained their health.

The glass addition to the museum didn't try to become part of the former structure; more the opposite, it highlighted the old against the new. Jacobo explained that the original building had been commissioned by King Philip II during the Spanish

Golden Age and how at one point he had been king of Spain, Portugal, Naples, and Sicily. And because he was married to Queen Mary I, he had also been king of England. I suspected that Jacobo knew so much about royalty because of Patricia.

Guernica had its own room. Jacobo walked to the front while I stuck near the entrance. Despite its scale and powerful imagery that drew you in with faces deformed by pain and crying for help against the shadowy dark background, I was more interested in looking at Jacobo. I tried to imagine how I would feel had I first seen him there in that moment. Tall; bony like a bird; his hair, long and messy, that he combed to one side when it fell in front of his green eyes; his long, thin arms, crossed in front of his chest when he became absentminded. And how he dressed, in worn-out clothes with holes in them, always trying to conceal his beauty, to not draw attention. Even when he was not wearing the watch, the BlackBerry sticking out of his back pocket and the espadrilles about to disintegrate that sometimes slipped off as he walked betrayed he was a rich kid.

I went up to him and stood by his side.

"Impressive, huh?" he said without lifting his eyes from the canvas.

"Very. Can I take a picture with your phone? I want to send it to Chus."

Without waiting for an answer, I put my hand in his back pocket and left it there for a couple seconds.

"Oh, hi there!" He turned his head slightly and opened his eyes wide.

"Hello," I said, sticking my tongue out and grabbing his phone.

. . .

ALMOST AN ENTIRE WEEK had passed since I had met Matías. It was impossible to gauge my chances of getting the job, but I was excited about the two more elaborate options that I had created, slight variations of a chocolate tart and a butterscotch pudding that had been all-time favorites at Le Bourrelet. I sent an email to Chef thanking him for putting in a good word and described my visit to the restaurant. He answered almost immediately, urging me to rehearse every dish because the consistencies and textures of the ingredients would be different. I imagined him in the office of Le Bourrelet, typing on his old desktop computer that he only used to send emails, its keyboard covered in grease.

My first reaction after finding out that we had been spied on by Jacobo's father was to never return to his house. But the only place I could rehearse the desserts was his kitchen, where the convection oven, industrial range, and ice-cream machine were the kind of professional appliances I needed. I told Jacobo how funny I felt about going back, the possibility of finally meeting his father, and then was happy to learn that his parents were still in Mallorca.

I researched bakery supply stores. All of them appeared to be closed in August, but as I was about to give up, a small local shop near Ventas popped up. The store and the woman who ran it were tiny, old, and grimy. When I opened the door, her head was resting on her forearms. The sound of small bells brought her back to life. She looked as if she had been sleeping for years. I toured the aisles overflowing with metal baking supplies covered in dust and found a dough mixer, a set of silicone spatulas, all kinds of piping bags, and even a Thermapen, the most accurate thermometer on the market. Despite having seen baking trays and adjustable cake rings in Jacobo's kitchen the morning

I made the chocolate sauce, I grabbed some croquembouche and pyramid molds for the chocolate coulant. Once my eyes adjusted to the lack of light, I became obsessed and dove into baskets packed with molds of different shapes and sizes. The prices were low, so low that with the money I had in my pocket to pay Jacobo back, I could have bought enough equipment to open my own bakery.

The day was scorching hot and the heat seemed to come directly from the center of the earth, through the asphalt, and into the soles of my feet. When the bus came, I hopped on and sat in the last row. The air conditioner was blasting, which felt a little extravagant for only three passengers. Grateful, I closed my eyes and felt the gears switching back and forth, the vibrations pushing me into a light sleep.

I woke up as we were leaving the M-30, the FDR of Madrid, moving toward the city center. The bus began a long descent down the Avenida de América as the urban landscape began to change. There were no more bridges covered in graffiti and tunnels full of junk, all I could see now were postcard-perfect streets, massive water fountains, and manicured patches of greenery embroidered with colorful flowers. The bus pulled over in the Castellana and I descended into the boiling fumes of the afternoon. Now that Lavapiés was home, the ancient limestone façades of the Barrio de Salamanca appeared even more magnificent. Walking through the neighborhood, even after having lived here for weeks, I noticed for the first time the stairwells covered with red, narrow carpet runners and the vigilant doormen sitting next to cheap plastic fans.

As soon as I entered the apartment, I looked for the photo of his father shaking hands with the king and compared it to the one with Matías. Occupying a prominent spot on the wall, placed at eye level, it was difficult to miss. I studied it closely. The image seemed to have been captured at exactly the same time, as if the official photographer of the royal family had the otherworldly faculty of taking identical photos. Both Matías and Jacobo's father were bowing in front of the monarch as he produced the same manufactured smile: distant and distinguished, yet friendly and warm.

Down the corridor, I heard the voice of Jacobo excitedly finishing a joke. At first, I thought that he was talking on the phone, but then someone laughed. As I approached the kitchen to drop off the bags, an older man with slicked-back hair, dressed in a navy blue blazer and orange chinos, opened the door of the living room. A wave of hashish poured into the hallway.

"Hi, I'm Juan Osorio," he said with an air of grandeur, the use of his last name a failed attempt to conceal his reeking seediness.

"Demetrio." I dropped one of the bags on the floor to shake his hand.

He bowed slightly. Was he making fun of me?

"Hi, D!" Jacobo yelled from the living room.

"Lovely to meet you. You're the baker Jacobo raves about." He stared at me with hustling eyes.

"I guess so."

"I love sweets, but unfortunately, I have to go." He glanced at me a second too long and headed to the entrance.

I entered the kitchen feeling dirty. As I began inspecting the drawers and cabinets, trying to memorize where everything was so I could return it back to its place, all I could think of was the possibility that Jacobo was sleeping with Juan Osorio. Moments like this made me question whether I would ever be able to trust him.

I unpacked the bags slowly, caressed the marble counter

with my hand, its seamless surface ideal for working with flour and chocolate. I turned on the convection oven and found the sound of gas igniting into flames comforting. Although my knives didn't require sharpening, I slid them swiftly back and forth across the gray stone, swish-swash, swish-swash, a ritual that helped to clear my mind.

The more I thought about it, the less I could see Jacobo's being into someone so preppy looking. I pulled out my notebook and recited the list of desserts. I was proud of the names that I had come up with, their Spanish sounds capturing their delicacy. Chef had taught me early on that the appeal of a dessert begins the moment a customer reads it on the menu. He took this to an extreme, obsessing over new names for weeks, oftentimes renaming dishes long after the menus had been sent to the printers.

Pouring cream and sugar in a stainless-steel bowl, I set the mixer at a high speed. I became absorbed by the grains of sugar slowly disappearing into the twirling cream while I considered whether it was proper to go into the garden to collect some marigold petals without asking first. I decided to wait for Jacobo and walked into the sunset light pouring through the window. The view, which had been exciting and full of promise the day of my arrival, was nothing like I remembered. The metal gates of the pharmacy and the supermarket, shut in the early evening, gave the street a gloomy look. Down below, Juan Osorio was unlocking a Vespa near the gate. After he kicked the pedal several times, the engine started and a rattling sound echoed through the empty block.

Jacobo entered the kitchen wearing an oversized NYU basketball shirt and his cut-off shorts with the zipper wide open.

He was carrying a box of watercolors and brushes of different sizes, a large drawing pad under his arm.

We kissed on both cheeks and then he went to the sink to fill a glass of water.

"What are you making?" he asked after taking a seat at a round table near the window, the copper light illuminating a sketch of amorphous shapes. Swish-swash, swish-swash. Jacobo stared at my flexing biceps and made a face, puckering his lips. I rolled my eyes and smiled.

"I'm going to make a bittersweet chocolate biscuit with hazelnut cream and a marigold ice cream with paper-thin candied yuzu slices. I was thinking of using some petals from your mom's flowers."

"That would be so cool," he said, and walked up to the stove, dipping his finger in the chocolate melting in a glass bowl on top of a saucepan.

"Careful, you can burn yourself."

The possibility that he had just had sex with Juan Osorio followed me around the kitchen like a dog at my heels. Despite my attraction to him, I still felt that, if I had to choose, I would rather become an unconditional friend and not another person to fuck. That, he could easily find, if not in Madrid, at least in the anonymity of New York streets or within the boundless creases of the Internet.

I remembered the gory drawings from his notebook, their sharp contours and broken flesh. Now, looking at the delicacy of the pastel colors and the care with which he was stroking the paper with the brush, I wondered how the same person could create such viscerally different images, how those opposite worlds collided inside him.

Jacobo took his watch off, which he had not been wearing since we arrived in Madrid.

"Can I try it?"

"Yeah, of course. It's too heavy for me." He placed it on the table, then rubbed his wrist. "Do you like it?"

"Do I like it?" I smiled. "It's my dream watch."

"No way, really? You don't strike me as someone who would be into watches."

"Because I'm not. I'm just into some Rolexes. I used to love going to Tourneau to try them on."

"Oh. That's funny. That's where I go to get it serviced."

I put it on, looked at it, then extended my arm.

"Looks better on you. You have bigger wrists."

"You think?"

The timer went off. I turned around to grab a baking sheet and covered it with parchment paper. I scooped and carefully shaped the dough into circles, hoping they would hold their form as they baked. I peeked at the chocolate cakes gradually rising in the oven while listening to the ice-cream machine freezing and churning. I walked up to the window. The sunlight had disappeared, and the street had become more crowded. The neighborhood, compared to the liveliness of Lavapiés, had a subdued energy. I saw an old lady draped in gold and pearls, slowly pushing a walker on the sidewalk. She made me think about the elderly couple who sat on plastic chairs in front of my building.

I glanced at the glass subtly changing colors as different pigments floated in the water.

"So, when is the trial?" he said without lifting his eyes.

"Trial?"

"Yeah. When are you baking for him?"

"In two days." I lowered the speed of the mixer to beat in the vanilla.

"You think you'll get it?"

"Who knows," I said, wiping down the counter. As I glanced at him, absorbed in the watercolor, I considered sharing that I had seen his mother at El Lucernario.

"How do you like it?"

I looked at what appeared to be two men made of geometric shapes, interlocked with each other. The meshing contours and color overlaps produced a beautiful golden hue. Only after a while I noticed that they were either wrestling or having sex. Random memories of our fight flooded my mind: the blood from his busted lip dripping onto my face, my fist hitting his cheek, his erection pressing against my butt while I sat on top of him, pinning his wrists to the rock. It occurred to me that this moment of raw and painful intimacy was the closest we had been to making love, the moment we had revealed our most vulnerable selves.

"Have you considered doing fine arts?"

"I did consider it, but my dad would never support me." He placed the watercolor back on the table. "Convincing him to let me go to Gallatin was a stretch. For him it's business or law."

WE WORKED UNTIL the kitchen grew dark and the only light was coming from the oven. I took the cakes out, let them sit, and put the ice cream in the freezer. Jacobo prepared gin and tonics using thick pieces of cucumber to lessen the taste of the alcohol, then went out to the garden. When I stepped outside and sat next to him, the coil of bug repellent made my sinuses throb.

"You were probably a mosquito in a previous life," he said, wetting his fingers and snuffing out the ember.

"Oh, thank you. I'll take that as a compliment."

Jacobo smiled and lit a candle. The night was still. There were no lights in the apartments across the street. I imagined most neighbors in their vacation homes, living temporary lives they wished were permanent, sleeping on beds that folded into sofas where they still rested better than in the comfort of their actual homes, far away from the stress of the daily grind. I wished we could go back to Cabo de Gata and lie on the beach under the stars and listen to the surf breaking on the sand.

I went to the kitchen and brought out the chocolate biscuits.

"Look at these beauties," he said, then raised his glass. "To getting the job."

"To getting *a* job," I said.

Jacobo broke off a piece of the biscuit and before his taste buds could have possibly processed the flavor said: "Wow, it's insane."

I took a bite. The consistency was right, but I had slightly burned the chocolate. I considered adding Himalayan salt to bring out the flavor and changing its name to Bittersweet Chocolate Biscuits with Salt from the Himalayas.

"So, what do you think?" He placed a piece of hashish on the table.

"Not bad, but I need to use a chocolate with a higher percentage of cocoa butter. It will make it a little less bitter. And I might add some Himalayan salt."

"Well, I'm going to make a joint with hashish from the Rif

Mountains, tobacco from pure American red Marlboros, and rolling paper from St. Mark's Place."

I slapped the back of his head. "Let's try the marigold ice cream before we smoke up."

The ice cream had attained the right smooth and creamy texture but the color, instead of the deep yellow I had expected, was off-white and not very appetizing. I served it in two dark bowls to create contrast and make it more appealing.

"I can't believe you made ice cream with petals. Mom's going to flip out."

"There's enough in the freezer for three more servings. Tell her that I'm naming this dessert after her."

"This is totally crazy. I can taste the petals! You're the best *pastelero* I've ever met." He stuck out his tongue, now covered in ice cream. "And the first one."

"Stop it."

"What? I'm not doing anything."

"You're such a tease."

"Me?" He laughed. "You have to be kidding me, Mr. *I don't think in those terms.*" He stood up and headed to the kitchen to refill our drinks.

The city was so silent, it seemed like we were the last two people on the planet. For the first time, I wondered if I had been wrong all along, if I should have pursued the only person I had ever had a real but inexplicable connection with. If I had missed my chance.

When Jacobo came back, he rolled another joint and curled up on the sofa, resting his head in my lap. This time, I didn't need him to be passed out to run my fingers through his hair. The stars, usually muted by a thin layer of pollution, were extraordinarily bright, and the sky was brimming with light.

.   .   .

I WAS IN a faraway place, lost in thoughts, most of them involving Chus and my days at Le Bourrelet, when I heard a distant "Hello." Opening my eyes, I looked around the garden and considered whether I had started to dream. Jacobo was breathing deeply, the candle still lit. A large mosquito that seemed made out of black thread was caught in the wax, fighting for its life. At the sound of a door shutting and a kid running through the hallway, Jacobo woke up, his face crumpled like paper.

"My parents."

Before I was able to turn his words into actual meaning, Jacobo put the bag with the hashish and the rolling paper into his back pocket and hid the ashtray of joint butts behind a plant.

"The American is here! The American is here!" Estrella yelled excitedly, stomping onto the terrace.

Jacobo acted cool. He pulled her up in the air, making her instantly scream with delight.

"Do the helicopter, please," she said, then yelled: "Helicopter! Helicopter!"

"It's too late, Estrella. We'll do it tomorrow." But they still moved away from the table, then Estrella kneeled, and he grabbed her by her ankles. Spinning her briefly on his feet, she turned like the blades of a mixer, her long hair caressing the grass. He put her back down. She smiled with her whole face, red from being upside down.

Patricia and her husband entered the garden, both dressed in light, camel linen clothes that accentuated their tans. The sluggish effects of the gin and tonics and the hashish were suddenly gone. I stood up with shaky legs and tried to look calm.

"Good evening." I opened my eyes a little wider to look more alert.

Patricia hugged Jacobo first, then me. "It's so lovely to see you."

"You too," I said.

"Hello." His father walked up to Jacobo and kissed him briefly on his forehead, an action that didn't correlate with my idea of him. "Your mom isn't feeling well." He spoke as if Patricia were not there.

"What's wrong?" Jacobo walked up to her, knocking over a chair.

"I'm Alfonso," his father said, offering his hand.

"Hello, sir. I'm Demetrio." As I shook his hand, I realized Jacobo's watch was still on my wrist.

"Tomás is on his way. Your mother's been feeling drowsy since Wednesday. We first thought it was from the new keel on the boat, but yesterday she got a strong headache that hasn't gone away. Of course, she refused to go to the hospital in Mallorca. I don't blame her. Island people are the worst." He spoke in a tone that expressed both exasperation and profound tenderness.

"Your father is blowing it out of proportion."

"Hold on. Here's Tomás. He's probably downstairs." Alfonso walked inside the house with the phone in his hand.

"Are those gin and tonics?" Patricia asked, pointing at my glass. "I'd love one." She pulled up a chair and sat next to me. "I'll wait for Tomás here. It's a beautiful evening."

"I'll make you one." Jacobo grabbed the empty glasses, a look of consternation on his face.

"I want to make them!" Estrella tugged at his shirt and followed him to the kitchen.

We were left alone.

"So, how do you like El Lucernario?" She patted her thigh as if shaking something off her dress.

I knew that Jacobo could have told her, but something in her voice suggested she was acknowledging seeing me at the restaurant.

"I actually haven't started yet. I just went in for an interview." She gazed at the Castellana.

I heard the distant sound of skateboards rolling down the street and a dog starting to bark.

"How're things?" she asked.

I looked down at my hands, then back at Patricia. I wished that my empty glass were still on the table so I could hold on to something.

"Are you feeling more at home?" She leaned back in the chair, her body relaxed but her eyes fixed on mine.

The silence became louder, so I began talking, thinking about my words as they lingered in the air, unable to bring them back.

"I don't know. It's confusing," I said. "I thought that moving here would make me feel different, that I'd have some sort of epiphany, that everything would finally fall into place. I was tired of being stuck at the same job and wanted the freedom to explore others. But I haven't. And now I'm as stranded as I was in America but without my uncle. I feel terrible for abandoning him."

Her eyes asked for more.

"He's got a chronic disease, and even though he was okay with me leaving, I shouldn't have. He'll never come back to Spain. And I can't visit him, at least not for the next ten years."

I prayed she wouldn't ask about his sickness, and dreaded

bringing the three letters into this house. I wondered if she knew about Jacobo's sexuality, if so, how comfortable she was with it.

Patricia leaned toward me. That simple movement, the physical expression of care, made me look away.

"I don't know your uncle. But I'm sure he understands your need to leave the country. Wanting to live without the fear of being expelled is enough of a reason. Besides, your life began here. You *are* from here."

She spoke solemnly. I wasn't sure whether her words were looking to console me or if she truly believed that being born here made me Spanish. I was feeling as foreign as I had the day of my arrival, even though I now navigated the streets with familiarity and interacted with the locals more fluidly. I had accepted that I would never be home, because home, if I had ever had one, could never be found.

"Are your parents alive?" she asked, looking at the city as if the question were floating in the night.

For a moment, the images of a mutiny in Carabanchel I had watched on the Internet entered my mind. The corridors were engulfed by flames. Thick gray smoke poured through windows, then floated above the prison like a crown. I wondered if the fire had been visible from where we were sitting and imagined fire trucks outside the prison with their hoses pointing at the windows of El Palomar.

"My mom died when I was sixteen. My dad was never in the picture."

I stared at Patricia until she turned her head. Looking into my eyes with a piercing intensity, she placed her hand on my thigh. An instant calm overcame me.

"Is your headache any better?"

"It's not, but at least I'm home. And the floor doesn't move," she said, rubbing her temples. "I hate boats."

Jacobo arrived with the gin and tonics and two scoops of ice cream.

"Demetrio made this with your marigolds." He passed her the bowl.

My heart was beating fast.

"That's incredible," Patricia said.

She took a bite and, with her mouth closed, made a sound of pleasure.

"It tastes wonderful," she said.

"Did he tell you he's rehearsing some desserts for a job interview?" Jacobo asked.

"No, he hasn't."

"I'm going to include it in the menu. Helado de Maravillas de Patricia," I said, changing the name from what I had written in my notebook.

She tucked a tress behind her ear. "You're going to name it after me?"

"You bet I am."

"You're such a darling."

"Have you heard of El Lucernario, on Jorge Juan? It's supposed to be exquisite," Jacobo said.

I could overhear Alfonso speaking on the phone in the living room, his voice getting louder and louder, the sentences turning into expansive monologues. It was clear he was used to giving orders.

"No, I haven't," she said elusively, looking at the sea of city lights, losing her gaze in them.

16

It was shortly after I started at El Lucernario in its fairly young kitchen, caught in a great storm of Michelin stars, that my life quickly began to resemble the one I had left in New York. I had assumed that the ability to move freely from job to job would renew my passion for a profession that had provided me great comfort for so many years. But I felt just as restricted and unhappy as I felt working at Le Bourrelet the last couple of months and kept reminding myself that I had no reason to feel restricted or unhappy.

The pace of the kitchen was less hectic than Le Bourrelet's, though it was hard to know for sure because Spaniards took their vacations seriously and the city in August was deserted. As I was changing into my shorts, Emilio, the sous-chef, who was friendly to me but hard to read, insisted that I go with them for a nightcap to celebrate my joining the restaurant. All I wanted was to get home, because the following day Jacobo and I were having a picnic by the lake at the Palacio de Cristal. But I said yes and acted as if nothing would make me happier.

When I headed to the back door, I caught a glimpse of Emilio and some food runners snorting lines on the back of a cast-iron pan. I waited for them outside, on the loading dock, marveling at the similarity of two kitchen cultures thousands of miles apart.

"Why would you ever leave New York, man? I don't get it," Emilio said as we began walking down the street. "It's such a dream city."

Listening to the question, I momentarily considered whether Chef might have shared with Matías my reason for leaving. But I couldn't imagine him doing that.

"I don't know. I was kind of burned out. It's such an intense city. I needed a break."

As I was finishing my thought, Emilio began talking to someone else, clearly uninterested in what I was saying. I looked around, comforted that no one had noticed my being ignored. One of the washers, whom I had seen scrubbing a pot with such fury that I made a joke about how he was going to make holes with the brush, walked up to me.

"Hello, Chef. I'm Amir," he said, knocking his heart gently with his fist twice, then extending his hand. He couldn't have been older than sixteen.

"Nice to meet you, Amir."

"Welcome to the restaurant. I've heard you're from New York!"

"I'm actually from here but yeah, I lived in Manhattan most of my life. How long have you been at the restaurant?"

"Not long. It's my first job in Madrid."

"Very cool. Where are you from?"

"Ouarzazate. Four hours away from Marrakech."

"Oh, that's awesome. Do you like Madrid?"

"I do. It's a great city. People are nice. But I miss my town, it's so beautiful." His eyes lit up. "It's near the Atlas Mountains.

Do you know the Atlas? It's very, very famous. *Gladiator* was shot there. Have you seen it, with Russell Crowe?"

"I have," I said, laughing, jealous of the longing in his voice. I wondered if I would ever feel an attachment to a place again.

"You should go one day. My family will host you. They are farmers. We have a good house."

"That's very sweet. Thank you."

By then we had arrived at the bar. There was nothing remarkable about it, just another hole-in-the-wall.

"What can I get you?"

He smiled. "I don't drink."

"You don't drink alcohol. But you do drink other stuff, right?" For some reason this made him laugh.

"Yes. Fanta naranja."

WE SPENT THE WEE HOURS submerged in beer and whiskey and in and out of thick white clouds of hashish. As people kept asking me why I left a restaurant like Le Bourrelet and a city like New York, I found myself saying that the reasons were to reconnect with my culture and learn about Spanish cuisine. I only hoped that by repeating it many times, it would become, if not true, at least believable enough. When the opportunity presented itself, I snuck out without saying goodbye and spent the hours before dawn walking the streets of Lavapiés.

Crossing Tirso de Molina, I noticed a kid curled up on a bench who looked like Amir. He had disappeared shortly after drinking his Fanta from a straw, the two dimples on his face making him look even younger than he was. I refused to believe that on days after long shifts, having to be back at the restaurant in five hours, Amir didn't travel to the bed-room community where Emilio had mentioned he shared an apartment with other immigrants. I rambled around the neighborhood fighting the thought away, and when I heard the familiar sound of the garbage truck betraying that in a few hours my alarm would go off, I headed home.

Sleep refused to come. The image of the kid lying on the bench came in and out of focus and at one point the face became unequivocally Amir's. The possibility he was sleeping on the streets kept me awake, then pushed me out of bed. I got dressed and rushed down the stairs of my building. Some people in my neighborhood were already on their way to work. By the time I arrived at the square, the day had fully broken. The bench was empty and the area pretty desolate, except for two talkative policemen leaning on the hood of their patrol car, the sharp chirps coming out of their radios puncturing the stillness of the morning.

AS I WALKED AROUND the stands of the Mercado de la Paz, I wished I had woken up earlier so I could have bought pro-duce to prepare something special for our picnic, but I woke up late, and all I could do was conceal my sluggishness by buying overpriced gourmet tapas and two nice bottles of wine. The Palacio de Cristal was inside the Retiro. I had bad memories of the park; it reminded me of our first fight after I mistakenly thought I had been locked out of the building. I wondered if the idea to meet there wasn't a coincidence, if it was a way for Jacobo to convey we had come full circle. As for me, I felt that both fights had brought us closer, the sharp-edged words and bloody fists breaking something open, a sudden level of intimacy that otherwise we might have never reached.

I followed Jacobo's directions through the park. The sun was high in the sky and the swaying treetops made the light shimmer. Surrounded by a small lake and a lush and verdant garden, the glass-and-iron structure looked so light, it was hard to believe that it had been standing there since the 1800s. Jacobo was lying down on a blanket, shirtless, his head resting on his palms, his gaze lost in the sky. I stopped a couple of feet away to admire his long, smooth torso and lean, toned muscles. Part of why I found him so attractive was because he seemed to always be trying to disguise his beauty. Up until now, everyone I had met who was as gorgeous as him had capitalized on their looks, which I had always found terribly off-putting.

Two guys were also checking him out. Suddenly feeling territorial, I walked up to the blanket and laid on top of him.

"Oh, hi!" he said, shocked at my body pressing on his.

"Have you been waiting for long?" I said, rolling to the side and sitting down, giving my back to them.

"I got here early. Trying to see if I can get rid of this Morticia Addams look before I go back to school. Wait, you look bigger."

"Bigger?"

"I mean, more muscular."

"Do I? Nah," I said, thrilled he had noticed I had started working out again, even if only for a week. "I'm lifting again. This is what I usually look like."

"So jealous. I wish I could put on some muscle. But I can't."

It was sizzling hot again despite having cooled off the last couple of days. I wanted to take my shirt off, but I worried he would think I was trying to get him excited. I began unwrapping the tapas instead. "You look great the way you are. Muscles are for guys who aren't beautiful, like me."

"Oh, stop it."

"I'm serious."

I was able to find two bottles of a Verdejo that the sommelier had been raving about the night before, which I thought would pair well with the costillas de ternera I got at the market. I poured two glasses and passed him one.

"To your new job," he said.

"And to finding each other."

"Yes. Por el destino," he added.

We drank the first bottle quickly and halfway through the second, I peeled off my shirt and pulled down my shorts slightly so the elastic of my jockstrap would show. He covered the sun with his palm.

"Oh là là," he said in a mocking tone, fanning his face with both hands.

I stuck out my tongue.

"I wouldn't mind if you stayed," I managed to say after he laid his head on my chest.

"Yeah, I wouldn't mind it either." The breeze made the tops of the trees rustle. "But I can't."

"Why not?" I began petting his hair.

"I don't know. I just can't."

"Give me at least one reason." I pressed my fingers on his neck, giving him a gentle massage.

"For starters, I would lose my scholarship, probably immediately."

"Your what? You have a scholarship? Why?" An uncontrollable anger was suddenly boiling up. How was the world such a place that someone of his wealth could get a free ride to college when others had to join the fucking army? I sat up and relocated his head to my lap, convinced he could feel my heart pounding rapidly.

"It's not need-based. It's an academic scholarship, based on merit."

"Oh, okay. That makes sense," I said, getting ahold of myself, knowing it made no sense at all. What I found most troubling was not learning about another way in which the rich protected their wealth, but the fact that using the word *merit* made them feel they actually deserved it.

CHUS AND I HAD BEEN playing phone tag for days. When we finally connected, I was buying Tupperware at a Chinese store where everything cost one euro.

"Oh, Deme. I can't believe your email. It sounds terrible."

"I know, it was horrible. Believe it or not, it's all better now."

"How's that possible? What happened after you got back?"

"We didn't speak for a couple of days. Then we found out that his dad had hired a private investigator to follow us. Can you believe that?"

"Of course I can! That's very much fascist behavior."

"Anyway. We saw each other again, and I realized how much I like being with him. But still, it's complicated. Listen to this. Yesterday, for example, we spent the afternoon in the Retiro, literally on top of each other. I really thought this would be the moment when we'd finally make out. I was really feeling I had finally got over my hang-ups, but then he brought up that he's at NYU on a merit-based scholarship. Can you believe it?"

"Yes, of course."

"That he's getting a free ride?"

"Deme."

"Deme what? I can't believe these people."

"Why?"

"What do you mean, why? Because rich people shouldn't be getting free rides anywhere!"

"But, Deme, that's just how the world works. It's not the kid's fault."

"Well, all I know is that if I were rich, I would pay for my own education."

"But you didn't want to get an education in the first place."

"Chus! That's a different story. That's not the point."

"Well, he's not doing anything wrong. Merit-based scholarships are just that: merit-based scholarships. If you had gone to college on one, which you could have because you're very smart, you would feel differently."

"Actually, I can assure you I wouldn't. Gosh, you're so annoying sometimes. In any case, I just can't explain it. I like him a lot, but I feel we're not compatible, like we're from two different planets. It's all too much and too complicated."

"Listen to me. I know you too well, and I can feel it. There's something special between you two. You know it's special when it makes you feel the way you're feeling right now. Don't shy away from it."

"I don't know that I can do that. But thanks for listening."

"You're welcome. I love you."

"I love you too."

THE DAY OF Jacobo's departure, after insisting I wanted to see him off, he picked me up on the way to the airport. Sitting in the back of the car, he asked the driver to put the radio on, then make it louder until the voices were so high, it was impossible to hear each other or even my own thoughts. I wondered if he did that so the driver could not report anything to his father. The Spanish journalists were having a heated discussion; I couldn't understand why they were always yelling. I missed the soothing voices of NPR.

Terminal 4 emerged in the distance like an apparition, its shiny red beams like bird wings. Jacobo squeezed through the front seats and switched off the dial himself as if wanting now to concentrate on the image outside the window. In the deep silence that took over the car, I heard echoes of my conversation with Chus.

Jacobo moved through the airport with ease. The few times that our eyes met, he glanced away. The rhythmic, soothing announcements from the PA system heightened the inevitability of his departure. I followed his steps, and as he turned his head back to make sure I was trailing behind, I questioned whether he would have preferred to be alone.

The check-in area was a mess, the lines long and unruly. People stood among enormous suitcases, some of them wrapped in plastic like sandwiches. They were speaking loudly, their excitement palpable. Jacobo ignored the crowd and walked up to a counter. As we stepped onto a soft red carpet, I realized he was flying first class.

"There were no more seats in coach," he said, as if he had access to my thoughts.

"No need to apologize. Nothing wrong with going first class."

"Business."

"What?"

"I'm flying business, not first. And I'm not apologizing. I'm just saying." He smiled widely to soften the edges of his words. From the moment we got into the car, I sensed that he was trying to distance himself from me. First putting the duffel bag on the seat between us, then forcing other voices in so we couldn't have the conversation that maybe he suspected I wanted to have.

The woman behind the counter was clearly flirting with him and he was following through, putting on an act. I detested his fabricated masculinity, his Spanish mannerisms that buried his American self.

"Thank you." He checked his boarding pass and slid his passport into his back pocket.

We walked around the terminal, our patterns altered by the trajectories of others. I avoided looking at my watch but kept glancing at the time displayed on the flight boards, a constant reminder that the end was near. At one point, annoyed that we were so distant, I purposely fell behind and got lost in the crowd to see how long it would take before he noticed my absence. I kept an eye on him, and when he finally turned back to a sea of travelers, I enjoyed seeing his worried face, his eyes momentarily showing panic.

At a newsstand, we looked through magazines and newspapers in silence. I couldn't focus on anything I was seeing. Jacobo bought a copy of *El País* and a skinny global edition of the *New York Times*. I flipped through the pages of *Saveur* and grabbed the last issue of the *New Yorker* even though I never read it. He insisted on paying for both.

A full hour before he was scheduled to depart, we headed to security. At the checkpoint, we stepped to the side. Jacobo didn't lift his eyes from the floor. He switched his bag from shoulder to shoulder and then put it between his feet.

"Okay," he said.

Now that our separation was imminent, standing under a gigantic glass dome through which the late summer light poured in, I knew this was it. I struggled to find the right words. Rolling the magazine into a tube, I started swatting at my leg.

"You're driving me nuts, Deme."

"Oh, I'm sorry. I've been meaning to say something for a while."

He gave me a distant look, as if he had already taken off.

"You know I really like you, right?"

"Yes, I kind of got that." Under the words, he was saying, *That's not enough.*

"I know this is going to sound crazy."

"I'll be the judge of that." For the first time that day, he smiled.

"I know it's strange to say this because you're leaving and I'm staying. But I wouldn't mind going steady." I ordered my tears to stay put, but tears don't follow orders.

"Damn. That's great timing." He began to laugh and cry at the same time. Both sobbing and laughing, my tears, at least, were mostly of fear and sadness. I grabbed the back of his neck and pulled his mouth toward mine. As we began kissing, I could taste his salty lips. I squeezed his nape. He put his hand in his pocket.

"We're making a scene," I said.

"*You're* making a scene."

We smiled and dried each other's faces.

"So, what do you say?" I knew I had no right to insist.

"Going steady happens after dating for a while, doesn't it? I'm gone until Christmas, Deme. It's four months."

I knew it was too much to ask.

"I know, I know. It's a long time."

"It is. Here's what we should do. Let's take it one day at a time. How about I fly back for Columbus Day weekend, and we see then?"

"That's fair."

Jacobo held out his hand. I gave him a pat on the back of his head and kissed him again. We hugged. We hugged for a long time.

"Have a good flight." I peeled my chest away.

"Thanks. You too." He rubbed his eyes. "Sorry. I meant good luck at the restaurant."

For a moment, I fantasized that we were both going back. I saw us boarding the plane, the flight attendants welcoming us with smiles that would later be erased as tiredness crept in. Sitting by a window, I would look at the suitcases going up the belt, entering the gut of the plane. I imagined eight hours suspended in nothingness, though this time I would know what awaited me on the other side. I could visualize the final approach to New York City, its buildings at the water's edge like tall weeds of a swamp.

"Are you okay?" Jacobo asked.

"Yeah, I am. Promise me you'll take it easy with the partying."

Jacobo gave me the finger. I grabbed it quickly and bit it hard. He screamed so loudly people turned around. During our last hug, we didn't stop laughing. I liked feeling his bony torso shaking against mine.

"I should go, or I'll miss my flight."

"I wouldn't mind if that happened."

He said nothing. Grabbing his worn duffel bag from the floor, he gave me a quick glance and shook his head. "I can't believe you, Deme." His eyes were watery again. "See you in October."

As he was about to hand his passport to the security guard, he turned around.

"Keep it until I get back," he said, unfastening his watch.

"You're crazy. I can't."

"Come on, it's just a watch. And it looks better on you anyway." He grabbed my arm and put it on my wrist.

Overwhelmed, I looked at the dial and said: "Six weeks, starting now." I smiled apologetically and waited for him to go through security. After crossing the metal detector, he was pulled aside and patted down. While the officer felt his waist with the back of his hand, Jacobo turned his head to me and stuck out his tongue. I laughed so hard that tears started rolling down again. As he walked up the belt to collect his bag, I noticed a big hole in one of his socks. Unwilling to untie the laces of his sneakers, he struggled to put them on. I said to myself that if he turned back, it would mean he was interested in me, that things would work out. But he entered the escalator with his gaze down and slowly began to disappear, first his legs, then the torso, and finally his head with the sunglasses holding his hair back. I felt my phone vibrating and opened a text with a smiley face. Overcome with sadness, I responded with the same dumb smiley face. I waited in the same place until the security guard looked at me with pity, then wandered around the terminal until I found myself back at the newsstand, where I grabbed a copy of *El País*.

I decided to indulge myself and took a cab back to my apartment. The traffic entering the city reminded me of the West Side Highway after a long weekend. I watched the meter rise with regular clicks, the numbers quickly approaching the amount of money I had in my pocket. When we finally entered the Castellana, and after watching the lights change from red to green and back to red again, I asked the cabdriver to pull over. He cursed me for getting out before arriving at the destination. Descending underground while checking my phone, I slipped on the stairs. As I lay on the floor with a piercing pain at the back of my head, I looked at the watch and checked it wasn't damaged.

17

ix weeks is not a long time, unless you count them in minutes. My new routine weirdly resembled my last couple of
weeks in New York. The long and taxing shifts left me with little energy to do anything other than walk home in the middle
of the night and fix myself a drink that would put me to sleep.
Now that Jacobo wasn't around, Chus and I started a weekly
ritual of long phone conversations that mostly revolved around
Jacobo and whether my loneliness was pathological, part of
how I experienced the world. Otherwise, I argued, there was
no explanation for why I had suggested giving the relationship
a try the moment Jacobo was leaving the country.

Now that I knew what it felt like to be truly in the world,
spending my days in a windowless kitchen depressed me. After
living most of my life in a city whose tall buildings kept the
sun away, traveling through vast, open spaces and endless and
deserted roads that disappeared into the horizon made me
yearn to be outside. This awakening, I realized now, could only
have happened here, in a country that I could not be expelled
from.

One night, I crossed the empty dining room readied for the
next day and left the restaurant through the main entrance as

usual. Triana was sitting on the stone bench across the alley. She was wearing a pleated short skirt with blue and red stripes that resembled a school uniform. Out of boredom, we had begun texting a couple of weeks back, but we seemed more interested in making dates and canceling them at the last moment than actually seeing each other. Most of the time, these plans were hatched late at night, when she was out with her friends and the alcohol freed her fingers.

Even though it was a pedestrian street, Triana turned her head to both sides as if to make sure there were no cars coming. I had just finished a twelve-hour shift and had been wearing the same shirt for the last couple of days. My armpits stank. After Jacobo left, my social life had been reduced to a few interactions with people in the neighborhood and broken conversations with Amir, who every now and then slept on my sofa to avoid the long commute home.

"What a surprise." I tried to sound more excited than I was.

She kissed me on both cheeks and ironed the pleats of her skirt with her hands. "I was in the neighborhood."

"Cool. I'm happy you came."

We began walking without a destination, letting ourselves go, neither of us taking the lead. It was a late Saturday night, and there were crowds pouring in and out of bars, kids partying, and large families sitting at outdoor tables squeezing in the last remnants of the day. Compared to New York, a city that lately had become wealth obsessed, where old people became invisible or pushed out, I enjoyed seeing them as part of everyday life, reading the newspaper and sipping coffee, strolling through parks with their grandkids, or playing petanca. Their lives were not threatened by their lack of productivity.

They didn't have to worry about being shipped away to forgotten nursing homes in the Rockaways with uplifting names to lessen the guilt of those who had confined them.

As I was lost in these thoughts, we found ourselves near my apartment and ended up at the Wall, a local dive bar that played music from the sixties. I ordered a tequila soda for me and a beer for Triana. I was surprised by how many people I recognized from the neighborhood, people who acknowledged me by raising their eyebrows slightly as we crossed paths on the street and who were always ready to strike up a conversation.

At one point, as the bar got crowded and people closed in around us, Triana began moving her hips to the rhythm of the music. She was dancing with a tall kid whose black, curly hair reminded me of Alexis. For a moment, I was under the impression she was picking him up. After I observed them for a while, not knowing what to do with myself, Triana waved at me and introduced me as Jacobo's friend. I tried to follow the conversation, but his accent was thick, and he was slurring his words. Hearing Jacobo's name for the first time since he had left made him real again.

Growing up around Caribbean Latinos, I was hyperaware of my stiff body and lack of rhythm. Still, I started to dance so I would have something to focus on. At one point, her friend asked if we were going to El Amanecer. I thought he was asking me something related to the sunrise, which, given his drunkenness, seemed fitting. He then pulled out his wallet and handed me two VIP passes to an after-hours club near the Puerta del Sol.

Four tequila sodas later, after I was introduced to most of the people in the bar, the entire dance floor appeared to be one large group of friends. I was struck by the robotic way Spaniards danced, but by the end of the night, I was jumping with them in disjointed, stilted moves. At around three in the morning, the bar began to empty, and soon after, the lights were turned on and we were politely thrown out.

I can't remember the exact moment Triana and I decided to go back to my apartment. Climbing the stairs, realizing that the photos of the trip were taped on the walls, I felt the urge to turn around, but I remained calm and decided to act drunker than I was, dropping the keys to the floor, buying time to come up with an explanation.

"I'm sorry. This lock acts up sometimes."

After fumbling with it for a while, Triana put her hand on my shoulder.

"Here, let me try."

Before she could reach the doorknob, I opened the door.

The moment we entered I knew that coming to the apartment had been the wrong decision. Triana walked over and stared at the photos. I filled the silence with silly jokes that failed to make her laugh. She paced around the room, her lack of words heightening the sound of the creaking wooden floor. By the extreme zoom the photographer had used, it was evident that the photos had been taken without consent. I contemplated telling her the truth but felt an obligation to protect Jacobo's family. I went to the sink and turned on the faucet. Watching the water run calmed me down. I grabbed a bottle of Vichy Catalan, a salty sparkling water that tasted like the ocean, pulled two used glasses from under a dirty plate, and filled them up.

"Aren't they interesting?" I walked up to her.

She was looking at a photo of Jacobo and me peeing, playing

swords. The action hidden as our backs were to the camera, we appeared to just be looking into the horizon.

When Triana finally spoke, she sounded sober. "Who took them?"

I felt a vein in my neck throbbing and heard myself saying: "It was a project for an art class Jacobo was doing this summer."

I had spoken calmly and with a flat tone, as if I were telling her something obvious, something like, "I need to be back at the restaurant in three hours," or "I haven't done laundry in two weeks."

"He was taking classes in the summer?" It sounded like an accusation.

"I don't know. That's what he said."

I handed her the glass of water. We sat at both ends of the sofa, not ready to fully inhabit it. I decided to commit to my lie and wait for her next question. The stillness was menacing. There were usually sounds in the night of water running through the walls or pigeons cooing on the windowsill covered in white droppings. Now the silence was absolute. I could hear the air entering and exiting my nose. We didn't move for a long time. Finally, she grabbed a joint from her handbag and asked for a lighter.

The thick white smoke pushed the lie out of the room. After we passed the joint back and forth, I laid my hand on her leg. The pleats of her skirt were like tectonic plates, and sliding my palm back and forth reminded me of the hills in Cabo de Gata. I took long puffs and flooded my lungs with piercing smoke until I could no longer breathe. Triana kissed my hand and pushed it to her chest. She lay back and closed her eyes. I climbed on top of her and began rubbing myself against her body. She unbuttoned my jeans. The herbal taste of her mouth,

the pungent smell of smoke nested in her curls, and her long
and loud exhalations made my cock escape through the opening in my boxers. I hadn't had sex in months.

I turned off the light but left the blinds open. We kissed
each other as if we were both being pulled by the same under-
current. Triana kept her eyes closed. I shoved my pants down,
hauled her onto all fours, and entered her with the help of a
little spit. We moved in silence except for a few sharp intakes
of breath and isolated metallic howls coming from the sagging
springs of the sofa. We rocked like a boat approaching the
shore. I felt a rush coming looking at Jacobo, shirtless, with a
swollen eye, his face covered in dry blood.

A FEW DAYS LATER, Matías announced the condesa de Mon-
talvo was at table five. I knew that he was referring to Patricia because a week before, flipping through an interior design
magazine waiting to get my hair cut, I had read a feature on
her house in Mallorca. The kitchen buzzed with energy. The
new chef garde manger, a French girl with a buzz cut who had
recently joined us, began to prepare a tasting of hors d'oeuvres,
which featured a version of deviled eggs with padrón pep-
pers, a signature dish of El Lucernario. The fish chef nervously
inspected the lowboy for the meatiest piece of sea bass that had
arrived from Galicia that morning.

Only executive chefs visited the dining room from time
to time, a practice that had become more common with the
increased popularity of TV cooking shows and food docu-
mentaries. Sous- and pastry chefs rarely made an appearance,
unless family or colleagues were in the dining room. Chef was
surprised when I asked him for permission to bring out the

dessert platter to Patricia. He was even more surprised when I referred to her as a friend.

I went to the locker area, put deodorant on, and changed into freshly laundered chef's whites. I intended to sneak out discreetly so no one in the kitchen would notice, but I knew that once I was in the dining room, the food runners would quickly bring back word I was sitting with the condesa.

I had prepared a platter with my favorite selection, and when I saw Chef going into his office with the hostess, I took the liberty of including a new addition I intended to introduce: chocolate sage cookies with orange peels. Crossing the line that separated where the food is prepared from where it is enjoyed always made me anxious. This was probably true for most professionals in an industry where one is trained to believe one's only purpose in life is to make or serve food to be experienced by others.

A few guests glanced my way as I entered the dining room. Patricia was sitting at the same table where I had seen her the first time, alone. Even though she was still a little tan, her face had a yellowish hue, her head covered with a silk bandana. She was flipping through a magazine, and from the way she turned the pages, it was clear that she was distracted. Most of the sea bass was still on the plate, though the placement of the silverware indicated she had finished. As I neared the table, her cell phone began to vibrate and light up. I stopped a couple of feet away, and when it was clear that she was not going to answer it, I said: "Something wrong with the fish?"

"Oh, hi. No, no. It's lovely. I seem to have lost my appetite," she said as if running out of air, slightly pushing the plate away. "Can you sit down for a moment? Are you busy?"

"Thank you. No, I'm good. We're almost done with the shift."

A waiter came to grab her plate. I could tell from his face he was anticipating Chef's reaction to a barely touched dish. I placed the desserts in front of her and sat down. Her energy was low, her lips swollen and dried. She had a faraway look that I recognized. For many years after Ben passed away, Chus had those same eyes, eyes engulfed in sadness.

"These look so good," she said, making an effort to sound animated.

"Here we have a lychee jelly parfait with chia seeds, raw cream, and tapioca pearls," I said, slowly turning the plate. "This one here, an improved version of the bittersweet chocolate biscuit you tried in the summer."

"And these?" She grabbed one of the cookies.

"Oh. That's a new addition I'm planning for the fall."

"They are delicious." She bit into one of them. "Sage and chocolate?"

"Yes. Sage, bittersweet chocolate, and orange peels."

"What a great combination. I can taste the orange now, it balances the chocolate quite nicely," she said, sucking her cheeks.

"I want them to be part of the fall menu. But it won't be an easy sell. Chef hates simple stuff."

"Well, I love them." Her gaze was constantly shifting, as if keeping her eyes still would reveal the source of her pain. "Do you know my favorite?" Not allowing me time to answer, she said: "The marigold ice cream. I was elated to see it on the menu."

She took another bite as if performing the act of eating a cookie.

"I hope you don't mind me saying this, but you don't look well."

She glanced at me glassy-eyed and said nothing. The silence amplified the sound of silverware scratching the plates and the coffee machine whistling like a train about to depart.

"I'm ill."

While I searched for words, Patricia motioned to the waiter, signing in the air with an imaginary pen.

"What's wrong?"

She acted as if she hadn't heard me. I asked a second time, and she acknowledged my question with a gloomy smile. The bandana covering her head yelled cancer, the word so deafening I couldn't think of anything else.

"Please don't tell Jacobo I came. I'm exhausted. Can we meet on Thursday? I can explain then," she said in a low tone, pain in every word.

"Yes, of course. And no, I won't tell him."

We exchanged phone numbers and said goodbye. Neither of us knew what else to say. Or if we would ever meet again.

When I returned to the kitchen, the sound of machines spitting orders was fading out. The calm that usually followed a frantic lunch shift was heavier than usual. My thoughts were racing.

Inspecting the plates from food critics after they have finished eating is common among chefs. It can suggest the general direction of a review, especially if the food has been barely touched. But when I saw Matías at the pass examining Patricia's plate, I realized that his obsession was on a different level. My stomach was upside down. Jacobo and I were supposed to have a Skype conversation later that night, and as I cleaned my work area and prepped some desserts for the dinner shift, I looked for an excuse to cancel our chat.

I told my assistant I had a doctor's appointment and managed to leave the restaurant without bumping into Chef. It was strange not to feel I had to be the employee with the strongest work ethic, which up until then had defined my career. I had wasted too many years living with the fear of being deported, believing that, if I became an exemplary employee and one of the best pastry chefs in America, life would work itself out. That belief was now gone.

I walked back to my neighborhood with the excitement of keeping an important secret and the anxiety of someone who has lied and fears getting caught. The more I tried to find a pretext to avoid our conversation, the less capable I felt of hiding the truth from Jacobo. When I arrived at my apartment, I began mopping the floors compulsively, finding comfort in the mindless task. After I finished a second pass, the strong smell from the cleaner became so unbearable I had to open the doors of the balcony. The potent odor of grilled sardines and a light gray smoke flooded the living room. Thinking about which of the two smells was less disgusting, I heard the sound of a Skype call.

I let it ring, changed into a shirt with no bleach stains, and fixed my hair. After a short silence, the computer started beeping again. I pressed the green button and the screen filled with Jacobo's face. There was something familiar about the background, though in those first moments I was unable to determine what it was. A leg momentarily covered the camera and turned my screen a dazed blue. When the image stabilized, Chus was sitting next to Jacobo.

I was so taken aback that I opened my mouth and stayed completely still, faking a frozen image. I clicked on the red button and made them disappear. Paralyzed, I stared at the white orchid background on my computer and then paced around the apartment sweating profusely, listening to the beeping coming through the tiny speakers. After calming down, I called back. This time only Jacobo was on the screen.

"Hi. Are you at Chus's?"

Jacobo moved the camera back to its original position, and Chus entered the frame again. "Yes! Surprise! Can you see us?" Jacobo waved his arm as if I were across the street.

"Yes, yes, I can. Hi!" I yelled.

"How are you?" both said in unison.

"Okay." Too many words rushed into my mind, turning my thoughts into a mesh of disjointed half-formed sentences. Unable to articulate anything, I smiled.

Chus was on the brink of tears. He got emotional easily, no matter where he was or who happened to be around. It was known among the students that several times during the semester, reading a poem, he would have to stop halfway through to compose himself in front of the class. I remembered him sobbing inconsolably at the theater when he took me to see *Good Will Hunting*. Now I regretted finding his sentimentality embarrassing.

Trying to cover my initial shock, I yelled: "How are you?"

"We're good," Jacobo said. "We're very good."

"We just got back from grocery shopping. Tomorrow we're going to see a movie in Bryant Park." Jacobo pointed the camera to a tote bag, the neck of a wine bottle peeking out, the picnic blanket Chus and I used to lie on during long afternoons at the West Side Pier rolled up next to it. "They're playing *Casablanca*. Isn't that cool?"

Knowing how hard it was for Chus to leave the house, I was happy to see them bonding.

"By the way, I've installed Skype on your uncle's computer.

Let me add you to his contact list so you guys can talk later."
Jacobo passed his laptop to Chus, who held it as if it were a
newborn.

"Hi." I was happy to be sharing the screen only with him.
His hair, at least on the screen, appeared whiter and thicker
than I remembered it. His skin was sun-kissed. He looked
healthy.

"Hi, dear. I love seeing your face. You look wonderful."

"Have you been spending time outside?" I asked, even
though it was clear he had.

"Yes. I've been going to the pier again." He then went silent
and with his lips said: "He's so cute!"

I was distracted by the sound of a friend request.

"Ortegaygasset49?" I cracked up.

"Yes!" Jacobo yelled from what I assumed to be my old bedroom, where our ancient desktop computer had been sitting for
years under a thick layer of dust. The thought of Jacobo's seeing
the ramshackle twin bed I had slept in as a kid and that I had
grown up showering in the kitchen made me feel embarrassed.

"Very scholarly," I said.

"Well, Jacobo insisted on Gasset_hunk, but I decided
against it," he said, showing teeth.

THAT NIGHT I drank myself to sleep. I was jealous to see them
spending time together, even though it had been me who had
urged them to meet. I imagined Chus introducing him to the
New York he still cherished, walking around the neo-Gothic
City College campus on Convent Avenue where he had taught
for years, enjoying sugary baklava at the Hungarian Pastry
Shop in Morningside Heights. I could see them at the secret

bookstore on the Upper East Side that Chus still frequented every month to meet friends and visiting scholars. I could see Jacobo wanting to stay.

I woke up in the middle of the night with a sense of guilt and anxiety. I felt ashamed for having slept with Triana and couldn't help but wonder if I was trying to prove to myself I could be more uninhibited. I tried going back to sleep but every sound in the night echoed in my head. When the first light appeared, I became absorbed looking at the photos still on the wall.

After searching for the fountain pen that Ben gave me for my fourteenth birthday, I decided to write Chus a letter. As I relived the most meaningful events since my arrival in Madrid, they piled up on the page. I realized how lucky I was. The image of Patricia signing in the air asking for the check kept popping into my head. While I was distracted, the fountain pen resting on the white paper made dark blue ink smudges that looked like planets around a constellation of words.

Plaza Mayor was always crowded. I took a small detour as I walked to the restaurant and found myself in front of the Chocolatería de San Ginés, its tables full of locals fighting the wind with their newspapers and tourists studying their guides. I fantasized about working at the chocolatería, spending my days frying churros instead of stressing over complicated creations, and taking my breaks sitting in the square, looking at people go by.

As I lingered near the entrance, the old waiter whom I had ordered hot chocolates from months ago appeared at the door and acknowledged my presence with a smile. I nodded at him, and as he leaned over a table to serve a dozen churros, his back toward me, I snapped a photo with my phone. The image also

included a lady with her gaze lost in space and pigeons peck-
ing crumbs around her feet. It wasn't a good picture, but good
enough for Jacobo to remember our first night out.

The moment I stepped into the restaurant, I knew something
was off. None of the washers I crossed paths with made eye
contact with me. My assistant was nowhere to be found, and
given the frantic ways people moved, Chef was either arriving
soon or already there and in a bad mood. I wished I had the day
off so I could lie on the grass at the Templo de Debod, looking
at planes flying over Madrid.

"Do you have a minute?" Emilio said, motioning me to the
loading dock where he smoked his morning cigarette. The
main reason he talked to me, I realized now, was because he
had lived in London and enjoyed showing off his English.

We walked outside in silence. I could hear Amir scrubbing
the large stockpot that was used to make the family meal, farther
away the rhythmic sound of a broom. I closed my eyes briefly
and let these familiar sounds merge in my head. I enjoyed the
mornings in the kitchen when everything was quiet, unrushed,
when I could be immersed in my own thoughts, planning the
day ahead, a time I didn't need to be around others.

I looked at Emilio, but he kept gazing away. His face was
serious. He pulled out a Zippo with a Harley-Davidson logo
embossed on it and flicked the lighter on his jeans, a ridiculous
gesture he had probably learned from an American movie. I
leaned on the handrail so the sun would hit my face.

"I want to give you a heads-up," he said, and then took a
short drag. "Chef found out you served some cookies that
weren't on the menu. He was furious." He tapped the cigarette
as tiny ashes leisurely made their way to the floor. "Is it true?
You don't strike me as someone who would do that."

"Yeah." I knew the gravity of what I had done. Cooks were fired for less than that.

Emilio lifted his eyebrows.

"To be honest, and I know this sounds silly, I wasn't thinking."

Emilio didn't respond. He took a long drag from his cigarette and exhaled through his nose. I would have never imagined I could turn into that person, an employee whom a chef had a right to fire.

"I don't know how things work in New York," he said after a dramatic silence. "You can't do that kind of shit here."

At this point it was clear that Emilio had despised me from the very first day, maybe because he had sensed my lack of interest in becoming part of the kitchen family. Except for Amir, the only person I had befriended despite our rudimentary communication skills, I seldom talked to anyone.

"Good luck with Chef, man. You're going to need it." He looked at me with contempt and, wetting his fingers, put out his cigarette before walking back into the kitchen.

I remained there with my eyes closed and thought about the money I had in my bank account, enough to survive for the next four months. I pulled out my phone, hoping to find a message from Jacobo, and looked at the clock on my screen, still set to Eastern Standard Time. It was 4:15 a.m.

AT FAMILY MEAL, the gesture of Patricia's signing in the air played in my head at odd moments. I ate without lifting my eyes from the plate. The only time I looked up, I caught Emilio staring at me. In the afternoon the kitchen got hit hard. Every table seemed to be ordering the sea bass and the roasted duck, the two dishes that took the longest time to cook, slowing the kitchen flow. José Luis, the other sous-chef, whose pale face and red eyes betrayed his partying hard the night before, was getting sloppy. Halfway through the second shift, his station was a complete mess. As Chef stood at the pass inspecting plates heading to a VIP table, José Luis ran to the bathroom. By then, it was clear he was unable to keep up. A line cook had to take over and throw away two roasted ducks that had dried out.

Chef was enraged, but he managed to send José Luis home without adding more stress to the stations, now working at double the speed to compensate. The kitchen was dangerously behind. I helped the chef garde manger prepare some complimentary small appetizers that would alleviate the pressure on the grill, a gesture Chef appreciated. For a couple of hours, I forgot all the things that occupied my mind, and when we finally made it through the shift, everyone in the kitchen was exhausted, including Chef, who, after paying everyone double that night, locked himself in the office with a bottle of Calvados.

Heading downstairs to change, I checked my phone. Twenty-three missed calls. As I scrolled down, I saw most of them had been placed within five minutes. The idea of Jacobo's finding out about his mother made me feel queasy. Still buttoning my pants, I climbed the stairs with wobbly legs and rushed out of the restaurant as I heard Chef calling my name.

18

We talked on Skype through most of the night. Even though Chus had given Jacobo a sleeping pill, he couldn't stop crying. As the medication took effect, he began slurring his words, and his speech became less frantic. I wished I could have been next to him, but all I was able to do was provide him with words that he didn't seem to fully process and long stretches of silence. He made me promise to leave my camera on and stay awake until the pill knocked him out. When his eyes finally closed and his breathing became rhythmic and deep, I lay down next to my computer and watched his puffy face deflate into sleep.

Patricia's cancer had metastasized to her liver and beyond. She had been given no hope and four weeks to make final arrangements. I could not understand how the same doctors who had not been able to find the disease for years while it had lingered in her body would dare say how much life she had left. The cancer had spread throughout her vital organs and was slowly shutting her down. She had been taken to the hospital and most likely would not return home. I considered telling Jacobo about our encounter at the restaurant, but now it seemed irrelevant. I wondered whether his father would still be icy and distant, exuding superiority.

THE FOLLOWING MORNING, as I walked through Lavapiés on my way to work, the streets appeared to be noisier, filthier, the whole city layered with pestilent grime. I was prepared to face Chef, the possibility of getting fired becoming less frightening overnight. Death, I remembered from when my mother passed, had the otherworldly ability to reorganize the world around you.

The kitchen was hit hard again. Chef came in late and seemed to be in good spirits. After the second shift was over, he called me into his office. As I walked downstairs, I thought of Jacobo flying over the Atlantic, how much I had wanted him to return earlier and how sometimes life gives you what you want but never the version you have in your head.

When I knocked on the open door, Chef was busy with paperwork.

"Is everything okay?"

"Yes, all good," I said, playing dumb. "Why do you ask?"

He looked concerned and gestured toward a chair. "Take a seat. I've been wanting to talk to you. I was shocked that the other day you served some chocolate cookies that are not on the menu. That's a fireable offense." He paused to assess my reaction, but I gave no indication of my thoughts. I only nodded to signal I was listening. "You know I'm very happy with your performance, and I have to admit the cookies are excellent." He paused and seemed to be wondering if his words were having an impact.

"I want to give you more of a spotlight. I've discussed it

with the partners and we're thinking about doing a PR push to announce you taking over as pastry chef. We want your name to be on the menu, next to mine."

I looked around the office. A water stain on the wall reminded me of the southern tip of Portugal as I saw it from the plane when we approached the peninsula.

"So? What do you think?" His eyes narrowed.

"I appreciate your trust, Chef. But I need to think about it," I said a little too fast.

Chef was surprised. We both were. It suddenly dawned on me that I had not traveled thousands of miles, leaving my family behind, to live the same life I had in New York.

"I haven't been honest with you, Chef. I'm going through a rough time."

His eyes widened.

"One of my best friends has cancer. The doctors said she won't make it through the end of the month. It's not that I don't appreciate the offer, Chef. I do. I'm just unable to think straight right now." I hated myself for using Patricia as a shield.

"I'm sorry, Demetrio. You should've told me. You don't need to give an answer now. Take a couple of days off. Let's talk when you are back."

"Thanks, Chef."

We stood up and shook hands.

I returned to my station. The epiphany I had just had was both exhilarating and overwhelming. To calm down, I decided to make piruletas for Jacobo's sister with some leftover cake. After shaping the cake crumbs into small balls and as I waited for the chocolate to harden, I thought about the absurdity of using a cake pop to comfort a child who was about to lose her mother. When they were done, I put some in a plastic container for Matías's daughter and wrote him a thank-you note.

As the first orders were being called in, I left the restaurant through the service door. Out on the loading dock, I looked back at the cooks readying for the first shift as the sun hit my face. I stepped out onto the street. Amir was sitting on the sidewalk rolling a cigarette.

"Hi, Chef. Are you leaving?"

"Yes."

"Are you coming back?"

"You mean am I *ever* coming back?"

"Yes. Are you leaving us?"

"Why do you ask?"

"You're not happy here. I can tell."

He stepped closer to me and put his hand up as if it were a visor. Even after he had spent some nights sleeping on my sofa, we had not exchanged phone numbers. I took a pen out of my bag and wrote mine down.

"Here." I gave him the piece of paper.

He folded it multiple times until it became a tiny speck of white.

"Fi Aman Allah." He brought his right fist to his heart and knocked it twice.

"Fi Aman Allah." I repeated the words back to him without knowing what they meant.

JACOBO'S PLANE LANDED at 6:09 a.m., six minutes ahead of schedule. By the time I read his text message, he was already on his way to the hospital. I had to fight the urge to call him, knowing he was sitting next to his father in the car. I wanted to hear his voice, say I loved him. Instead, I texted back saying I was around if he needed me.

I had been in Madrid for more than three months and ventured out mostly through the same streets. Despite my long walks throughout the city, there were many areas that remained unexplored. Growing up in a city with a meticulous grid, where I had mostly moved in linear patterns, I was captivated by curves and winding streets whose unexpected paths never ceased to surprise me. I enjoyed discovering watchmakers, tailors, and tanners who had had the same address for centuries, whose storefronts glowed with a golden and lustrous patina, and knowing that the run-down shops weren't turning into hideous condos any time soon.

I spent the day thinking about my mother. I remembered her vaguely, as if she were part of a dream. In what seemed like a vivid memory, she was sitting on a rocking chair by a window, a white curtain blowing in the breeze, the sunlight streaming in. After running down a long corridor, I jumped on her lap. "¿Quién es este hombrecito?" she said, not recognizing me. I ran back toward Chus, who was by then entering the room. Hiding behind him, I peered at her from in between his legs as if they were iron bars of a cell. This memory, Chus assured me, could not have been possible, as he had fled Spain before I was born.

The last time we saw each other I was eight, but we talked on the phone almost every Sunday until she passed away eight years later. Chus lied about the cause of her death and convinced me that losing a parent at a young age would in fact make me stronger and give me a deep understanding of existence early on. For a while, I didn't forgive him for not having allowed me to mourn her the way I should have, but then I accepted that parenthood had come to him by accident.

As night fell, not yet having heard from Jacobo, I headed northwest and took Princesa, a regal, tree-lined street with wide, clean sidewalks. I stopped at every big intersection to follow my path on the dilapidated map, its sections now held together with clear tape. The hospital sat on the western edge of the city, near a roundabout where the traffic coming from three wide avenues merged into a circle. Made of concrete and massive, the main building looked like a mausoleum, a blue, lit cross crowning its top, and next to it, a small chapel with its own cross, not blue, nor lit.

I sat on a bench across the street and observed the ambulances going in and out of the emergency entrance with muted sirens, their urgent yellow lights becoming less so in the silence. Only when they were two hundred feet away or so did the sound come on, and by then, I could only hear them faintly, like voices in a dream. I waited until the twilight began engulfing the hospital, its glass windows progressively becoming prominent squares of white, pale, fluorescent light that turned the façade into a grid.

At least in the States, the hospital windows were locked. I knew that from St. Vincent's. I assumed that Spain would be the same, so when at around ten-thirty, a woman wearing an oversized blue hospital gown opened a window and climbed onto the ledge of the building, I wondered if I was imagining it. I held my breath and repeated to myself: Don't jump, don't jump. Please, don't jump. A momentary breeze picked up and the lower part of her gown began flapping like a flag. I counted the rows of windows down to the ground floor and tried to visualize the emergency number stuck on my fridge door, but I was too nervous to recall the right combination of ones and twos. I tried dialing 211 with no luck. After what seemed to be an endless moment, the woman began walking back. With my eyes fixed on her, I was unable to move until she entered the building again. Then the light in her room went off and my heartbeat gradually returned to its normal pace.

I considered texting Jacobo one more time, but I didn't want to stress him out. After an hour looking at the façade and ensuring that the woman hadn't changed her mind, I slowly made my way back home. Feeling exhausted, I couldn't stop thinking about her. I imagined her frail body inside a mesh of blue fabric, free-falling to the deadly dark gray asphalt of the parking lot. Was she back on the ledge of the building contemplating jumping? Had she reconsidered her options? Would Patricia be capable of committing suicide? Would I?

Before making a left turn and leaving the avenue to enter the winding streets of Malasaña, I looked back to the hospital. Far away now, the blue cross shined in the darkness, like a lighthouse for the sick.

THE NEXT MORNING, even before making my espresso, I rushed to the newsstand. Sharing a bench with a flock of pigeons, I inspected the metro section of the paper looking for news about a suicide and found nothing. I walked back to the apartment, opening and closing several times the last message I had sent to Jacobo, making sure it had gone through.

I took a long shower and shaved my stubble. I laid the button-down shirt I had worn to dinner the day of my arrival on the kitchen counter and lost track of time pushing the steaming iron against different planes of wrinkled cotton. When all the lines had disappeared, I put it on a hanger to cool off, opened the window and became engrossed looking at the fabric moving in the breeze. Then I texted Jacobo I was on my way.

The expansive hospital lobby reminded me of an airport concourse. Instead of moving in decisive patterns, people wandered around without a clear destination, waiting for news or gathering momentum to enter the elevators. I spent ten minutes in a stand next to the reception inspecting flowers that looked so lifeless they couldn't possibly lift anyone's spirits. I decided to walk around the block in case there was a flower shop nearby. Behind the hospital, a woman selling cheerful sunflowers on the sidewalk suggested I sprinkle them with holy water before giving them to my friend, the petals were the same color as Patricia's marigolds.

Back at the hospital, I asked for Patricia's room number at the information desk, which they politely refused to give me since I was not part of the family. Wandering around the elevators, I noticed a sign with two praying hands. I had never been a believer, but instead of randomly looking for Jacobo, I headed to the chapel, whose stained-glass windows I had stared at the night before. I pushed the door open and a gust of wind made the flames of the candles near the altar tremble. The space wasn't big, but the vaulted ceiling and low light gave it an expansive feeling. Below a massive bust of Jesus, a young girl with long blond curls was kneeling in prayer, her palms glued together.

I walked down the aisle, taking small steps, trying not to interrupt the conversations people were having with God. Sitting in the middle of a bench, I placed the bouquet on my lap and the cellophane made a loud noise. I started reciting an Ave Maria in a low voice and was surprised that I remembered most of the words.

The flickering flames betrayed the door opening. I stayed still, looking at the bright red wounds Jesus had on his forehead. The low light gave his face a sinister quality that brought back a long-ago memory. I was in a city—it had to be Seville—at a procession for Holy Week. Losing my grip on my mother's hand, I got swept up in a sea of people wearing white tunics and pointed hoods. As I began to experience the echoes of that horror, someone stopped near the bench; the wood, bending slightly, made a faint crack. Then I felt a leg touching my leg.

I kept my gaze straight ahead as Jacobo put his hand on my lap. Jesus was staring at us. I turned my head and saw his face unshaven, swollen, distorted with pain. The dark pouches under his eyes made them look even greener. He leaned his head on my shoulder. I hung my arm around his neck. His body felt bonier, emptier. The collar of my shirt was instantly dampened by tears. As he cried silently, the absence of sound made his pain seem even more profound. I held him tight. He put his other hand on my hip. I counted the number of thorns on the crown, but no matter how hard I tried to distract myself, I couldn't avoid getting aroused.

We stayed still for a long time. The wax falling from the candles formed a white mountain range on the floor, its peaks constantly morphing. At some point the little girl kneeling on the floor began sobbing. It was Estrella. Jacobo stood up, adjusted himself through the pocket of his jeans, and walked to the altar. I watched him calm her down and listened to their muffled voices, unable to understand their words. When she stopped crying, they walked toward me. I said hi but she didn't respond. Instead, she grabbed my hand and the three of us got out of the chapel together.

Out in the lobby, doctors walked through the corridors with firm steps and calm faces, faces they had probably rehearsed in front of mirrors to disguise the true meaning of their words. Visitors, on the contrary, floated aimlessly.

"Do you mind staying with Estrella while I look for my dad?"

"Yeah, of course."

"Do you like cake pops?" I asked her, tightening my hand around her tiny palm, instantly regretting my childish tone.

"Everyone does." She dried her tears with the hem of her dress.

I fished the Tupperware out of my bag and offered her one.

"Did you make them?"

"Yes. Just for you."

She didn't immediately react to my words.

"Thank you." Her voice sounded lighter.

We walked up to a row of plastic chairs screwed to the floor. Estrella sat on my lap facing me. Behind her, I could see Jacobo in the hallway talking to his father, who was dressed in a dark Wall Street suit.

"Does your mother live in New York?"

I opened the container, grabbed a cake pop for myself, and faked having difficulty unwrapping it. "They came out pretty good."

"Does she?" Estrella asked, looking intently at me.

"No, she doesn't live in New York," I finally said. "But my uncle does. His name is Chus."

Jacobo and his father entered the waiting area, their solemn faces betraying the severity of the conversation they had just had. They looked defeated.

"Mom says I've been to New York, but I was very young so I don't remember it." She bit the cake pop, a small piece falling on my lap.

I waved at them. If Jacobo's father was surprised to see me there, he didn't act like it.

"Hello, Demetrio."

"Hello, sir." I put Estrella on the floor and stood up.

"Thanks for coming." He shook my hand. "We really appreciate it."

"I'm so sorry," I said, and felt awkward about how trite my words sounded.

He gazed at me, confused, as if his eyes suddenly needed lenses to see me clearly.

There was a long pause.

"Thanks." A sad smile revealed the shadow of a young boy who resembled Jacobo. "We should go," his father said.

I couldn't tell to whom he was directing his words.

"Time to take a bath and go to bed." This time, he looked at Estrella.

She held my hand tighter and was suddenly on the verge of tears. Jacobo crouched down, whispered something into her ear, grabbed one of the sunflowers from the bouquet, and gave it to her. She gazed at the flower, uninterested. Alfonso lifted her up and she put her arms around his neck. We said good night. As he headed to the entrance, Estrella rested her face on his shoulder and looked back at us, my heart breaking into a million pieces.

We walked back to the chairs and sat down.

"How are you feeling?" I said, fighting away my tears.

Jacobo looked at the floor.

"I don't think I can handle this." His voice was trembling.

"Let's go for a walk." I grabbed his elbow.

"Okay, but we should stop by the room and leave the flowers first. Mom is awake. She'll be happy to see you."

He reached for my hand. I wasn't able to hear the sentences he pronounced next, as if the words, latching on to his vocal cords, refused to leave his body.

"Sorry, Jake. What?"

"My dad just told me that they're going to put her on a morphine drip to alleviate the pain. The doctor said that these might be the last hours before she becomes—"

The end of the sentence was drowned out by sobbing. I hugged him tight while he tried to speak, though no words came out. Strangers passing by looked at us, their gazes offering solace, knowing they could soon be us. Night was rapidly approaching, and some visitors were readying to leave while others arrived with overnight bags and pillows under their arms. Holding his waist, I guided Jacobo to the elevator. As we reached the tenth floor, my legs began to shake. I feared he would notice how scared I was. We took small steps, the hallways growing longer, his face more somber as we approached the room.

"Do you want to go in alone first?" I hoped he would say yes.

Jacobo nodded, opened the door, and disappeared into a light humming of machines. I leaned my back on the wall and slid down until I reached the floor. A group of nurses walked by. One of them was talking passionately, urging everyone to vote in future elections. Her favorite candidate was Zapatero because he was sexy and tall, she said, two qualities necessary in a president. She reminded them of their obligation as citizens to exercise their right, even if it meant casting a blank vote. The words came by fleetingly, but I held on to them in a loop, so other thoughts couldn't enter my mind.

Sitting on the cold floor, I couldn't avoid thinking about the days that followed my mom's passing, the long walks along the Hudson. Chus's silences. Thinking about my mother brought back the days spent at St. Vincent's, the days when there was nothing else to do but wait for Ben's last breath. I remembered the long nights curled up in beds where people had recently died and sitting on lonely benches next to visitors whose faces I couldn't quite recognize entirely, but whom I had seen around in the city or during our summers on Fire Island.

Jacobo came out of the room.

"She seems to be in horrible pain. I'm going to grab the nurse. She wants to see you."

He pushed the door open, and I had no other option but to enter. In the small reception area there were two armchairs, a half fridge, and a coffee table covered with interior design magazines. I spotted Jacobo's duffel bag on the floor and realized he hadn't been home yet.

The room was lit by a dull light. Patricia was lying down with her eyes closed, her forearms perforated with IV needles. I laid the bouquet quietly near a silk robe folded on the bed next to her. She looked transparent, as if a significant part of her had already departed.

"Hello," I whispered.

Looking out into the darkness of the parking lot, I saw the bench where I had sat the night before.

"Hello, Patricia," I said.

She opened her eyes, looked at me, and began to mumble unintelligibly, her fingers moving as if they were playing an invisible piano. I was afraid to touch her. But I managed to move closer and carefully hold her hand.

"Jacobo just went to look for the nurse."

The mumbling continued. She was trying to say something and made a gesture that indicated wanting to sit up. I propped a couple of pillows behind her back. Holding on to my arm, she struggled to pull herself up.

"Hello, darling," she finally said, some color returning to her face.

She moved her hand to touch mine but the IV pulled her arm back. I leaned closer to her. "How are you feeling?"

"Quite dreadful."

"I brought you something," I said, grabbing the Tupperware from my bag, grateful for an action to perform. I put it on the night table next to an army of vials. "They're strawberry cake pops. I'll leave them here in case you decide to have a pajama party in the middle of the night." I smiled.

"Did the cookies make it onto the menu?"

"They did. Chef talked to his business partners, and they want to put my name on the menu."

There was a subtle tightness in my stomach when I talked to her. I could feel the words leaving my body and then a strange hollowness. I waited for her reaction with great anticipation, and didn't understand where this maternal illusion came from, but every time we interacted, I experienced a childish desire to be liked.

"That's wonderful."

"Yeah, I guess so."

A strange quality in the air, a lack of smell, reminded me of a place I could not fully remember. Was it St. Vincent's? Where else had I breathed this odorless, cold air?

"Maybe I say this because I never quite had to do anything I didn't want to do, or because I'm ill and about to die," she said, linking her fingers with mine. "But life's too short to do something you don't want to do, my darling boy."

It was hard to believe that, as sick as Patricia was, she had perceived my lack of excitement.

"It's not that I don't like baking anymore, I do. It's weird but I used to love spending twelve hours a day locked in a room away from the world, and now it makes me depressed."

Another long silence. The electric humming of the machines attached to her made it clear that this could be our last conversation.

"There's nothing strange about wanting to experience the world fully. Don't forget why you left the United States."

"I know."

"Remember: You now have a responsibility not only to yourself but to your uncle, the responsibility to build a better life," she said, and then struggled to take a breath. "Life is now."

The words, encouraging and charged with hope, sounded like a farewell. I excused myself to go to the bathroom, and turning on the faucet, I drowned out the sound of my sobbing in the running water.

19

If he doesn't come in the car with us, I won't go," Jacobo yelled in the bedroom.

I heard his shattered voice while leaning over the sink, where I had been rubbing my hands on a towel long after they were dry. I walked back into the room as he was frowning and moving his head from side to side. Without saying goodbye, he threw the phone on the bed.

"I don't know who the fuck he thinks he is."

"Your dad."

Infuriated, Jacobo walked to the balcony. He began wailing. I went up to him and put my arm around his shoulders.

"I'm sorry, Jake. Remember he's also going through a very tough time."

The world outside the walls of the apartment hadn't taken notice that Patricia had slipped away during the night. On the street below, two men were battling with their horns for a parking spot until one of the drivers finally got out of the car, enraged. I pulled Jacobo in and closed the doors.

"You should try and get some sleep."

He walked up to the bookcase and grabbed a photo album. We sat down on the bed and started flipping through it. Almost all the photos were of Jacobo celebrating birthdays, graduations, and other moments that had been deemed worth capturing forever. Even as a preteen, when most kids, certainly me, went through an awkward period of pimples and metal braces and slightly disproportionate bodies, he looked handsome despite the boy-band spiky hair and baggy jeans that made him appear even lankier. Most of these moments had taken place in a house facing the ocean that I assumed was in Mallorca. There were other people around, but almost always Jacobo and Patricia appeared next to each other, inseparable. By the time we finished going through the album, I got the impression that Jacobo's life had been one endless summer.

Staying awake was a form of penance he was inflicting on himself. When he could no longer keep his eyes open and crashed, I stayed still, waiting, imagining everything that was to follow, the last look at a body no longer breathing, the hollow words full of good intentions. I wanted to be here when he woke up to the crude realization that no one could ever fill the void a mother leaves. I wanted to let him know that I was here. That I was here to stay.

ALFONSO HAD LEFT to make arrangements for the burial and Estrella was with her aunt, the house shrouded in darkness. I went into the living room and sat in front of a portrait of a young Patricia I hadn't noticed before. I looked around the room and saw her everywhere, in the curtains, in the chairs, in the sculptural objects carefully placed on the low marble table like planets orbiting a sun that no longer shined.

I heard distant steps and imagined Patricia coming through the door. For a moment, feeling like a trespasser, I considered occupying myself with a task. Gabriela walked ghostlike into the living room and placed a clean glass ashtray on the table. She wasn't dressed in her usual uniform but in a black dress that reminded me of the old woman who swept the stairs of my building.

"Hola, Gabriela," I said in a voice that fit the quietness of the room.

"¡Ay, Dios santo!" Gabriela brought her hand to her chest as if to prevent her heart from escaping.

"I'm sorry."

With the windows shut and the curtains drawn, Gabriela kept the world away. She held on to the arms of a cream-colored chair and sat slowly, as if testing whether it would support her weight.

"Did Jacobo take a sleeping pill?" she asked.

This moment could only exist in Patricia's absence, the effects of her death pushing us to behave in ways we couldn't have imagined, the literal disappearance of her body rearranging our places in the world.

"He didn't. But he finally crashed."

"How is he?"

"Broken."

Gabriela was calm, though her eyes were veiny, red, and swollen. I stood and walked up to her. Kneeling down, I grabbed her thick wrist and looked at the face of a tiny silver watch lost in the creases of her skin.

"How are you feeling?" I asked.

The question caught her unprepared. For a moment, she was unable to speak.

"I always liked la señora. After Jacobo left for America, the house was never the same. She spent too much time alone. El señor was always away. We became very close. Sometimes she would even ask me to have dinner with her at the table." She fixed her gaze on one of the dining chairs and seemed to be traveling back in time. "I've been working in this house for twenty years but now that she's gone, I don't know that I can stay."

Gabriela got distracted by the dust that had accumulated on the base of a bronze figurine, a lady holding an open umbrella.

"She was very good to me and to my family." She wiped the bronze with her sleeve. "Do you know if Jacobo is staying? Or is he going back to America?"

I said it was too early to know and that the family needed her now more than ever, that she should be strong for them. I was disgusted at myself for acting the way I did, for treating her like an employee and making her feel she had a moral obligation to them.

A short metallic squeal cut through the silence. Gabriela and I looked at each other without saying a word. I thought it was a hallucination, but then I heard another scream. Gabriela covered her mouth with her hands. I stood up and ran to the bedroom.

THE DAY OF the funeral, after waking up in Jacobo's bed, I pulled down the sheets of the bed in my old bedroom to make it look as if I had slept in it. I didn't want to add more tension between Jacobo and his father, who seemed to be slightly softening toward me. The few times we had talked, he had listened carefully, paying close attention to what I was saying, then asking questions for me to expand on. Whether the interest was genuine or not, I couldn't tell. We had spent the night with Alfonso's brothers drinking wine older than me. Nobody seemed to question the friend from the States, though I'm sure much had been suspected. In the time that we spent gathered around the table where I had met Patricia for the first time, her name was never mentioned. Alfonso seemed to be more preoccupied with the menu for the reception that was to follow the funeral than with how his nine-year-old daughter was coping with the loss of her mother.

I had attended mass twice in my life and both times left feeling like an impostor. I was nervous about attending the funeral because I worried people would be looking at my church protocol. Jacobo's extended family and his boarding school friends were traveling in from all parts of Europe. After Alfonso finally agreed that I could go with them, Jacobo insisted on driving in separate cars.

We left the house and followed them in the Mercedes, its mats still full of sand and memories. Every time the soles of my shoes made a scratching sound, I thought about hiking to the cove, the summer seeming more distant than it actually was. Estrella spent most of the time looking back and making faces through the rear window, and I tried not to get distracted and do my best to switch gears smoothly and keep the right distance so other cars wouldn't get between us. A couple of times, I forgot to step on the clutch pedal, and the roaring sound coming through the shifter made Jacobo wince.

"Sorry. I'm clearly not great at this."

"As long as we don't crash, we're good."

He had taken a pill, and the words coming out of his mouth were eerie and removed, their lack of emotion making every piece of information sound factual, irreversible. I knew it was the medication, but even so, I couldn't stop wondering if his iciness and detachment toward me indicated how he actually felt and wasn't a behavior engineered by people in white lab coats.

The traffic was heavy. By the time we arrived at the church, the parking lot looked like a luxury car dealership. I instantly felt out of place. We drove around to the back and parked next to a sign that read *Family of the deceased.* Before we even opened the door, the car was engulfed by a wave of dark suits and black dresses. Jacobo was slowly pulled away from me. I observed him at a distance shaking hands, kissing and hugging, and though he had sunglasses on, I knew he was fighting back tears.

I stood by the car, not knowing what to do. I worried that the cheap black suit I had bought at Zara would make people think I was Jacobo's driver.

"You clean up well."

I turned around. Triana was standing behind me, in a short black dress.

"Can you believe it? I saw her not long ago at a fundraiser for the school. She looked fine." Triana walked up to me, then started to cry.

As we hugged, the faint smell of marijuana in her hair brought back images of our sex. What had I been thinking? I was now terrified that Jacobo could find out.

"It's unbelievable how fast it happened," I said when her sobbing subsided, gently lifting her head from my shoulder. "We need to be strong for Jacobo." Once again, I felt strange ordering people how to feel.

"Did you tell him about us?"

I gasped for air, noticing the cheap fabric of my suit trapping the heat under my armpits. "Tell him about us? No?" I walked away, my heart racing as if instead of taking small steps, I was running for my life.

Gabriela and Federico stood side by side. Only now, seeing them without their uniforms, I realized they were husband and wife. I waved at them, but only Gabriela waved back. The crowd outside was slowly clearing as most people had already entered the church. Jacobo was by the entrance surrounded by a group of boys and girls our age. I figured it was a mix of friends and cousins. I recognized some of the guys from our first night out and the party at his house.

"How are you doing?" I said.

"Don't leave me. Don't leave again," Jacobo whispered into my ear. He pulled his sunglasses up so I could see his eyes full of tears. "Don't you ever."

We hugged. I pushed my hand into his curls and massaged his head slightly.

"You better stop," he said, smiling complicitly for the first time in days.

"I'm sorry. I didn't mean to," I said, embarrassed.

We entered the church and Jacobo put his arm around my neck as if for support. It coincided with the first sounds of an organ. The choir began singing the Ave Maria. We made our way to the front row, taking our time. Everyone looked at us. I thought about whether one day Jacobo and I could enter a church like this under other circumstances.

We stood next to his father. Estrella left his side and walked in between Jacobo and me. She grabbed our hands. When the music was over, the priest took the podium. We sat down and Estrella climbed onto my lap. Her father glanced at me, annoyed.

Patricia's brother went up to the pulpit. His British accent reminded me of her. I had met him the night before and from how he had talked to me, I had gotten the impression he knew exactly who I was. He was dressed in a tight black suit and had her same round face and vivid eyes. His hands were shaking. I expected he wouldn't be able to finish his eulogy. He focused on every word, making pauses to take deep breaths, like a swimmer who knows that only long, steady strokes can cut through turbulent waters. By the time he finished, Jacobo was shaking his leg, the photo of a young Patricia printed in the program, radiant and untouched by illness, now blurring with the sweat of his hands.

THE NEXT DAY, I was able to catch Chus before his class.

"It's so incredibly sad. And so fast!" Chus said, sitting in front of his computer. He looked healthy.

"I know. It's strange and kind of hard to explain, but Patricia and I had a strong connection," I said.

"Yeah, you mentioned that."

"From the very first day. It was as if we had known each other for a long time. Has that ever happened to you?"

"Yes, it has. That's how I felt when I first met Ben. How's Jacobo doing?"

"Devastated. He's been kind of distant, and I don't blame him. I understand the pain. It doesn't seem that long ago that I was finally able to get over the loss of Mamá. It's such a weird coincidence that we both lost our mothers so young. Don't you think?"

"Yes, I guess so."

"I don't know, I have a funny feeling about it, about us. I don't think he's really into me."

"Deme, stop. You're delusional. The guy can't get enough of you. He's obsessed, kept asking about how you grew up, what shows you liked, what kind of guys you were into. He even asked to see photos of you as a kid."

"I hope you didn't agree to that."

"Of course I did! You were adorable."

"Oh gosh, how embarrassing." I took a sip of water. "I don't know. Maybe it's the pills he's been taking that are making him look, I don't know, vacant?"

"The kid just lost his mom, Deme. What do you expect?"

"No, I know. I just really, really like him. On a different note, the dad's finally come around."

"Never trust those fascistas."

"Wait. He actually invited me to go to Mallorca with them, they have a house there. But I declined. I don't want to intrude."

"I'm glad you did. They need their space. Listen, I'm going to get ready for class. But keep me posted."

"I will. I love you."

"I love you too. And send Jacobo my love."

I SPENT THE NEXT couple of days drifting through the city worrying that Triana would say something and anxiously waiting for Jacobo to return my call. I convinced myself, or tried to, that his silence was a consequence of needing time. Or maybe he was with his family in the middle of the sea on the boat that I had seen in the photographs. One afternoon, kneeling in front of the washing machine, absentmindedly looking at the foam, I was brought back to reality by a short buzz. I walked to the bedroom to grab my cell phone, hoping to find a missed call from him, but instead there was a blocked caller ID on the screen. My first thought was that something had happened to Chus.

After reminding myself that he had looked healthy a couple of days back, I called my voicemail and listened to a message in a strange blend of American and British English. A voice that identified itself as a lawyer urged me to call back. I tried to remember the name of a British pro bono lawyer I had met at an after-hours on Avenue D and with whom I had exchanged phone numbers years ago.

Even though returning to the States was not a possibility, every now and then the thought entered my mind. Would I go back if I had the chance? Listening to the Arabian folk music playing faintly in the distance again, I looked at the plants that needed watering and the unpaid bills on the kitchen counter indicating this was slowly becoming my home. Unable to find an answer to what maybe was not a yes-or-no question, I dialed Jacobo once again. This time the call went straight to voicemail. I imagined him on the boat, lying on its prow stargazing, trying to get in touch with his mother. The night of her departure, Patricia had assured him that her soul would eternally exist floating in the cosmos, turned into positive energy, which I found both beautiful and heart-wrenching.

I waited anxiously for Jacobo's call all day, and at dinnertime, I couldn't restrain myself from dialing his house. The phone rang for a long time. Finally, Gabriela's voice came at the other end of the receiver. She sounded sleepy.

"Hi, Gabriela."

She didn't respond.

"Is Jacobo back?" I knew that they were not supposed to return for a couple of days. "It's Demetrio."

"Hi, Deme," she finally said. "No, they're not coming back until Sunday."

"They're still in Mallorca?"

"Yes. Jacobo called about an hour ago to give me their flight number, so Federico can pick them up at the airport."

Knowing that Jacobo was reachable and ignoring my calls, I experienced a sudden need to hang up but still managed to ask her how she was doing. The moment she began to talk about how much she missed Patricia, unable to focus on the words, I excused myself, saying I had to take something out of the oven. We wished each other good night, then I lay on the floor.

I was convinced that Triana was the reason for his silence. I worried my walking away might have upset her and maybe a call had been made in retaliation, a call where she explained the things we had done that Jacobo and I hadn't done yet.

I left the apartment and went back to some of the places where we had forged our memories. I sat on a terrace facing the Reina Sofía, mesmerized by the glass elevators pulling people up toward the clouds, and listened to each of Jacobo's voicemails. I had forgotten the sound of his voice before it was altered by death, his frisky tone and playful words full of double meanings attempting to seduce me. I regretted my lack of courage, how long it had taken me to get over my hang-ups, my inability to act. Summer was already a version of us that only existed within the confines of our memories.

Jacobo's absence, now that he was in the same time zone, felt more present. It made the separation more voluntary. I kept forgetting that I had been invited to go with them, that it had been I who had decided to stay. His silence made the sound of Matías's offer more enticing and too good to pass up. Wasn't this the kind of opportunity I wanted to be able to pursue while I was at Le Bourrelet? The reason I left?

I paid for my coffee and decided that time would go by faster if I went back to work. On my way to El Lucernario, I took Gran Vía and checked my phone every time I stopped at a crosswalk. I had two bars of battery left and was considering whether to go home and get the charger when a number began flashing on the screen.

"This is Demetrio," I said, though I never answered the phone that way.

"Demetrio Simancas?" the voice asked.

"Yes. This is he."

"I'm Lucas Isasia. I represent the estate of Patricia Smithson."

20

I never made it to El Lucernario. Sitting on a bench on the Paseo del Prado, I looked at a traffic light changing colors until I convinced myself the call hadn't been a prank. In her will, Patricia had left me Las Brisas, a rural property in the province of Cádiz with ten hectares of hills and fruit trees. From what the lawyer said, the house was not in great shape, most of the old corrals were dilapidated and the stone walls barely standing. But the property bordered the beach and could be easily sold. There was already a buyer in case I was interested.

"You won't believe this," I said to Chus the moment he picked up the phone.

"What's wrong?"

"Nothing's wrong. For the first time, nothing's wrong." I paused and thought about what I had just said.

"What is it?"

"Patricia left me a house."

"What?"

"What you heard. She left me a finca. The lawyer said it's a house with about ten hectares of land, which I don't even know how many square feet that is."

"Oh my god, Deme. A finca is an estate. Ten hectares is massive. It's like five city blocks, avenue blocks."

I tried to visualize the distance between Washington Square and Astor Place. "I can't even wrap my head around it."

"What did Jacobo say?"

"Nothing. He's been MIA for days. I wonder if that's the reason he hasn't been answering my calls."

"I doubt it, Deme. He is probably destroyed. His whole world's shattered."

"Yeah, I guess so. But not even a text message?"

Chus didn't respond. "So, what's next?"

"I need to meet the lawyer and sign some documents. I'll keep you posted."

"Okay, call me from the computer soon. This is going to cost you a fortune."

"Yeah, let's do that. I love you."

"I love you too."

THE NEXT DAY, before heading out for breakfast, I turned on my computer and checked an email from the secretary of the law firm that included a detailed description of the property and a screenshot of a map. I searched "Las Brisas and Cádiz" and found an article in the society pages of a local newspaper about a wedding that had taken place at the finca a couple of years back. From the black-and-white photos, I couldn't quite get a sense of what the place looked like.

After calling Jacobo one more time, I went to La Pecera, the restaurant of the Círculo de Bellas Artes. The food was unremarkable but eating under centennial frescos made the steep bill worth it. I now attributed Jacobo's silence to my getting Las Brisas. I re-created some of my exchanges with Patricia, and each time a scene played in my head, bits of our conversations would surface, like pieces of driftwood slowly making their way up from the bottom of the sea.

I walked through the Cortes neighborhood until I found myself in front of Atocha. Like a sleepwalker, I went into the train station and wandered through the mist of a man-made indoor jungle with incredibly tall palm trees reaching for the sunlight. The glass ceiling soaring a hundred feet above had the shape of an inverted hull. The warm, humid air made it difficult to breathe.

Not until I stood at the ticket counter did I realize I was heading to Las Brisas. Most people waiting in line were pink-skinned tourists next to big rolling suitcases and shopping bags, their faces a mix of excitement and bewilderment. There were also some executives, day-trippers dressed in formal suits, carrying slim leather attachés, who stared at their watches impatiently, sighing from time to time. I pretended to be listening to all the different options for Cádiz, fighting an internal voice that warned me to not visit the property before signing anything, and finally bought a ticket for the next train.

A man sitting on a bench, wearing sunglasses, snapped a photo in my direction. I told myself not to be paranoid but couldn't help walking around the station to see if he was following me. Among the lush vegetation, I found a pond with tiny turtles diving in and out of algae and sat down on a bench. I became distracted looking at the fleeting rainbow that appeared intermittently as the sprinklers turned on and off. By the time I got to the platform, the train was about to depart.

The cars were sparkling white and so sleek and futuristic looking they seemed to have arrived from another planet. Shortly
after I found my seat, we began moving, and a couple of minutes later, the train bulleted out of the city.

I followed our shadow projected onto the landscape until I
became dizzy, focusing on the trees next to white stucco houses
in the middle of the fields that, as we moved south, became
a dry barley yellow. I had never traveled so fast on a train. It
was unnervingly quiet. At one point, the possibility of crashing entered my mind, and trying to calm down, I noticed low,
almost imperceptible, soothing music clearly aiming to soften
those kinds of thoughts.

A fear that Jacobo believed I had somehow manipulated his
mother came over me, and soon I was unable to think about
anything else. I kept reminding myself that this had been
Patricia's last will, that I had never acted in a calculating way.
Wanting to calm down, I went to the dining car, sat at the bar,
and emptied a couple of overpriced, tiny wine bottles.

At some point, it seemed that the speed of the train had
decreased considerably, and I blamed the alcohol for having impaired my perception. But then I overheard the waiter
telling a passenger that the high-speed tracks only ran until
Seville, and we were now traveling on the old rails. I walked
back through the aisle to my seat, holding on to the headrests,
and as soon as I sat down, I fell asleep.

CÁDIZ WAS the last stop. The station, small and rickety, had
not been painted in years. The floors were covered with a thin
layer of dirt. People were sleeping on benches or lying on the

floor and didn't seem to be going anywhere. I crossed the main hall and walked up to the ticket counter. The attendant, a young woman breastfeeding a baby, informed me that the last train back to Madrid was in four hours. Since there were plenty of seats available, she suggested not buying a ticket so as not to pay a rescheduling fee in case I decided to stay longer.

Outside the station, a group of cabdrivers, gathered around a water fountain under the shade of a tree, were engaged in conversation. After standing next to the taxi-stop sign, fidgeting with my phone, I walked up to them. They seemed uninterested in me, even though I was the only customer in sight. I waited for a while and finally interrupted them to ask who could drive me to Las Brisas. When I handed a piece of paper with the address to the only driver who had made eye contact with me, he said it was too far from the station. I told him to name a price and he responded that he was a cabdriver and not anyone's private chauffeur. The answer provoked a unanimous laugh. He then pointed to a guy at the other end of the parking lot and suggested asking him. The kid was about my age, maybe a bit younger. He had dark hair that was cut short in the front and left long in the back. His tight jeans made his high-tops look even larger. Smoking a cigarette, he was leaning on a ramshackle car with tinted windows and doors covered with red flame decals.

I decided to go back into the train station. After I fought with a rusty vending machine for a bottle of water, a can of Coke Zero banged against the metal tray. I sat down, defeated. Glancing at the screen of my phone, at the battery bars full of hope, I said out loud, "Call me back, call me back, call me the fuck back." I flipped the phone open and sent Jacobo a single, lonely question mark.

The kid who had been leaning on the car entered the waiting

area and looked around. When he saw me sitting on a plastic chair that was making the back of my thighs sweat, he grinned and walked up to me. He was short and stocky with rippling biceps. I wondered if I would be able to fight back if he were to mug me.

"¿Buscas taxi?" He had tiny, crooked teeth and a strong accent that sounded like Gabriela's.

I looked at him, unconvinced.

He extended his hand. "I'm Raúl."

"Demetrio." I gazed at his faded blue jeans, which were so washed out the contours of the pockets underneath had made white marks on them.

"Where are you going?"

"Right outside Zahara de los Atunes." I used the words of the cabdriver, trying to show that I knew my way around. I handed him the piece of paper with the address. He glanced at it and bit the tip of his upper lip.

"Las Brisas?"

"Yeah."

"What for?"

"It's my friend's," I said, still incapable of believing I owned a house. Chus and I always wished we could have bought one of the apartments in our tenement building, which, back in the eighties, were being sold for thirty-eight thousand dollars. Now they were worth a million.

"It's about forty kilometers from here. I'll take you for sixty-five euros."

"Thirty?"

"Fifty. Do you have any bags?"

"No, I don't." I looked to my sides as if to prove my point. "Let me run to the bathroom before we go."

The restroom smelled putrid, a mix of stale urine and spoiled food. I entered a stall, locked myself in, and hid one hundred euros in my sneakers. Then I walked to the sink and splashed my face with cold water, avoiding the eyes of a man who seemed to be spending the afternoon washing his hands.

MOST OF THE JOURNEY was on a two-lane uphill road that became more winding. We ascended a stretch of hills and the car struggled to maintain its speed, the engine roaring louder and louder. What I first had taken for massive black boulders interspersed throughout the grass were majestic Spanish bulls with velvety black coats lying on the ground. The sharp curves kept unwrapping rolling hills covered in green shrubs, and even though we were moving at a considerable speed, I began to relax. The sun was hiding behind the only cloud in the sky, and when it came out again, I marveled at Patricia's ability to touch my life even after she was gone.

Raúl pointed at a space that had opened in between two hills where the light bounced off the white marshes with an intense splendor. He turned down the flamenco music to say that those were the Salinas de San Fernando, the biggest salt beds on the Atlantic coast. A strong breeze began to blow loose the top layer, its white speckles creating a thin film of transparent mist.

"Have you been to jail?" Raúl lowered the music even more.

I considered lying. "No, never."

"Good, because it's not fun. Let me tell you."

My throat tightened.

"I just got out. I was locked up for one hundred and fifteen days," he said. "And all its nights."

Raúl spoke differently now, with a raspier tone. He slipped down the seat to pull something from his back pocket, making the car swerve into the opposite lane.

"But I have this." He handed me a piece of paper. "Now if there's a problem with the cops, I only need to show this letter. With this, I'm untouchable," he said, raising his voice proudly.

It was a release statement with his full name, the address of the jail where he had spent time for theft, and the contact information of a penitentiary social worker. Fixing my gaze on the letters made me dizzy, but I read it from beginning to end. Nothing in that letter made him untouchable.

"Very cool, man," I said, wanting to open the door and throw myself onto the rushing pavement.

We had been following a low wall made of uneven stones for a while when Raúl released his foot from the accelerator and the car began to slow down. We stopped next to a cattle gate that had once been blue. I considered asking him if there were bulls grazing on the property but decided not to prolong our time together.

To turn the motor off, he disconnected two wires from underneath the steering wheel. It was only then I noticed there was no key in the ignition. Now that the rattling sound of the engine had stopped, the silence was overwhelming. A bird began chirping loudly, its cadence like a car alarm on a hot sleepless New York night.

"Here we are." Raúl opened the car door.

I glanced at the unwelcoming rusty chain tied around the gate and faked a smile.

"Thanks, man."

As he bent slightly forward to stretch his lower back, I grabbed my wallet and counted the bills, fearing that a police

car would drive by and catch me giving money to someone driving a stolen car, as I was about to trespass on private
property.

"I'll give you my phone number," he said.

I must have made a strange face because he added: "In case
you want me to pick you up later."

I wrote down his number, put the paper in my back pocket,
and told him that I would text him. We said goodbye and shook
hands awkwardly through a small opening of the window. He
then hot-wired the engine, smiling casually, but it wasn't an
apologetic smile, it was genuine, as if the action were funny in
and of itself. Flamenco music began blasting again. Skidding
on the dirt, the car disappeared behind a cloud of dust. I waited
by the side of the road until the last rumbles faded out. In the
silence, I could hear every sporadic sound amplified, the chirping of birds, cicadas, and what I assumed to be lizards running
in the underbrush that had come to welcome me.

21

Making sure no cars were approaching, I jumped the low wall, the fatigue from the journey replaced by an adrenaline rush that flooded every part of my body. I began following an old dirt road, its two furrows covered with green weeds suggested that no vehicles had passed for a long time. To the left, there was a narrow path that zigzagged uphill and looked like a shortcut, but there was something soothing and welcoming about the wider road. Walking on the dry mud, I inspected the tractor marks and thought about the different wheels that had gone up that lane throughout the years, the old footprints erased and replaced by newer marks.

The landscape emerged before my eyes with a certain shyness. What I noticed first were the lush shrubs near a river, with trees that were taller and a more vibrant green than those on the other side of the drive, farther from the water. I was tempted to take a detour but an inexplicable urge to reach the summit pulled me up. I made a mental note to visit the valley later on and hoped to see its view from the top. As I climbed up the hill, feeling my socks slowly dampening, I thought about the impossibility of owning part of a river because rivers couldn't be owned, no matter what a deed said. Now that all this land would soon be under my name, all I wanted to do was preserve it forever.

After a long ascent, the hill flattened and turned into an expansive plain with lemon and orange trees in perfect rows, their elastic trunks bent from carrying too much fruit, some of which had fallen underneath, rotten and pecked. I walked through the field and saw, behind the tree line, a cortijo, a white stucco house typical of Andalucía. From the conversation with the lawyer, I had assumed that it was quite dilapidated, and though it looked like it hadn't been inhabited for a long time, and on some parts of the façade the white paint had faded completely and the brown stone showed underneath, it seemed structurally sound.

The main door was locked. I walked around the outside, which was covered in tall wild weeds, peeked through the windows, and saw white sheets covering the furniture. The back of the house had an interior courtyard with a black metal gate. It was ajar. Built on the wall opposite the entrance, next to a row of logs covered by moss, there was a wood oven. The ancient black marks of the flames made me think of the different generations of families that had gathered around the fire, the many loaves of bread that had been baked there throughout the years.

I lay down on the floor, its thick stone cool on my back. Staring at the passing clouds, I imagined Jacobo looking at the same dimming blue sky but from the open sea. My first thought was to turn the cortijo into a dessert restaurant. In the latest issue of *Gourmet,* I had read a long article about a Norwegian chef who only served dishes with ingredients he sourced from his organic garden. The idea of creating a dessert menu with fruits, flowers, and herbs grown in Las Brisas felt like a continuation of what I had started with the Helado de Maravillas de

Patricia. I knew that the south of Spain was a preferred holiday destination for Europeans and there were significant seasonal restaurants dispersed all over the coast. I wished I had a map to see how far Las Brisas was from Marbella, a popular tourist destination that had to be nearby. After the initial excitement, the more pragmatic questions began to eclipse the anticipation of starting a business. Where would I get the money to fix the cortijo? My lack of industry contacts would make it hard to even open a small pastry shop in Madrid, let alone a restaurant in rural Andalucía. I began playing with different amounts in my head, the cost of equipping a kitchen and installing convection ovens, remodeling and furnishing a dining room, buying dinnerware. I calculated numbers in dollars, based on New York prices, knowing what a futile exercise that was. I wondered what Jacobo would think about these plans and what he thought about the will. What he thought about me.

THE SUN HADN'T gone down completely, yet a massive, almost full moon was beginning to climb on the opposite side of the sky, capturing its faint amber light. I was still dazed from a dream I was trying to recall, from which I had woken shaken and stunned, when I heard the distant sound of an engine. At first, I assumed it came from a nearby road. But then headlights illuminated the treetops next to the house. My stomach churned. I stood up and looked through the metal bars of the patio. I held my breath for a couple of seconds and then Raúl's car came into view. I was suddenly wide awake.

I ran out of the courtyard, scratching my elbow on the gate. As I bent over, I noticed an oxidized sickle lying on the grass. I grabbed it and circled the house, looking for a place to hide. A door opened and shut in the distance, the engine still running. When I finally regained sight of the car, from behind a pile of hay bales that had gone brown from the sun, I saw Raúl sitting in the driver's seat.

No matter how hard I squinted, I couldn't tell what he was doing. Had he come to pick me up? After my eyes adjusted to the darkness, I saw the fiery amber of a cigarette illuminating his unshaven face. Then he backed up the car, turned around, and began moving down the lane slowly.

I stood, paralyzed, long after the red brake lights had vanished behind the leafy trees, long after the rattling engine had faded and the sounds of the night had closed in around me. I stepped out from my hiding place into the open field, a regained calm extending through my body pushing me to a state of complete bliss.

The moonlight lit everything around me, the sky brushed with thin orange clouds fading into the horizon. I looked up at the stars, wishing I knew the constellations. As I walked unsteadily in the field, I remembered a trip I had made with Chus and Ben to see Comet Hale-Bopp soon after I turned fourteen. We woke up at four in the morning and headed to Cold Spring, a small town in the Hudson Valley. A scientist friend of Chus's had assured him that, away from light pollution, we would have a clear view of the comet. Waiting in the main concourse of Grand Central Terminal to take the Metro-North, Ben pointed at the zodiac mural on the ceiling, tracing the tiny bulbs representing the constellations. He said that the stars had been rendered incorrectly by the Vanderbilt family, which, at the time, we assumed was part of Ben's propensity to condemn everything done by the upper class, or Americans in general. From early on, I observed that people whose families had been in America for generations were more inclined to criticize the actions of their country. It was like an earned right. I wondered if after living in Spain for a while, I would eventually feel empowered to do the same.

Looking at the dissolving amber clouds, I remembered my extreme disappointment when the comet didn't appear. The twirling orange particles floating in the sky now seemed to connect to the other end of that moment. I stared at the horizon, engulfed in stillness, and sensed Patricia watching over me.

It was ten o'clock. At some point, I had considered spending the night at Las Brisas. Now there was no other option. On the walk back to the cortijo, I counted stars and smiled at the impossibility of the task. It had become a favorite pastime during my summers on Fire Island, a way to entertain myself while Ben and Chus went to the beach after dinner to drink wine from red plastic cups.

I must have walked with my head up for a long time, because when I looked down, I was close to the house. Solid, electric light was coming through the front windows. I wished I had brought along the sickle I had left next to the hay bales. My first thought was that Raúl had come back and forced his way in, then I considered that maybe a caretaker lived there. Defenseless in the open field, I tiptoed toward the trees, hid behind a bush, and pulled out my phone. The battery was dead.

I stepped out carefully, trying not to make noise. The sudden thought that maybe Jacobo's father had come to Las Brisas to empty the house made my heart sink. I considered leaving the backpack with my wallet and keys, but I couldn't see myself walking without an ID on the side of a country road in the middle of the night. Even though for the first time, if I were to be stopped, my lack of documents wouldn't be anything other than a momentary misunderstanding.

I waited. There were no sounds coming from the house. I decided to grab my bag and walk down through the forest, away from the main path. The shrubs and weeds were so dry, it was hard not to make noise. I missed the mushy dirt near the riverbank that had absorbed the sound of my steps. The moonlight was now almost as bright as daylight. I could see the backpack where I had left it on the floor against the wall farthest from the gate. As I picked it up quietly, a wave of smoke floated over me.

My knees were suddenly incapable of supporting my weight. I could sense Raúl observing my movements. I felt the one hundred euros in my sneakers and hoped they could be a passport out of the situation. Flooding my lungs with air to puff my chest so I would appear bigger than I was, I turned around.

"I thought you had left," Jacobo said.

I breathed out, my body shrinking back to its normal size. Speechless, I looked at him and felt an overwhelming calm, every muscle giving up, like strings unwinding from a guitar.

"Hi, Jake."

Jacobo took a long drag from a joint. Tiny orange pieces of hashish fell on the dry weeds. He held in the smoke and showed no emotion. We looked at each other like strangers. He then exhaled a white dagger and walked back to the front of the house. In the pure night air, the smell was sharp.

I stood in the courtyard and looked at the stars. The distance I had been imagining between us was real. I couldn't tell if his behavior was a consequence of the grief from losing his mother or because he now saw me as some opportunistic grifter who had taken advantage of his family. The excitement that I had experienced exploring the land and dreaming about my new life turned into a deep, irreversible sadness.

I considered Patricia's leaving me the property some sort of cosmic reward. Still, I decided to tell Jacobo I was not going to accept it. Whether I would ultimately follow through, I did not know. In some way, I knew I had no right to this gorgeous land. Yet I had never experienced such an instant fondness for a place, a landscape that was novel and magnificent yet strangely familiar and welcoming.

Suddenly, the whispering of the leaves was interrupted by a thunderous sound and what seemed to be glass shattering.

"Get out! Out!" Jacobo yelled.

I ran out of the courtyard and made my way to the front door. In the few seconds that it took me to reach the entrance, I imagined Raúl and Jacobo rolling on the floor. I expected the worst. Raúl was much stronger than him, and his prison time had surely hardened his punches.

By the time I entered the living room, the noises had stopped. I walked into the kitchen. Jacobo was sitting on the floor, broom by his side, a cute little dead mouse next to him. I kneeled down and put an arm around his shoulder. With teary eyes, he looked at me and began sobbing.

"Can you pick it up and throw it outside?" he said, laughing through tears.

"Of course," I said.

I put the mouse in a black plastic bag I found in the kitchen and left it outside the house. When I got back into the living room, Jacobo was curled on a sofa under a white sheet.

"I'm sorry I didn't call you back. The doctor gave me more pills to get through the next couple of weeks and I took them all in three days."

I sat next to him and peeled off my sneakers. Covering my feet with a cushion, I hoped he wouldn't notice their smell. "I was worried about you."

We both looked at the ashes left in the fireplace. I wondered if he was also thinking about Patricia. The right words, if they existed, were far away.

"How was Mallorca?"

Jacobo didn't respond. An owl hooted. It was probably perched high in a tree outside, but the silence was so intense that it sounded as if it were in the room. I heard it again, always with the same pitch and duration. It seemed to be intending to convey something.

"I've been trying to reach you for days."

Jacobo kept looking at the ashes, but a slight movement of his face indicated he was listening.

"I don't want you to think I did something unethical. I'm as surprised as you are about the will. Your mom and I—you know this—had an instant connection." The blurry image of Patricia's face printed on the funeral program popped into my head. "It was like I didn't have to explain anything to her. She seemed to—"

Jacobo began crying again and pulled his hands up to his face. As I looked for words, I hoped the owl would make a sound.

"I'm sorry. I shouldn't have brought her up."

Jacobo turned his head to me and uncovered his eyes, which were red and swollen. As he began to speak, tears rolled down his cheeks.

"It was Mom's idea to leave you the finca. We talked about it. She had considered leaving you money but then decided that she wanted to give you a place." He paused as if he were reliving the moment in his head. A pensive, gloomy smile was drawn on his face.

"And how do you feel about it?" I asked.

"How do I feel about what?"

"About me getting this place."

"I agree with Mom."

"I'm thinking about opening a dessert restaurant," I said, instantly regretting being so tactless.

"I thought you were feeling funny about your job," he said, puzzled.

"It's not the job I can't stand. I love baking, I still do. It's the being in a kitchen locked up from the world most of the day that I can't see myself doing again. I was talking about this to your mother at the hospital. And today, walking the fields, I imagined what it would be like to live permanently up here, open a bakery maybe. It's such a special place."

Jacobo didn't react. My eyes landed on the fireplace again, joining his gaze affixed on the ashes.

"What did your dad say?"

"He was against it, he still is. But it was Mom's last wish. And besides, this estate belonged to her family, so he has no say. There's nothing for you to feel guilty about."

My body was filled with a momentary lightness. Looking now at Jacobo, I had the urge to wrap my whole body around him.

"If you're hungry I can go see if there's something in the kitchen."

"Sure," he said, curling up into a ball.

As I held the armrest to pull myself out of the sofa, Jacobo grabbed my hand. "Remember saying goodbye at the airport?"

I opened my eyes wide.

"I'm here now."

I hugged him and kissed the back of his ear. Even though I had imagined this moment differently, I wouldn't have changed it for anything. I thought again about how life sometimes gives you what you want but never the way you expect it. I took off my hoodie and placed it over his chest. He grabbed one of the sleeves, pushed it to his nose, and breathed in deeply.

There were a package of spaghetti and a can of tomato sauce in one of the cabinets, along with other basic provisions. When I went back into the living room to share the news, excited to cook a meal for him, he was in a deep sleep, a light and rhythmic whistle coming from his nose. I sat next to him and admired his beautiful face with dark circles under the eyes that had been there since he had arrived from New York. I took off my shirt and lay next to him.

NO MATTER HOW many deep breaths I counted, how hard I tried to make my mind go blank, sleep didn't come. The thought that I had become a homeowner overnight and that we were finally in a relationship was too much to process. Unable to slow down my racing thoughts, I got up from the sofa, tucked Jacobo in, and began to look at the cortijo not for what it was but for what it could be. The main living room was big enough for fifteen tables and connected to a decent-sized dining room where we could fit another five or six. The sparsely furnished kitchen could be expanded toward a patio that was now used as storage, the corrals transformed into outdoor dining space. The possibilities were endless.

When it was apparent that I would not be able to trick my mind into sleep, I walked outside. The sun had started to rise. The mixture of moon and daylight twinkled on a thin layer of dew, making the tawny lemons shine with an uncanny quality. I grabbed Jacobo's denim jacket resting on a pile of firewood, and put it on. Slightly damp, it clung to my chest. I stood on the esplanade in front of the house and looked at the long, winding lane from which I had arrived. The moisture, brightening every corner of the field, brought out the most pungent aromas of lavender, thyme, rosemary.

I walked to the back of the cortijo and experienced a familiarity, as if I had bonded with the land overnight. I noticed an old stable made of gray stone and thought about what kind of animals had lived there in the past. Next to it, a narrow, overgrown trail meandered into the woods. I looked back at the house, my house, and began the slow descent down the hill, hoping to find the beach. Never in my life had I experienced such joy.

I followed the path for a while as the first rays of sunshine filtering through the treetops muted the last traces of moonlight. The vegetation on both sides of the trail was thick, impenetrable, a tangle of brown and green bushes extending through the slope. After hitting several cobwebs along the trail, I grabbed a stick to clear the way and wondered when the last time was someone had gone down this path.

At one point, as I walked through the dense woods, deprived of sunlight, the wind brought a salty, wet smell. The shrub mantle extending around me began to slowly open up and I could see small, light brown patches of earth through the thinning vegetation. The dirt soon turned into sand.

I stepped out of the green tunnel through which I had been traveling and was welcomed by an intense, pure white light. The sun had risen. I could feel its heat through the thick, luminous fog. My depth of field was so limited that it took me a while to realize I had begun climbing a dune. The distant, rhythmic waves crashed on the shore like the crackle and hiss of a vinyl record that had hit a locked groove and begun to loop.

After walking down to the other side, I reached a long, deserted beach. A group of young gulls was gliding across the sky. I sat down on the sand. The fog, lifting up like a veil, allowed the light to become more radiant, revealing the coastline of Morocco in the distance. I imagined people across the ocean and all around the world embarking on new journeys, crossing borders and oceans and deserts. And dreaming of other lives.

Acknowledgments

One can only guess where stories come from, what is lived, what is dreamt, what is just a figment of the imagination. I daresay this novel originated on a summer afternoon my friend Yigit took me to the Big Sur Bakery after a hike overlooking the Pacific Ocean.

This book exists in large part thanks to the vision of my editor, Shelley Wanger. Her incisive editing and care have not only made it a better story but have also made me a better writer. Thanks, also, to the extended team at Pantheon for believing in this novel and for helping usher it into the world.

Thanks to my agent, Maria Cardona, who pushed and pushed and pushed so you could read these pages.

My graduate studies at Columbia marked the beginning of a life I cherish and protect every day. During that time, I had the opportunity to work with remarkable colleagues and professors. Deborah Eisenberg and Stacey D'Erasmo helped me unearth what few could: the possibilities that exist within me. To everyone in the School of the Arts, and to them especially, my deepest thanks.

To Lambda Literary, thank you for all you do, and for providing community, time, and space at a crucial moment.

Thank you to Forsyth Harmon, Scott Hunter, Clare Smith Marash, and Satoshi Tabuchi for their intelligence, their encouragement, and their generosity reading and rereading.

I am indebted to New York City, a place without, quite possibly, I would not be the writer I am today. Thank you to Carole, Jacob, Jose, Nestor, Pix, Rory, and Tim for showing me that family isn't always blood.

Thank you to Anthony Roth Costanzo, the hardest-working artist I know, for always being there and seeing who I truly was before anyone else did, including me.

Eloisa Díaz, colleague, friend, sister. Gosh, the world is so much better with you in it.

Lastly, thank you to Anthony W. Thornton for his love and willingness to read many iterations of this story, for his insightful comments and notes. And for the magical years.

A NOTE ABOUT THE AUTHOR

Javier Fuentes is a Spanish American writer. A 2018
Lambda Literary fellow, he earned an MFA in fiction
from Columbia University, where he was a teaching
fellow. Born in Barcelona, he lives in New York.

A NOTE ON THE TYPE

This book was set in a modern adaptation of a type designed by the first William Caslon (1692–1766). The Caslon face, an artistic, easily read type, has enjoyed more than two centuries of popularity in the English-speaking world. This version, with its even balance and honest letterforms, was designed by Carol Twombly for the Adobe Corporation and released in 1990.

Typeset by Scribe,
Philadelphia, Pennsylvania

Printed and bound by Berryville Graphics,
Berryville, Virginia

Designed by Cassandra J. Pappas